LOOSE CANNON

Loose Cannon

Short Fuse II

A Novel by
Brent D. Seth

Loose Cannon

Copyright© 2020 by Brent D. Seth

This is a work of fiction. All names, characters, places, and events are products of the author's imagination, or are used fictitiously. Any resemblance to real people or events is unfortunate and coincidental. All rights reserved.

Cover Art by Diren Yardimli

ISBN: 9798553874742

I wish to acknowledge my friend Kristoffer Gair for his enormous contribution to this book. Not only did he help with the details, he kicked my ass when I felt like giving up. I can never repay the debt

And

For Leo

1993 – 2012

Still the center of my universe

Chapter 1

Three months ago, by my perspective, I was a middle-aged grocery clerk in central Illinois. Driving home one night, I got in a car crash and subsequently woke up, young and healthy, aboard an alien spacecraft, with no knowledge of how long I had been there, or why. I soon discovered the extent of my physical modifications and found myself caught between two hostile empires in the grips of a centuries-old cold war. Within weeks, that cold war turned hot, with me at the center. Me, Jason Miller, the most average guy in the whole galaxy.

The war lasted only a few hours, but the amount of damage done in such a short time is nearly incalculable. Wars have a tendency to do that, but in this case, the entire galaxy altered substantively. The full effect of which was yet to be fully felt by my friends or me.

My friends. We started as mere allies, former slaves who shared a common goal: survival. But in the course of that war, we gained an appreciation for each other, even a genuine affection. Three months later, reduced from freedom fighters to fugitives and vagabonds, that affection was wearing thin.

We roamed the galaxy in a commandeered war machine, searching for... Well, we really didn't know. Home? Maybe. But in our absence, home would now be something quite different from what we remembered. More than anything, it seemed, we were on a quest to find a quest.

Destiny is fickle. Some individuals spend their life chasing dreams or ambitions. Sometimes, destiny crashes through your front door, spits in your face, and sets fire to the whole neighborhood with nuclear weapons.

Our destiny came abruptly and seemingly out of nowhere. And we were in the middle of nowhere when it arrived.

The emptiness of deep space between the spiral arms of our galaxy is as barren as it is cold, but with a solitude that, for heavily hunted individuals like my friends and I, is comforting. Out here, there was nothing but a few sparse particles, noble gasses, bits of various dark matter and lots of radiation—nothing at all to constitute a threat. After everything I've seen, this equated paradise.

I sat in the Captain's chair of our vessel, piloting through a direct interface between the ship's systems and myself. In a sense, I was the ship; I felt the hull as if it was my own skin, its sensors had supplanted my eyes and ears, and the engines were indistinguishable from my own beating heart. Before my body of flesh and blood was a sprawling console with lights and switches. I had no need of manual controls; my fingers, despite the numerous hours I had spent in command, had never touched most of those buttons.

This vessel, formerly an Ullinarian assault craft, traveled through the empty region along an inward, helical path. I had a terrific, almost intimate, view of the central region of our galaxy thanks to this course. The light was brilliant, subdued only slightly by the intervening lanes of dust and ice like wispy clouds under a full moon. In order to fully enjoy this sight, it was necessary to travel through the shallowest layer of hyperspace; only a single spatial membrane separated this ship from the four-dimensional universe of accepted reality. This allowed for only modest velocity, slightly greater than the speed of light. In terms of interstellar travel, this was slower than waiting for a check from the IRS.

I wasn't concerned about speed, or lack thereof, although my companion Tony would be furious if he knew I was sightseeing again. We had no reason to rush. Pretty much everything these days amounted to little more than killing time, especially with no clear destination in mind, and no fear of our own mortality.

This is why the first volley of plasma bolts came as such a great surprise. I must have let my mind wander too far to have missed such a large contingent, seven attackers on an oblique approach. The sleek, orange/while skin of Ullinarian scout ships was unmistakable; my current life began in one of those. They were fast and maneuverable but, individually, had low offensive capability, especially compared to a ship like mine.

I banked hard, taking only a glancing blow to one of my aft thrusters. It was not a critical hit, but still painful and enough to collapse our hyperspace envelope. We careened into normal space and I struggled to maintain a stable course with the remaining thrusters. The attacking ships exited hyperspace in a much more controlled manner than my own arrival, and resumed their onslaught.

I called for help through the ship's interior speakers and, one by one, felt the consciousness of my companions joining me inside the computer. With our minds sharing the same space, I could feel their emotions as if each were my own; fear, confusion, and considerable anger. No doubt about the source of the latter.

What the hell've you've been doing?

I could try to defend myself, but as part of the computer, Tony had the same access to the sensor logs as I did. The simple truth is I wasn't paying attention, and everyone knew it. We had to deal with the situation and find a way out.

Sharing consciousness within the machine is both seductive and terrifying. Maintaining any sense of individuality, although instinctive, requires considerable effort. Trying to work together required an equal amount of effort too, otherwise… chaos. Our ship veered in one direction, thrusters obeying the will of one pilot, and then someone else tried to lunge in another. We fought each other as well as the ships firing on us.

Another barrage seemed to catch me square in my chest as a second wave of scouts exited hyperspace in a flash of blue. We still had a superior vessel, and if we acted together, we were more than formidable. I forced my mind to relax despite the stress and succumb to the lure of our technology and allowed my individuality to melt.

Four operators became one and our ship sprung to full potential. Cannons flared, and we wove between assailants effortlessly like minnows in still water. The ship sustained damage, but automated repairs were already underway, and our collective technical skills bypassed those areas needing greater service.

Our digitally enhanced minds interpreted the enemy fleet's attack pattern and extrapolated their strategy. They herded us in a specific direction, intent on incapacitating us just enough for capture, but not destruction.

No scout ship, or even a dozen, could net an Arrow class assault vessel, and the attacking fleet knew this. Unfortunately for us, they were not alone, as became evident when another distortion in local space heralded the massive form of an Ullinarian Dreadnaught, slipping into view.

"Can we jump?" One of us, or perhaps all of us, asked in unison. A response came in the form of a mental impression of a swiping yellow paw. The engines were damaged, several critical systems were on the verge of failure, but thanks to our brilliant mechanic, we still had one last opportunity for escape.

Our ship veered portside to face our left flank. The enemy matched course to challenge, but instead of engaging, we made a hard right and accelerated. The Dreadnaught fired on empty space as we plunged into the deepest layer of hyperspace.

The ride was not smooth. Our damaged engines pushed harder than even optimal conditions would recommend. I attempted to warn everyone else, but found my consciousness impotent, shoved aside, and back into the isolation of my physical body.

I looked around the command deck through my own eyes. Tony was there, leaning over the controls, his hands making enough contact with the mechanical infrastructure to allow his mind access to the computer. He was so still, anyone unfamiliar with our enhanced nature might have mistaken him for a mannequin or corpse.

"I'll drive for a while, thank you," he announced through the ships com system. Even though his voice was mechanical and displayed no emotion, the rattling bulkheads revealed the anger present, which the computer could not simulate. And even though he appeared absent, I knew he was watching.

"Well, I can—"

"Just go and check the damage. I got this," he snapped, flatly.

The hatch opened with a violent grind as if to underline his statement.

I decided to comply with Tony's *suggestion* and give him time to cool down, so I followed the designated route into the deeper portions of the ship. This had originally all been one big compartment, but before beginning this voyage, we partitioned several areas with a clever use of hospital-grade blankets. It kinda looked like a kid's pillow fort installed aboard the ISS. They were actually old filament sheets from gamma filters that I had stol—er, liber—*removed* from the space station we recently visited...and all but destroyed. Since they no longer had a use for them, I gave the fibers a new life. The people of that station were hopefully having a similar experience.

The next compartment was our main living quarters—although the actual appearance made a mockery of the word *living*. The Ullinarians, former owners of this vessel, are not the kind of people you would ask to decorate your new home. What they lack in aesthetics, which is considerable, they made up for with a strong penchant for cruelty. One side of the chamber had once housed a set of integration beds, storage units for technologically enhanced slaves who performed most of the work in running the ship. I spent years in such a state on another vessel, so it had been my great pleasure to remove those atrocities. And since the Ullinarians themselves also lack a sense of personal comfort, crude hammocks made from more gamma filter replaced the original crew bunks.

The room lurched violently, forcing me into one of the hammocks, as our vessel jumped into even higher gear. This ship, despite its disturbing past, was an uncompromised model of engineering wizardry. We had artificial gravity, inertial compensators, and a dozen other systems that could neutralize any sense of motion. However, all these systems were dependent on the competence of the pilot. Just like a rear-view mirror and turn signals, they only work if you use them. Furthermore, we had just escaped from a firefight, the results of which were, as yet, undetermined.

"You left Tony in control by himself?"

I disentangled myself from the makeshift hammock and turned to the speaker.

Oola, another member of our crew, kneeled on the floor by an open inspection panel, humming softly to herself. Oola was an Olemsi; she had orange skin and what looked much like a helmet of dense, pitted green flesh that could almost have been a shell where one might expect to find hair on a human female. Two tiny black eyes were set above a short trunk of a nose and her lips were also tiny and very pink. Her name was actually Oola Oola, her preferred address. No one called her

Oola Oola. And after weeks of correcting us, she finally stopped calling herself Oola Oola. Frustration? Defeat? All of the above? It didn't matter. Nobody was going to call her by her full name. Just like Tony and me, the Ullinarians abducted Oola and enhanced her with nanites. Also like me, she had been a database. There were dozens of different species the Ullinarians used for slaves, but the details of these species were one of the few things they had not seen fit to program into our heads. The only clues to our origins among the piles and piles of navigational data at my disposal were planets labeled *acquisition points*. I had the location for over three hundred such places, but no idea of what kind of materials to acquire at any one of them. Now that the Ullinarian Empire was essentially closed for business, we had been systematically surveying these planets.

"He insisted," I explained, taking a seat near Oola. "We're light-years from anything; I don't think we have to worry."

"We might," she said, indicating the open panel. "That incursion, caused some serious damage. Almost every system is signaling critical. We really should go easy on the engines."

I scoffed. "Yeah, you tell him."

She didn't respond, which was itself a response. Instead, she continued to survey the hatch's interior. More accurately, she was watching our mechanical engineer who was doing the real work. From my position, I could see him, immobile, assessing damage through direct interface. To most humans, this would seem a truly bizarre scene; a tabby cat, smaller than the average male feline, attempting to repair complicated alien technology. Stranger still, he was really good at it. Leo had been my best friend since I found him as a kitten. He was an extension of myself, a surrogate child. The same could be said for Fido, the last member of our gang.

"Where is Fido?" I asked, losing this train of thought.

Oola continued humming, but in the form of coherent

words. "Cleaning the latrine."

"Again? He was doing that when I began my shift."

She paused from both her humming and observation and looked up. "Still. I think he successfully removed the smell weeks ago. He probably just wants something to do."

"There's probably enough work coming our way to keep him busy," I shot back just as my cat snapped to life and bounced from the hatch. He meowed as his observations began to post on a near-by monitor. Despite his upgrade and implanted knowledge far beyond his evolutionary placement, Leo was still a cat. I couldn't understand his speech any more today than before our abduction and, when not interfaced with a computer, his behavior was still that of a loyal pet and best friend.

The computer readout he had prepared, however, was another story altogether. A list was building before our eyes of damaged machinery, fried circuits, and even a few missing pieces of our hull. No ambiguity here. My little sightseeing excursion was going to cost us more than just some lost time.

I knew that Tony, still merged with the ship, would see Leo's diagnosis and reach the same conclusion. In fact, even before the display had fully rendered, the ship lurched once again, even more drastically than before, indicating an abrupt stop. Perhaps leaving Tony in command had been a bad idea after all; in the emptiness between spiral arms, he just slammed on the brakes.

"Guys, get up here!"

I expected a verbal attack from Tony and, indeed, might even have deserved one. His voice resonated from every electrical device on the ship. The computerized voice didn't allow for any emotion to show through, but somehow, he still sounded oddly cordial. In fact, he almost sounded amused, which became more pronounced the next time he spoke.

"Hurry! You won't believe what I found. It's really cool…

*

Loose Cannon

Oola and I joined Tony on the bridge, as requested. I was personally more concerned with his sudden stop than whatever *cool thing* he discovered. Even for a vessel as sophisticated as this, a reckless pilot could render serious damage, especially since the transfer from hyperspace to normal space is a complicated and dangerous maneuver. More disturbing was the realization we had already reached the nearest spiral arm, telling me that in only a few minutes, we had crossed hundreds of light years of empty space. Tony had indeed been driving fast, at least twice the recommended speed of this craft.

The view from here was one of thick dust lanes, pushing outward from the hundreds of old-age stars that had burned through their fuel and blown themselves to bits, leaving behind a continuing shower of charged particles and ionized gases. The view was, of course, spectacular; exactly the kind of thing I would slow down to appreciate, but certainly nothing that would interest Tony.

He was still leaning against the console where I left him, his face frozen, eyes open and staring. Just as his appearance would suggest, no one was at home. His mind remained inside the computer, from where his voice came once again and the smile, missing from his physical body, continued to be easily recognizable.

"Check this out," he said mechanically. "Space Spam."

With a mental flip of a switch, the speakers played an audio transmission, previously heard only by the pilot, now shared with the rest of us. Tony had been right about one thing, it was very much like suspicious emails from that elusive Nigerian Prince, or more closely resembling those annoying robo-calls so common during election years.

"Attention Liberated Upgrades…
The fall of the Ullinarian Empire has created
many exciting business opportunities for you!

> *Your abilities are needed in the vast, expanding free territories of the former Ullinarian Empire.*
>
> *Are you lost, alone, confused?*
>
> *Come to the nearest Rovalorian outpost to discover the rewarding opportunities waiting for you…*
>
> *Attention Liberated Upgrades…"*

The message began to repeat. Tony switched off the sound and exited the computer, his face coming instantly to life and swelling with an enormous grin. Personally, I found the transmission more than a little threatening, and I could not understand why Tony did not feel the same. We had been evading raiders for weeks, and this kind of broadcast seemed like an obvious trap. Perhaps too obvious; it was almost like something Wile E. Coyote would concoct to snag a meal. The only things missing were a printed sign reading *free birdseed* and a giant anvil suspended by rope.

"Isn't that a hoot?" Tony laughed and wiggled his eyebrows. "Should we take a look?"

"Spam?"

I was stunned—by Tony's suggestion, not Oola questioning spam. I worked in a grocery store for twenty-two years, and I still questioned spam. Not only had Tony been engineered for strategy and defense, but he had also been a police officer before our abduction. If anyone ought to see through such a transparent ploy, it damn well should have been him.

"*Are you insane?*" I demanded. "Were we not attacked just ten minutes ago? By people using Ullinarian ships? And now you want to accept an invitation from Rovalorians to join others, presumably also with Ullinarian ships? Really, the Rovalorians? They were the strongest ally of the empire—the last people we should trust! And I'm sure if anything remains of the Empire, they're trying really hard to rebuild what they lost. To do that, they'll need slaves. What would be better than former slaves, already upgraded, that they can scoop up and return to service?"

Tony shrugged and reclined in the chair like a man settling in to watch an episode of The Golden Girls. "The Ullinarians didn't really trust any of their allies; especially the Rovalorians. I bet they're just trying to build their own empire before the Ullinarians can rise again."

"Are you willing to take that risk? What do you think, Oola?"

She stood behind Tony, clearly missing both the humor and menace in the transmission. Not surprising; from what little she had told me about her home world Olemsi Myucuc, it was obvious their development had not reached the point of advertising, mass communication, or even organized commerce. She understood these things only because of her implanted knowledge and recent experience. Despite that knowledge, however, she still lacked a natural capacity for suspicion, or at times, even good sense.

"It could be safe," she mused, her head dropping to one side and resting on her shoulder. "You did a great deal of damage to the empire; their military must have been nearly eliminated. And you severed their control over all slaves. Whatever remains of the empire, if anything at all, must be nearly impotent."

I grunted, disgusted. "Yes, *I* destroyed their empire. Me! Those who remain would do anything for a piece of my scalp!"

I could tell by the looks on their faces they were not entirely convinced. For that matter, neither was I. The program I designed and unleashed was as destructive as it was viral. It must have scrubbed away most of the empire within seconds of its transmission. In my head, that sounded much nicer than *killed,* which is far more accurate. It was also accurate that there had been many non-Ullinarian races within the empire and horribly subjugated by them. My attack wouldn't have harmed them directly but certainly, the sudden disappearance of their Masters would have ushered in a bucket-full of calamity. Would that be enough for them to seek revenge? Or would they, in the case of the Rovalorians, launch a campaign to possess the weapon, me, who had set them free? Overall, nothing about any possible scenario I could imagine seemed promising.

And those concerns didn't even include the recent ambush. Someone attacked, either looking to capture me, or our ship. That alone should be enough to demand caution. Unfortunately, it was also enough to garner a certain level of necessity.

"Have you seen Leo's list?" Tony asked, surprisingly diplomatically, at least coming from him. "There's a bunch of busted shit we need to fix, thanks to you. Unless you know of a Wal-Mart close by having a sale on anti-tachyon couplers, we got no other choice."

That was a difficult point to challenge. Although I had only glanced at the list in question, I'd seen enough. Even those repairs we could manage ourselves required accessing the exterior hull. Performing an EVA in deep space is dangerous at the best of times, and I certainly would not allow my cat to walk on the roof.

There had to be a viable, and safer, alternative, and my nanite-enhanced brain raced through the few possibilities at hand.

"What about that abandoned base we passed a few weeks ago? It must have had some kind of repair depot."

Oola's head flopped to the other shoulder. "Are you referencing the one with all the corpses and failing reactor?"

"Good point." That was my only suggestion, and obviously, it wasn't going to solve anything. No one offered further argument. In their minds, presumably, the question was settled. The weight of their collective stares, however, continued the pressure.

"Fine," I conceded at last. "We'll give your idea a shot, but we must take precau—"

"No shit," Tony shouted, already interfacing with the ship to set course. He continued through the mechanical voice of the computer, "with all the damage you caused, we already have our pants down, and it seems we're all out of K-Y Jelly."

"Really?" I glared. "That's where you're going with this?"

"What is *kay why jelly*?" Oola asked.

"Don't." I rolled my eyes. "Just don't."

Chapter 2

The approach to our unknown destination—which still annoyed the crap out of me—was long, but only because I demanded caution and, surprisingly, everyone else consented. Well, *mostly* everyone else consented. Tony insisted my concern was unnecessary because we already proved the superior firepower of our stolen vessel, and thus had no reason to "*act like little old ladies.*" Oola sided with me, though begrudgingly, and broke the tie. Leo was busy washing his tail during the debate and abstained from the final vote.

Tracking the beacon to its source was as simple as following road signs in a town with only two streets. Unfortunately, those two streets led us a considerable distance across the former Ullinarian border. I remained deeply hesitant about this course of action, but Tony and Oola were unmovable. Of course, neither of them were directly responsible for the collapse of the Empire. They helped, no doubt about that, but they were not the ones who designed and finally delivered the fatal program. All on me. My cyber fingerprints packed the insides of every Ullinarian corpse strewn across the galaxy.

I suppose, by my own statements, I should have felt more confident. The program had been fatal, or nearly so. To imagine that the few Ullinarians still living would go to this much trouble over my skin seemed not only paranoid, but also self-centered. Those survivors, and I knew there must be survivors, by now would have more important things to worry about before revenge—like providing themselves with food and shelter without the aid of their technology. I'd removed the infrastructure from their society; kicked their entire way of life out from under them. And, goddammit, they so had it coming.

The Ullinarians were all bastards; slavers, invaders, sociopathic tyrants… so no one would count on people like this to behave rationally. Self-preservation or revenge? Which one would it be? No amount of logic could assuage my fears, and by the time we jumped to normal space, I expected a welcoming committee comprised of fusion torpedoes and concussion rays.

I was wrong. Instead of facing armed resistance, we found ourselves facing something so much worse: traffic.

All sensors registered no aggressive activity, even though local space provided abundant opportunity. We arrived at what I would equate to a major intersection in any large city. There were dozens of ships coming and going. Most of them were Ullinarian, and some were from other societies previously under the thumb of their fallen Empire. But not a single one of them was firing at us; in fact, they seemed to take no notice whatsoever.

I heard a new signal; a short-range transmission regarding approach procedures. The automated instructions came to us in the form of a data stream, not an audio or visual message. Whoever sent them knew exactly who and what we were. This, I was embarrassed to admit, reinforced Tony's assertion that the invitation might just be sincere. The Rovalorians would know all about Ullinarian upgrades, how to contact us, and our inherent value. They must also know controlling us was no longer as simple as it had been. Maybe they really were willing to offer an exchange for services rendered. And maybe an alternate universe existed where people were stupid enough to elect a tacky game-show host President. I wasn't buying that either.

Whether or not the *Rovalorian*s were sincere, there were plenty of other people looking into it. The traffic here wasn't like Veterans Parkway at rush hour; it was the San Diego Freeway during the apocalypse—but faster. We struggled to conform to the specified approach patterns while the hyper-space backwash from ships jumping in and out of normal space constantly dragged against our hull.

All four of us were plugged-in. Like every Ullinarian ship, our assault craft required a minimum of three enhanced operators for optimal performance. A single pilot could manage basic travel, but these circumstances required everyone. Well, not quite. Tony's talent with pulse cannons wasn't really called for with no one shooting at us. I wasn't really doing much to help either. All my attention focused on signs of treachery, while Oola, who was really flying the ship, constantly tried to wrest the sensors from my control. Meanwhile, my beloved cat Leo was doing a fine job regulating the shields against pressure wakes generated by local turbulence.

"Just remember to keep our story straight," I reminded everyone silently. With all our minds inside the computer, communication was almost easier than thinking.

"We know," Tony complained. "We all have memories as good as yours!"

He was right, of course. A multitude of tiny, interconnected computers enhanced all our memories. But again, I was the one with the big, neon target painted on my bare ass. Knowing how well they might remember my instructions was no guarantee of their possible judgment.

"We can discuss judgment later," Oola insisted, her mind to

mine. "I seem to recall a certain revolution…"

Sorry. In my nervous state, I had failed to guard my thoughts from observation. Like I said, communication was easier than thinking and sometimes they bled together. Oola was certainly correct about one thing; several of my recent decisions were far from perfect. Indeed, I had caused more damage and cost more lives than I could ever begin to calculate.

"I'm getting new instructions," Tony reported, sounding thankful to finally have something useful to contribute. "They're requesting I deactivate all weapons. No, they are *insisting* I deactivate all weapons."

"What about the other ships?" I mused publicly. From my position behind the sensors, it looked to me as though most, if not all, the other ships in the area were fully armed. But, I had to admit, none of them were nearly as formidable.

There was only one assault vessel among all the ships in the vicinity. The others consisted of scout ships, freighters and even a few passenger transports. Ours was the only craft capable of destroying everything within half a parsec.

I considered the implication of disarming. In recent days, we had had several altercations with… raiders or bounty hunters. We were never sure, but it was likely my presence on an assault craft could be common knowledge. Likely, in fact. *Services rendered* might be less valuable than a hefty bounty.

"They're getting impatient!"

I knew despite my anxiety that Tony and Oola really wanted to try this.

"Okay," I submitted through the static of our shared minds. "Take the cannons off-line, but leave the interceptors hot. That should convince them we're peaceful, but still capable of defending ourselves."

None of my comrades argued. Tony disarmed the cannons and the nagging calls from our destination ceased. They must have known as well as I that interceptors had little offensive potential. I recognized this was a good faith gesture on their part and struggled to keep that thought hidden.

We continued the specified approach, which led us deeper into an accretion disk of an infant solar system. Most of the rock fragments were no larger than a baseball, but the average distance between them was less than a few thousand feet. Following the approach pattern remained critical; the transmission guided us through a narrow channel, something astronomers on Earth would call a Kirkwood gap, generated by the orbit of something much larger, presumably our destination. I was still hoping for a lush, green world with fresh water and perhaps a sunny beach.

But it was not to be. The only massive objects revealed by my sensors were molten proto planets and dense ribbons of super-heated dust and gasses. Some of the asteroids were large, though not enough to qualify as true planets. The largest was only a couple hundred miles in diameter. I could read several of these in the immediate vicinity, and all of them were emitting energy signatures, suggesting mining operations. What I had recently experienced as fear now congealed into a dull sense of dread. There weren't going to be any beaches, rainfall or even sunshine.

I finally caught a glimpse of our destination, and it was worse than anything I might have anticipated. Several of the larger asteroids had been strung together to form one massive industrial complex. I could see reactors, factories, and ore processing plants projecting from the asteroids like the inflamed pimples that ravaged my face as a teenager. A metal framework tied the various bits of moon-sized rocks together and doubled as docking slips.

This looked to me like the worst of everything. My scans revealed much of the complex was located inside the asteroids themselves, meaning the lack of a planetary surface had not supplanted the presence of caves. And as far as the bits built above ground, the lack of any atmosphere, or even windows from what I could see, meant it was even more enclosed than the last floating assemblage of tin cans we had visited.

"Hell of a holiday." I grimaced. "Looks like the only thing we might find here is a bad case of scurvy!"

"I have received our docking assignment," Oola reported, ignoring my complaint. "Beginning approach."

She was doing fine by herself, so I disengaged from the computer. Everyone seemed remarkably accepting of my absence while they continued to guide the ship towards the indicated berth. Only Fido, who was curled-up in a corner like a loyal cocker spaniel, seemed to notice my change in position. He looked up with his one big eye, appeared to determine nothing was amiss, and returned to his slumber.

I stepped up to the small viewing port and looked out at the complex with my natural eyes. I could see everything when interfaced with the ship and all its glorious technology: all wavelengths of light, magnetic field lines, chemical compositions, temperature, and sometimes even the age of an object relative to its rate of decay. Without this technology, I felt damn near blind, but somehow looking through my own eyes was still something special, a connection to my previous life and my own humanity.

There was nothing to appreciate in this case, however. My unenhanced view was even more garish than what I had observed through the sensors. It was all rocks and metal; factories spewing waste materials into space like gargantuan robber barons of the early twentieth century, farting toxic by-products on their mission of greed and consumption.

I knew I was going to have to table my attitude. My compatriots had made it perfectly clear they wanted to investigate these so-called *opportunities*, and now that it seemed reasonably safe, I no longer had grounds for any legitimate objections. I would simply have to keep my mouth shut and make the best of it.

There was another argument favoring this endeavor, which

no one voiced, but likely shared by all of us. Three months of being cooped up in this ship, confinement, boredom, stress, and not just a little sexual frustration, was wearing on all of us. Distraction, even if that meant employment, offered some measure of relief.

The docking procedure lasted longer than it should have. I suspect upgrades like myself once operated the mooring mechanisms but were now under manual control of beings less suited for the job. I sat on the floor with my Gorlack friend Fido. His was the most alien of all the species encountered so far in my new life. They were about the size and shape of a small horse, but with six legs, each with fully articulated hands or feet—depending on need. They had no internal skeleton, giving them great flexibility, with free-floating organs visible through their semi-transparent, slightly pinkish, skin. His head was a large, nearly featureless, orb with a single eye, anchored to the rest of his body with a long neck. Though very much alive, Gorlacks were never the products of nature but rather a perverse act of biological engineering. Built and bred for strength and adaptability. Their brains were of little interest to those who enslaved them. Over the months I spent with Fido, I had learned their intellect had gone wildly underestimated, probably why they were so eager to launch their own revolution.

We played chess to pass the time with pieces I had cobbled together from spare parts. For a creature whose spoken language was so abstract that even my nanites couldn't translate, he had a good grasp of the rules and strategies of the game. In fact, he was winning.

"Gloop," he said, indicating check. His big eye turned to me, revealing both pride and a sense of apology.

"Hmm." I surveyed the sheet of fabric with the checkerboard pattern drawn on it. A few possible moves were open to me, but each one led to the same conclusion.

The sound of the final docking clamps locking onto our

hull spared me the humiliation of losing the game to an alien who learned to play only last week. Everyone not losing at chess disengaged from the computer and started moving about the cabin, ignoring me. Only Leo came to my side and observed the board. I don't know how much he understood about the game; since his upgrade, he understood more than most cats, or even humans, so I had to assume he too knew I had already lost.

"Well?" I prompted, since they seemed unwilling to offer information. "What now?"

Tony still ignored me, but Oola was at least willing to answer. Her species was short on many traits common to humans, including suspicion, deceit, sarcasm and humor. Perhaps resentment was also among those things lacking.

"We are preparing to be boarded and inspected. A local representative will speak with us."

"Does this mean you're done bitching?" Tony asked, finally acknowledging my participation. He didn't wait for my response, though, before marching to the airlock at the far end of the ship, passed the barriers of curtains and makeshift furniture.

I nodded, not that he could see the gesture. "Yes. Yes, it does. What are the conditions out there?"

"High humidity, oxygen, argon... nothing harmful. But the sodium vapor sounds unpleasant."

The reason for the salty air became all too obvious as Tony welcomed the Rovalorian inspectors aboard. I knew almost everything about this species and their society, but like everything else in my implanted memories, the knowledge resided just below the threshold of consciousness until the right stimuli unleashed a torrent of awareness. I greeted their arrival with a kind of blasé surprise, shocked only by my own lack of surprise.

Rovalorians definitely deserved an award for the strangest life form in the galaxy, second only to Gorlacks. They stood about four feet tall on short legs with big wide feet. Their torso, covered in a kind of simple gown, was tubular, almost like a bowling pin, and covered in thick scales in a rainbow of colors. Their arms were long and ended in well-articulated, delicate webbed fingers. Atop the slender part of their torso were heads too small to accommodate anything except their large clam-like mouths; even their eyes protruded almost entirely outside their tiny skulls. It would be hard to believe by their appearance that this species were some of the most brilliant engineers in the galaxy. The reason for this was simple; their brains only began in the head while the bulk of their considerable cerebral mass ran the full length of their spine. They were definitely the smartest walking fish you could ever hope to meet.

Leo was licking his chops while they scanned the command deck. Only when the scans were complete did one of them give us the slightest notice. The fish waved one of his or her boney hands, and indicated we should all stand before it as a group. I decided it was male, a totally arbitrary conclusion. I didn't know how to sex a fish on Earth, and I didn't know how to do it here. Not like I was going to ask him to dinner and a movie either way.

"I am Agent Scheleene. You will report to me for the duration of your stay. Who is captain of this vessel?"

I had been down this road before. Tony and Oola had no qualms about bullying me into following their foolish schemes, but when confronted by anyone in authority, they always turned their heads in my direction. Typical. Once again, they elected me leader without any consultation on the matter.

With I sigh, I gave the big fish a little wave.

Scheleene said nothing and instead tapped a few buttons on his computer pad. He then stepped forward and, to my horror, stabbed a fat cylindrical device that I hadn't even realized he carried, against my collarbone. I felt the pinch of a sub-dermal transfer, and the resulting lump left behind by the marker.

"The implant will give you access to most of the station and allow us to track your movements. We can remove it upon your departure. What's your name?"

"Jason Miller," I said, rubbing the still-stinging implant site.

He entered my name on the pad. "Have you chosen a designation for this vessel?"

"No, we never thought about that," Tony said, his mind apparently already cooking-up something. "How about *Bad Ass*...Or *Balls of Steel*...?"

I balked at being associated with a ship, or anything else for that matter, called *Balls of Steel*. But before I could object or offer a better suggestion, Scheleene added the information without opinion.

"You were a database?" the agent asked, continuing his entries.

"Yes, and the same for Oola."

The fish looked up to see who I was talking about. He surveyed and tagged the female Olemsi, he returned to his pad.

"My name is Oola Oola."

He made the correction and then looked at Tony. I could see the fish visually measure the circumference of Tony's massive biceps, rock-hard pecs and brick-like torso. "Tactical?"

Tony nodded and got tagged.

"Is there a mechanic?"

I pointed to the floor. "He's sniffing your feet."

"Oh." Scheleene seemed amused, but not terribly surprised. "We haven't seen one of these before. Is he an Earth creature?"

"Yes." To me, this was an exciting question. For the first time, I was beginning to think Tony and Oola had been correct to bring us here. "You know about Earth creatures?"

"Certainly." Scheleene nodded his tiny head. "We've had

many people from your planet through. Only two or three of them were not human; I think they're called dogs."

Scheleene continued talking while he tagged Leo. "You are about to ask if I can direct you to your Earth. That is usually the first question I get from new arrivals. Earth, or Olemsi-Myucuc, or Tapperlon, or wherever. Our Ullinarian navigational data is in the mainframe. You should know by now that we can't keep anything from you once you're interfaced, so you are free to use whatever information you find. All we ask is you perform certain duties and leave the system intact... Where did you find a Gorlack?"

"Ah..." I froze. After all the trouble I had gone through to make up a cover story and then rehearse it with all the members of my group, I was the one who almost went blank. "We found him."

If that didn't sound lame, I don't know what would. Fortunately, Oola was much more composed and took the lead.

"All of us awoke in a storage facility," she lied, remembering the plan with grace. If the Rovalorians knew her species as well as I thought I did, then her telling this story would give us even greater credibility. "We were among dozens of unassigned upgrades and a few prisoners, including the Gorlack and several K'Nostrons[1]. The Ullinarians were already dead when we woke. The other upgrades were unwilling to accompany us when we took this ship."

Scheleene accepted the story and entered it into his computer. He had probably heard it before with some variations. If everyone's personal details were on record, I would be able to get a fair picture of just what had transpired across the Empire since the liberation.

"You chose your ship well. This is the first assault craft we

---

[1] K'Nostrons: A species of intelligent, anthropomorphic plant, created by the Ullinarians as their first foray into building a slave-based work force. The K'Nostrons eventually rebelled, grew into an Empire of their own, also dependant on slaves in the form of Gorlacks. Their botanical name, if one exists, should be *Invasius Shitheadicus*.

have seen since the war and the *data bomb*."

"War?" I asked, trying to sound casual.

The fish nodded. "The Ullinarians and K'Nostrons finally went to war after centuries of preparation. It only lasted a few hours before the *data bomb* destroyed the Ullinarians and freed you upgrades. We assume it was from the K'Nostrons, but then their Gorlacks saw the opportunity and revolted. Again, all of this is in our main computer, so you will have the chance to catch-up on everything."

"I look forward to it," I gushed, in all sincerity. But honestly, I was more interested in the phrase *data bomb*. It obviously referred to the invasive programs I devised and transmitted throughout the entire Ullinarian Empire, an event that both allowed liberation and wrought genocide.

"Exactly how do these *opportunities* you advertised work?" Tony asked through the translator given to him on TBNL[2]. My nanites were capable of instantaneously translating all languages known by the Ullinarians, but Tony, as a mere weapons component, did not receive this particular ability. I only hoped the Rovalorian would not ask how or where he obtained the device.

"The newly formed Rovalorian Central Authority is trying to regain control of all facilities within our territory. Since the Ullinarians used bio-upgrades for all functions, we are converting everything to manual control, but we can't do it from the outside. We need your assistance to make these transfers. As payment, we can provide you with information, supplies, fuel… anything but weapons."

"Moral objection?" I asked, incredulous.

Scheleene's tiny head wobbled. "We have been dominated

---

[2] TBNL: A deep-space colony consisting of many alien races, unable to settle on a name for their collective refuge, so TBNL, an acronym for *To Be Named Later*, became the accepted designation. This is where the *Balls of Steel* crew sought sanctuary, and subsequently destroyed when Jason Miller instigated cosmic war centering on the colony. Oddly enough, the former residents of TBNL, now abandoned, regarded this disaster as the best possible outcome.

by one race already. We won't provide another with anything that may one day be used against us. All we want is to restore what's rightfully ours and live in peace."

I had no way of telling whether or not that was true. And even if their desire for peace was true today, it may not be true tomorrow. Either way, it was not my concern—unless I found myself in a position where I might have to make a moral choice of my own. And when it came to making moral choices, my scorecard was less than sterling.

There were hundreds of questions burning in my brain, and I hoped those answers would be found in the Rovalorian computer.

Chapter 3

My first impression of the facility was like a visit to the seashore—with lots of exceptions. The warm, damp, salty air was the same as I remembered from my visit to the Caribbean coast of Mexico. But the visceral sense of tranquility was short-lived. For one thing, the docking strut was gloomy, with a heavy atmosphere and a thin film of rust coating everything. All the structures rose from low mass asteroids, so artificial gravity supplemented the natural conditions. Furthermore, it was ramped-up far beyond that of our vessel, or even the Earth. This made for a sluggish sensation, further adding to the bleakness of these surroundings.

The dock was essentially an enclosed, reinforced tube running between rocks. Scheleene led the members of my group down the passage to an expansive cavern, hollowed from the pores of a large asteroid. This had been the product of great skill and advanced technology; the walls were a mix of arched metal ribs and living stone, reaching several stories overhead. The chamber was brightly lit, too brightly, almost to the point of sadism, emanating from no perceptible source. Within the harsh glare, noisy crowds of sentient beings bustled about on various, and in many cases, incomprehensible business. Many voices echoed off the walls like distant thunder, spoken in a multitude of languages and contexts so it was impossible for even my enhanced brain to process.

Despite the cavern's level of structural sophistication, it more closely resembled a wharf-side dive in one of those small countries no one ever heard of until a violent uprising makes the evening news. Grime and rust coated every surface and a bouquet of noxious odors permeated every breath. Dozens of *people* worked around the chamber as boxes and equipment were transported through a stockade of gates and security desks, all staffed by Rovalorians.

Scheleene led us through a security point without objection from the clerk. "This is the exchange hall, our main port for new arrivals. Avoid the tunnels marked with a red frame; those are for robot transports. Here, take these."

The fish handed Tony, Oola and me each a device that looked like a thick credit card. As soon as it touched my fingers, I could feel the silicon crystals beneath calling for me to interface. I resisted, waiting for further instructions.

"We have tasks for a mechanic, but can your cat hold one of these?"

I instructed Fido to help Leo, and to stay with him. Even though I couldn't trust these people yet, I knew for certain I could trust my Gorlack.

"Keep these with you at all times," Scheleene instructed, reluctantly giving the last card to Fido. "These contain your designated tasks, where to perform them, and the amount of credit you'll receive upon completion. The card will also record your earnings, which you can spend at any of our facilities."

"Our vessel sustained some exterior damage," Oola stated without recrimination, but I detected a jab anyway. "Is remote repair available?"

"The Dock Master can arrange that for you. Contact information and fees are listed."

"Well. I guess we'll get started. Thanks." I had already seen as much of this filthy hellhole as I cared to. The sooner we completed some work, the sooner we would get the information we came looking for.

Scheleene left us. Fido held Leo's instructions while my cat interfaced. With a satisfied meow, Leo trotted off with Fido close behind, like a cat on a mission.

I gathered the rest of my group into a little circle. "Let's not get distracted. Remember, we're looking for our homes, and any information on the Gorlack revolution. And if at all possible—"

"We already know this," Oola scolded politely. "You do not have to tend to us like children. I will speak with the Dock Master."

If Tony had an objection of his own, he failed to voice it. Instead, his eyes lit up like two exploding suns and his right index finger stabbed through the air towards an unknown target.

"Tits!" he screamed.

So much for avoiding distraction. Oola and I both turned to face the direction of the arrow (actually, by this point, there was more than one arrow pointed across the room, both originating from Tony).

Indeed, there was a pair of breasts entering the chamber, attached to an attractive young woman with shaggy dishwater hair. Her clothes were a mishmash of alien cultures, much of which may have been purchased here or at a similar facility. She had come from one of the other docking corridors and now chatted with the fishy gate clerk. Their banter seemed friendly. Obviously not her first visit. A collection of aliens, some species I recognized and a few I did not, were already pushing carts of metal cases away from what I assumed was her ship.

"I'm going in," Tony announced to no one's surprise. I could smell his testosterone surging, mixing with the salt in the air like a cocktail of approaching disaster.

Before I could warn him back, Tony launched himself into a near run across the crowded reception area.

"My mistake," Oola lamented.

We watched from across the room as Tony made contact. The woman faced him stoically as he leaned across the fish's desk, trying to look casual as he chatted-her-up like fresh meat at a singles bar. I couldn't hear his sales pitch, but when his target erupted with laughter, I had a good idea what he might have said.

When the Rovalorian behind the desk, who had also been watching the exchange, began laughing as well, Tony's head sank and he slinked back to us. His face was a bright red hue; apparently, humiliation is one thing our nanites are not qualified to fix. He'd resumed his casual demeanor by the time he reached us, but I could see how much effort it was taking to stay casual.

Tony cleared his throat. "She's… um… busy."

Oola's head tilted all the way to one side so that her ear rested on one shoulder. "I am unfamiliar with your species' mating rituals…was that common?"

"No!" I shouted, enjoying myself a little too much. Then I considered my own success in that regard back in my previous existence on Earth. "Actually… it is."

"Well," Tony's eyes flitted around, refusing to settle on any one thing, an obvious attempt to shake off his embarrassment. "I guess we can't let the cat do all the work, so let's get to it."

I held the card to my forehead and interfaced. This was much different from what I had experienced before, and come to expect. I received a quick rush of data instead of falling into a great ocean of information. It was more like reading a postcard than merging with a network or even a single computer.

The data... *injection*... dumped a menu of options into my brain. Just as Scheleene said, each option listed a specific task, directions, and value. I chose to take them in order.

"So, I'll see you guys back at the ship," I said, resisting the urge to warn them once again about... everything. But more than worrying, I needed information, and the only way to get it was by doing my job. Funny... I had a job. No matter where you go in the universe, unless you were born rich or royal, you have to punch a fucking clock.

I followed subway passage one-one-three as if I'd been doing it all my life. There must be a map and full schematic included in the... program. I didn't need the enhanced processing speed provided by my nanites to recognize the inherent danger. The card didn't just inject data into my head, but an actual program, accepted, and now running by my own consciousness. The Rovalorians definitely had a good grasp of this technology; indeed, they might even have been the ones who initially designed most of it.

I worked my way through the crowded chamber, pushing through crowds of multiple aliens. The variety of species here were even more diverse than the collection of refugees on TBNL. Even the most ambitious Earth-born biologist would go insane trying to catalogue all the physical attributes on display in this room alone.

Despite my curiosity of the surrounding figures, only one appeared even remotely curious about me. The creature was a fearsome construction, shorter than me, but brutishly thick. His head and arms were the color of sand, covered with tufts of hateful gray hair. His eyes, squid-like, irregular shaped pupils circled in red and yellow, fixated on me with the same dedication of a wolf stalking a rabbit.

My nanites quickly identified the figure as a Benzonite, followed by a flood of detailed information about the species and home world, which I forced to the back of my brain. I focused only on his scrutiny of me. His gaze was intense, and although he made no move in my direction, his twisted eyes followed my every step.

Implanted instructions led me across the busy dock to another massive corridor, the center of which was a red strip where a robotic train transported the heavier cargo. Before entering the corridor, I glanced back to the exchange hall. The Benzonite was still watching, but again, didn't seem inclined to follow me. Maybe I was the first human he'd ever seen, or perhaps he just thought I looked appealing in a culinary way. Or maybe I was just paranoid, and shouldn't give this another thought.

I decided to just get on with my work and followed the walking path that ran alongside the train, only to face a grisly discovery a few hundred feet in.

The contoured bed set into the stone walls was a familiar sight; my adventure in this strange world began in such a device. However, the dried, bloody stain, where the former operator's head once rested, was an addition.

I knew there had been a lengthy period, nearly half an hour, between my first and second... *data bombs*... when the Ullinarians, in facilities like this, had an opportunity, indeed even a mandate from their point of view, to start executing their liberated slaves. The reddish brown stain was the only memorial that poor upgrade would ever have; his or her name erased from history.

Just how much blood was on my hands?

Fortunately, I didn't need to climb into the bed. I held Scheleene's card in one hand, placed the other against the machinery and interfaced. This is where the Rovalorian's knowledge really showed itself. The implanted program told me what I was supposed to do, but not how to do it. This was the despicable genius of nano technology; my creativity and experience were tools no artificial construct could ever duplicate.

The former operator of this terminal had controlled eight

mining drones, now tethered to the side of this rock gathering dust. I had to enable them for manual control. This was promising; maybe the fish people really did want to continue without the need for slaves.

I spent nearly an hour restructuring all the drones assigned to this terminal. The card gave me ten credits, probably the galactic version of minimum wage. Fortunately, my nanites kept a complete record of everything I did, so the following stop required far less effort. Another sawbuck and I moved on to the next.

By the time I reached the end of the super corridor, I had earned over two hundred credits and completed half the duties on my schedule. The gravity was much lower here; I had traveled the full length of this particular strut and was now near an adjoining rock, apparently converted to ore processing. There was one last terminal to modify, but I heard a woman's laughter before I even had a chance to disengage.

It was easy for me to access the local sensors from this location. From my position inside the network, I could see myself, standing next to the grisly operator's bed like some ridiculous mannequin while a pair of blue-collar working fish hung out with a human female, the same woman Tony had struck-out with a few hours ago. She was joking with the Rovalorians, yet staring at me.

Avoiding her stare was easy cooking. I just pretended to work, even though the task had become routine and was finished almost as soon as I arrived. Unfortunately, this woman was likely as familiar with this kind of thing as I was. She turned and waved at the nearest security camera after a few minutes of watching me.

While interfaced, I was incapable of blushing, but would have done so had it been possible, especially after she pointed at herself, mimed talking with her right hand, and then pointed directly at the camera. Then she nodded and smiled, apparently expecting a response. I might have continued to feign ignorance, except that she left her company and came to stand at the end of the bed.

"Oh shit," I mumbled to myself, and disengaged.

Turning to face the woman, I was prepared to apologize for whatever insensitive, idiotic pick-up line Tony might have used, but I never got the chance.

"I saw you earlier in the exchange hall," she said. "You were with that twit in the cop costume."

Not sure whether this was a question or not, I merely nodded.

"And there was another person with you. An Olemsi?"

"Yes. We call her Oola."

The woman nodded as if she had just uncovered some tremendously important secret. The look on her face seemed impossible to decode. I could tell I had just revealed something, but for the life of me, I couldn't begin to guess what.

"My name is Betty," she said, revealing nothing beyond face value. "I used to be Betty Flannigan of Sioux Falls, South Dakota, but now everyone calls me Captain Betty. They grabbed me in 1962. What about you?"

"Jason. Jason Miller. I was abducted in 2015."

Her lower lip curled inward and she frowned, as if disappointed I didn't give the response she wanted. If there was something more, she shrugged it off. "I've met several other humans in the past few weeks. So far, I haven't met anyone abducted before 1940 or after 2021. I'm not sure what that means."

That is *information I can use*, I thought, and considered the implications.

"I can't be certain," I said, "But it feels like I was in service for more than six years."

Betty nodded. "No kidding. That's what I've been trying to deduce. As far as I can see, there are a few possibilities: either people were abducted after 2021 and I haven't met them yet, or for some reason humans became less desirable, or the Earth became… unavailable."

That gave me a shiver. I could think of only two reasons why our species might have become unavailable for harvesting by the year 2021, and neither of them was particularly optimistic. Self-annihilation seemed most likely based on everything I remembered from the day. With this new reality, however, I knew of one other, possibly more likely, explanation was the K'Nostrons had expanded in such a way that Earth, and her abundant supply of water, had come to lie within the borders of their Empire.

I put my fears aside and asked the one question foremost in my desire to know the answer to. "Have you figured out the location of the Earth?"

She snickered, her eyes bright and even a little wet. "No! Nor have I been looking. At the time of my capture, I was over sixty and living on a farm in the middle of nowhere. My husband was a lazy, racist drunk who knocked me around every Sunday after church. I don't give a damn about Earth, and have no interest in ever going back."

The amount of venom carried in her otherwise melodic voice surprised me, but, at the same time, I understood. After all, South Dakota… maybe the only spot on planet Earth that could make central Illinois seem picturesque. Except maybe Oklahoma. Or Kansas. Or fucking Nebraska… Suddenly, but only momentarily, I didn't care about finding Earth either.

"I don't know what else to do with myself." The words escaped my mouth before I realized I even spoke them. Usually, I could keep my personal thoughts and feelings closer to the vest, especially with strangers. But it was true; my main reason for seeking my home planet was that I didn't have a better idea.

Betty smiled and nodded as if she recognized my existential crisis. There was no way she could understand the full depths of my position.

"Life isn't so bad here, once you get used to how things

are. People like you and me are in a great position; we're desperately needed by a number of different cultures.

"I was fortunate," she continued. "I woke in a freighter with only a small Ullinarian crew who didn't know what to do about us. They died from the second transmission before they received instructions from base. Now it's my ship and the Rovalorians pay me lots of money to transport minerals between here and home world.

"Don't be afraid of your potential, or your abilities. Make the most of what fate has given you. What kind of ship do you guys have?"

Don't be afraid... I wanted to laugh. This woman meant well, I understood that, but if she only had half an idea of what she was talking about—or rather, to *whom* she was talking. Afraid? Just what kind of abilities does she think I might fear? The ability to manipulate two empires simultaneously and kicking their imperial Nazi asses' right out of existence? Oh yeah, I've already done that.

"Arrow class assault vessel," I informed her, pleased by the sudden look of awe on her face. Now I get why so many old men drive red corvettes. "Long story."

"I would love to hear it. Meet me for a drink later?"

Now was my turn to look surprised. No one ever seemed to show interest in me during my existence back on Earth. I sometimes thought I might be invisible. However, both her tone and expression seemed to carry no undertones, sexual or otherwise. It was in fact so very casual that I couldn't help but be suspicious, especially after her total dismissal of Tony's advances.

"I guess so." My lame response probably revealed considerably more than I would have intended.

If Betty divined anything from my words, she didn't let it show. "There's a bar in the upper gallery of the exchange hall. It's just a hole in the wall, but that's all they have here for socializing. I'll be there later. Drop by when you get the chance.

I may be able to make you an offer; your ship's firepower could expand my business opportunities, and make both of us a lot of money."

She turned and sauntered back to her associates. Money? So far, in this brave, new world, I had launched two revolutions, one colossal war and committed genocide on a scale that would be the envy of every despot in human history. If money was really my primary concern, I'm sure I could get that without anyone's help. This current endeavor, this job, was more a ruse to gain intelligence rather than the accumulation of wealth.

This led me to conclude that Betty might have something of value after all: information. Even though I had awakened some weeks before her, I've tried to keep outside the margins of galactic activity ever since. Well, *hiding* from the rest of the galaxy would be a better description.

I was gaining some useful intel from the outpost's mainframe, but it was mostly dry statistics, trade routes and schedules, and the best places to acquire qweellie beetles[3]. Navigational data, so far, included little more than warnings. I've already plotted every neutron star in the galaxy, and a few potholes.

Whenever possible, never rely on a single source. Captain Betty's direct experience could provide a wealth of details the Rovalorians might conceal. I would have to think about meeting her while I continued my duties.

---

[3] Qweellie Beetles: Flying insects indigenous to the first moon of Dipturia, and inadvertently spread across the quadrant. Rovalorians regard the qweellie as a much sought-after delicacy, served at spawnings, funerals, cosmetic sales parties and trade conventions. Naturally, they taste like chicken.

Chapter 4

I worked for nearly twenty hours before *clocking out* for the day. Reprogramming interface stations was tedious, but the experience of interfacing was, as always, seductive and emotionally satisfying. That aspect of the nanites was one of many ways the Ullinarians managed their slaves. It's hard to fight bondage when the chains are so addictive.

On my way back to our ship, I stopped at the local equivalent of a cafeteria. It was nothing more than a small room filled with automated dispensers. Nothing fancy. Nothing to write home about, but the absence of Guy Fieri[4] and his stupid hair made up for the lack of creative kitchen staff. I paid five credits with my data card and received a tube of flavorless, yet surprisingly enjoyable, paste loaded with copper and silicone that my body required for nanite replication. Indeed, the Rovalorians were masters of this technology.

I purchased a few extra tubes before resuming my way to

---

[4] Guy Fieri: Obnoxious television host and professional eater, prone to wearing sunglasses backwards.

the ship. The exchange hall was just as busy as the last time I passed through; suggesting this outpost was a major hub in whatever strategy engaged the Rovalorians. At least the creepy Benzonite had left, though I still wondered about his fascination—if indeed, his fascination was real and not just a product of my paranoid imagination. I had only observed him once, so I concluded the latter must be the case.

Upon entering the gangway to my ship, I reconsidered.

The Benzonite was standing by the access hatch. He wasn't watching me. He hadn't even seen me yet, but he was definitely trying to gain entry. I didn't know if any of my friends were aboard or still out working around the outpost. Regardless, this registered as an obvious threat, though it might have nothing to do with the data bomb or me. As Captain Betty had alluded, this vessel was an enviable piece of artillery, and possibly the only one of its kind in the service of former slaves. Of course, I had altered the ships computers in such a way that no one could do so much as turn on a light without my permission. Presumably, everyone on this facility familiar with liberated upgrades would know that.

I wish Tony were here. At least my absent companion's physique was substantial enough to provide some intimidation to the massive creature picking my lock. As for me, I was an old man in the body of a weak, skinny young adult. My stature wouldn't intimidate a newly hatched leper cockroach—which became a serious point of concern when the Benzonite finally noticed me watching.

He whipped around to face me, his tufts of gray hair rising to double his apparent size. Not only was he impressive in mere mass, but his body was clad in armor and several tools dangled from his belt, any of which could deliver a lethal blow.

I was prepared to retreat to the exchange hall and summon Scheleene, or any Rovalorian for help. They *had* guaranteed our safety, and I was prepared to test it. Fortunately, the situation abated without conflict. I started to step back from the approaching thug when I felt a brush against my shin and heard the sound of a familiar, yet unintelligible, greeting, followed by sloshy footsteps.

"Meow."

The Benzonite stopped. His protruding hairs went from erect to sweeping backwards in a surprisingly cat-like manner. But it wasn't the arrival of my cat that stopped him, but rather that of my Gorlack who, despite his gentility and kindness, was one fearsome motherfucker given the right incentive. The Benzonite turned abruptly and thundered down the gangway in the opposite direction.

"Gloop. Gloop-gloop?"

"I don't know what that was about," I said, guessing the question. "But from now on, I want you to stay with the ship."

Fido's response was a quick, six-legged gallop to the hatch where he assumed an alert posture. I had nothing more to worry about regarding intruders or thieves.

Neither of my other friends were around when Leo and I entered. The peace and quiet was delightfully refreshing, especially after the controlled chaos of the outpost, but I couldn't help but be concerned after that brief encounter. If the Benzonite connected me with our ship, certainly he would do the same with Tony and Oola.

Perhaps I could track them down using the facility's computer. I'd already discovered that interfacing with the local equipment did not lend the same kind of access I had achieved on TBNL, far from it. During my workday, I had divided my interface time with performing the job, and searching for information, of which I had obtained very little. Scheleene hadn't been completely honest. Their computers did have abundant data, but buried behind firewalls and layers of convoluted obfuscation. Whether from my experience aboard TBNL, or just a human proclivity to cheat, I was able to push passed some of their safeguards without notice. I was willing to go much farther.

I slipped into the command chair and, with Leo in my lap—as it should be—joined the digital bliss of cyberspace. First thing I did was check the condition of the ship itself. As I hoped, there was no evidence of interference or access from the Benzonite or anyone else. Robot mechanics were conducting the external repairs arranged, and presumably paid for, by Oola. Their work was progressing quickly, which left me partially relieved so I then turned my attention to the outposts' sensors. I couldn't get so much as a temperature reading, but my own sensors penetrated the nearest regions of the facility. I could see Fido, keeping himself amused by sweeping the corridor as he guarded the hatch, and much to my relief, I spied Tony and Oola approaching, their arms burdened with numerous silver boxes.

"Where have you been?" I asked, disengaging from the computer when my companions entered the command deck. "And what are you wearing?"

"We've been shopping!" Oola declared, almost glowing. "There are shops in the gallery above the exchange hall. Tony has been telling me about your planet's *Malls*. What a brilliant idea. We traded grain for items we couldn't make ourselves. This is much more fun."

Both Tony and Oola each wore a one-piece garment constructed of a shiny brown material, that appeared so loose from the waist up, one could use that area to store canned goods, and so tight below the belt that nothing was left to the imagination, which, I had to admit, looked good on Tony. He assured me it was quite comfortable and, allegedly, fireproof.

"What's better," Tony added, "lookie here, no translator."

Now, that was a surprise. "How?"

"Just like my iPhone back home. I bought an app, downloaded, and boom! I can now understand every language. Except for Gorlack. By the way, did you know Fido is outside scrubbing down the gangway?"

"Do you think that's wise?"

Tony shrugged. "It *is* dirty."

"No! Downloading an alien program into your brain?"

"We've been doing that all day, you know. Is there really a choice?"

Fair point; we had been allowing alien programs into our heads all day, but I was concerned about that as well. He was equally correct in that we didn't have much choice. The entire predicament was all just a means to an end, only I was still uncertain whose means to what end.

"Did you find any useful information? That is kinda the reason for being here."

Oola's head flopped to one side, her species' version of a shrug. "Some. Probably nothing you haven't found. Although, I was speaking to a Tartarlan trader—the embargo is over since there is no longer an Empire to enforce it—and they've begun trading with liberated Gorlacks. It seems the Gorlacks are fond of alcohol."

Well, I thought to myself, *who isn't?* "Anything about Benzonites?"

"Benzonites..." Oola repeated the name. "Their planet was surveyed by the Ullinarians some time ago, but no actions taken. The population posed a greater threat to the K'Nostrons so were ignored. Why?"

Obviously, Oola knew exactly as much about them as I did, which came as no surprise. I replayed my encounters with the unnamed Benzonite. Neither seemed concerned.

"Probably just another trader," Tony suggested dismissively. "Asshole probably got a hard-on for this sweet-ass firecracker."

Oola was visibly confused, so I translated. "The Benzonite might want to take our ship. I was thinking the same thing. I told Fido to stay on guard just in case he tries to steal it."

The Olemsi shook her melon colored head. "I don't think that's a concern. One thing I did learn from the traders is that they trust the Rovalorians. Security here is reliable."

I remained unconvinced, especially knowing Oola's proclivity for naivety. "Nonetheless," I warned, "watch for that Benzonite, and keep your distance."

They agreed and continued unpacking their haul.

Cradling sleepy Leo in my arms like a baby, I plopped back down in the command chair. So far, the entire day spent searching for useful information had been a near total bust. I still had no navigational data that might lead me back home, and almost nothing about the current state of the Ullinarian Empire. Perhaps it was time to abandon covert snooping, and simply ask someone with a bit more experience.

"I can use a drink," I announced and stood, carefully placing Leo in the warm depression my butt left in the command chair. He stretched and yawned, then nestled himself into a tight yellow ball.

Tony looked-up from adjusting his voluminous sleeves. "Where are you going?"

"I have a date."

"A date? With who?"

"Captain Betty. You know, that pair of tits who turned you down. Don't wait up."

I had no sexual interest in Captain Betty, of course, but the look of quiet rage on Tony's face as I exited the ship was priceless. And I was more convinced than ever that keeping this date was the right course of action. Even though I had awakened weeks before Betty, she had been interacting around the galaxy for some time now. The best intelligence we'd gathered so far came from Oola's small talk with traveling salesmen.

Outside the ship, I passed Fido frantically cleaning the corridor. His one big eye was alight with glee as three of his six feet scrubbed the rust and grime with bits of old cloth. I left him to his OCD and made my way to the exchange hall, still a throng of activity. This was indeed a 'round the clock facility.

Brent D. Seth

I recognized Scheleene inducting a new group across the room, two Olemsi and several furry aliens who my nanites identified as Cretellians.

The route to the upper galleries consisted of a ramp carved from the asteroid's flesh, winding like a corkscrew around and up from the floor of the exchange hall. As I climbed, looking for my rendezvous, I passed many of the shops my friends had mentioned. I could understand their excitement. Considering everything we had seen and experienced since awakening, these shops were a new blast of exotic inducements.

At a midpoint in the rising passage, I took a cursory glance at the room below. My eyes met the severe intensity of the Benzonite staring back.

We remained locked in eye contact and I felt a knot form in my gut. The wisest course of action might be to leave this facility the very second our repairs were complete. We hadn't accomplished anything else so far except possibly exposing ourselves to danger. However, the choice to stay or leave became inconsequential once the Benzonite turned away and entered a corridor labeled *Shuttle Transfer Point*.

A drink sounded even better now. I shrugged off the creepy sensation and followed the route to the very top. Betty had been correct; this place was, quite literally, a hole in the wall. Beyond the circular, chiseled opening, a narrow passage plunged into the depths of the asteroid and widened into a dome-shaped chamber. On the surface, this place seemed like any tavern you might find in the seedier side of any large city. I heard clinking glasses and the low drone of whispered conversations. I smelled the tang of alcohol and sweat. The dim lights, resulting from neglect rather than any pursuit of ambiance, helped obscure the dirty floor, tattered furniture and scurrying, well-fed insects. A specter of heavy smoke wafted through the compartment, pungent and pervasive.

I spied Betty sitting at a table by herself, close to a group of feathery ammonia breathers—the source of the noxious cloud.

She appeared oblivious to the various odors, so I quickly hid my own disgust and approached.

"I'm glad you could join me. Care for a drink?"

I glanced at the glass she was holding; it looked half-melted, her fingers were leaving an impression in the material, literally, and the contents smelled corrosive. Betty summoned a blue-skinned waiter and I ordered something a little safer. It scurried off and I turned my attention back to her.

We made small talk, mainly concerning the duties I had been performing. It was a strangely innocuous conversation considering we were the only two humans meeting in a wharfside alien bar, but it didn't take long before Betty took the next step.

"So, Jason," she began between swigs. "How were you picked up?" It seemed like a simple question, certainly one easily answered. Thanks to my mechanically enhanced memory, I could recall nearly every experience of my entire life with more accuracy than filmed documentation. However, the answer was problematic. She probably assumed my recent history would be similar to her own, and that of any other liberated upgrades she may have encountered in recent weeks. Betty could have no idea just how deep my involvement in galactic affairs was, or how much her current life depended on those actions.

I had come to this facility for information, and I wasn't getting it by being sneaky. This woman likely knew as much about what was going on around the galaxy as anyone else, so I decided to take the risk.

"I was driving home in late November..."

An entire day, local time, passed while I spilled my guts. We drank gallons of alcohol and watched the tavern's staff change shifts twice. Betty asked a few questions along the way, but mostly she just listened and drank. I finally completed my story, rendering Captain Betty nearly speechless. Her mouth hung open, almost as wide as her bulging eyes. There were now thousands of people like us, former slaves, roaming the galaxy. She probably never expected to meet the person who set her free. Moreover, if Betty had thought about these events, and I can only assume she had, her guesses would have had no similarity to the reality sitting across from her. And who could blame her: a gay, scrawny (formerly old and fat), stock boy from nowheresville Illinois, destroyer of empires...?

"It was you?" Betty asked, after several minutes of contemplation. "You are responsible for the Data Bomb *and* the Gorlack revolution?"

"Shh," I warned, looking around the bar to see if anyone heard. Ambient noise levels were high, so I felt reasonably safe. "Fido was responsible for his people's revolution. But, yeah, otherwise it was me."

Betty drained another glass and shook her head. "I've been trading across this sector for weeks. I've heard lots of speculation on who might have been responsible, but none of its even close. Don't get me wrong, I'm thrilled to be free, but..."

I ordered another round of drinks while she digested the revelation. Confiding in Betty had been a risk. I knew that from the beginning. Now I was going to find out what possible benefits that risk might bring.

"Damn," Betty declared, slamming another drink as soon as it arrived. "Do you know how many people are looking for you? Hell, there's a bounty on your head so large I'm considering turning you in myself."

"But you won't."

My confidence was false, but well placed. After a moment's scrutiny, Betty agreed.

"No, I won't. In fact, I have a better idea. You see, I've stumbled on something that could pose a threat to us both and everyone like us. Interested?"

I could already see another river of alcohol in my near future, another story waiting to be told. This time, I would be the passenger with another decision to make upon conclusion. Before the trip began, however, a small yellow visitor leapt into my lap. Leo purred and butted his head against my belly until I submitted and scratched his neck.

"Oh," Betty cooed. "This must be Leo. What a sweetie."

I'm sure the pride showed on my face like a full moon in December, but I was verbally accosted from behind before I could utter a single word.

"Have you been here this whole time?" Tony barked, understandably annoyed. "We thought you were dead. I could just kill you."

"Sorry."

"Sorry? Is that the best you got?" Tony snarled, and then pivoted towards my companion. His anger flipped to flirtation in a single heartbeat. "Hi there, gorgeous."

Oola sidled up behind Tony, her nostril flaring. "We have been working hard to supply the ship while you have been drinking your own earnings. I do not find that a wise use of our credit." She spoke in her typical calm demeanor but didn't fool me. I could see the venom behind her orange face.

"I can cover the tab," said Betty, addressing my jury. "The Rovalorians pay me a fortune."

"Or I'd be happy to cover *your* tab," Tony had obviously forgotten me, which stung a little, especially as I watched him swell south of the equator. "I'd love to hear about all your exciting adventures with the Raviolis…"

A flush of red passed over Betty's face before her nanites could enact corrective measures, but I saw it. Her expression also made it perfectly clear to me that she wasn't going to continue her story until we were alone.

"Here's my card," I offered, squirming under Oola's shame-inducing scowl. "Get whatever else we need and change the rest for hard currency. There are still a number of places around the galaxy that accept Ullinarian crowns."

Oola snapped the card from my fingers and made a noise in the back of her throat. She stomped away and gestured for Tony to follow. He was more interested in stalking Betty, but a grunt and nod from me gave him a little push.

He glared at me, and then stared at the floor, defeated. "Fine. We want to leave within the hour." Despite his pouting, he managed to shoot another coy smile at Mrs. Flannigan before slinking away.

"He's an idiot," Betty observed, watching Tony's departure. "But I have to admit, he's got a nice ass."

You should see him in the shower. I thought, also watching their departure, including the specific part Betty had highlighted. "Anyway, you were saying?" I wonder if my own nanites failed to resolve my blush fast enough.

"You've probably noticed how guarded the Rovalorians are. I'm guessing you've discovered those cards try to extract more information than they share. Since you're still roaming free, you've obviously blocked them from anything important."

I nodded. "Not everything, of course. I've even allowed a few false memories. Do you trust them?"

"Mostly. I think they're just concerned about self-preservation. Many races formerly subjugated by the Ullinarian Empire have seized their chance to gain power for themselves—"

"Yeah, I know! Raiders have attacked us a few times. Fortunately, I have a pretty fierce ship."

Betty smiled. "No shit. I decided to let you in on something when you told me you have an assault craft. I was going to tell you anyway, honestly. I've been warning all upgrades I meet, but now that I know what you've done in the past…"

"Wait," I stopped her, feeling as if she had already dropped a bomb and both of us barely noticed. "What was that about a warning?"

Betty took a deep breath and held her hands above the table as if trying to force it to levitate. I could tell with her eyes closed she and her nanites were processing information. There was something else, though... she was bracing herself.

"The Ullinarians aren't dead, not entirely. They should be, every one of them, but some survived."

"Good." I was relieved to hear that. Genocide is one thing I would never want on my resume, and to hear some of them survived by no means relieved my sense of guilt, but it was a small consolation.

"No, it isn't good!" Betty almost spat across the table. "They may be resurging, and as they increase their manpower, they'll try to regain their position. Now that the Gorlack revolution seems to be gaining momentum, there might be no one left to restrict their ambition."

"And the Rovalorians know this?"

She nodded. "I've told them everything I know. I've also loaded the information into the facilities mainframe, but they keep hiding it."

As if anticipating my next question, she continued. "They must be making plans of their own, and don't want anyone to suspect the Ullinarians are rebuilding their forces. They certainly wouldn't want upgrades to join the other side."

"Rebuilding their forces? That means abducting people, right?"

"I'm not sure. But they've invaded one of the worlds where they used to gain components—a world without the means, or inclination, to resist."

The temperature inside the bar seemed to drop twenty degrees, and the chattering patrons sounded as Gods, declaring judgment for my recent crimes. More destruction was in progress, like a colossal storm pushing in from the sea. An alien world, yet unknown to me, was falling prey to tyranny at this very moment, and despite the distance, I was once again at the center of it.

"I've been warning every upgrade I meet about this for their own protection," Betty added, not allowing me the time to digest the news. "But now that I know you were behind the data bomb, I'm hoping for a little more."

"What?" I coughed on the suggestion. Leo twitched in my lap and readjusted before falling back to sleep. "You want me to… do what… more killing?"

Betty took a data card from a stack in her pocket. She sat frozen; her empty stare aimed in my general direction. I knew she interfaced with the card, compiling her memories and associated information into an easy report. What she was not doing, however, was explaining to me why I should intervene. As far as I was concerned, I had done enough damage already.

"Everything's here," she said, snapping back to life and offering the card. It lingered on the table, just a few inches from my hand. Curiosity alone made the small plastic strip desirable, only my fear and guilt prevented me from reaching out.

"You have to do something about this situation," Betty told me in short, clipped sounds. Annoyed? Possibly even a little desperate? "In a way, it's all your fault, so you should feel obligated. You've also got the only ship I know of that might have a chance to actually accomplish anything. I command a freighter. Who's better equipped? At least go and see what's really happening there. Maybe it's not as bad as I think."

My eyes darted from the table to Betty. We both knew her last remark was bullshit, and as far as incentives go, very lame. However, my curiosity persisted like a bad hangover. I slowly reached for the card; my fingertips tingled at the feel of the plastic and lure of the knowledge just beyond. So easy. So close. So tantalizing. Yet, I pushed the card away, which took every measure of self-control I possessed.

Betty remained still, making no move towards retrieving the tiny computer. I had a feeling she wasn't finished, that she had another ace left to play. It's exactly what I'd do. And if I had placed a wager on that suspicion, I would have won.

"It's your choice," she said, shuffling the deck. "But someday you'll have to face whatever's rising from the ashes of their Empire. And when you do, you will have to explain to your friend Oola why you did nothing to save her home when you had the chance."

I almost choked; her last hand had been all aces. Here I sat, worrying about smearing a little more blood on my hands; all the while Betty had a few buckets in reserve. I'd already committed genocide, and now it looked as if I were going to have to destroy Olemsi-Myucuc.

Chapter 5

I was half-dazed when I stepped onto the gangway, still trying to decide what to do about the big, stinking turd Betty slipped in my pocket. Of course, I accepted the information; I had already interfaced with the card and my nanites processed, indexed, cross-referenced and filed the data. There was so much to examine, but most of it boiled down to reports of Ullinarian convoys of various ships and materials traveling to Olemsi-Myucuc, but few accounts of anything traveling back. It seemed as if the survivors were colonizing that world in full, but to what end remained unknown.

Also unknown was how any Ullinarians survived at all. Their species utilized nanites to enhance themselves, as well as turn other life forms into technological components and weapons. I knew all this. I'd taken advantage of it by reprogramming those very same nanites to destroy their Ullinarian hosts at a cellular level.

At the time this action took place, I tried to comfort myself by assuming some of them would survive, those farthest from the point of transmission. I never truly believed that would happen, but I tried to. I wrote my murderous program, which everyone now called the *data bomb*, and broadcast it through hyperspace; it traveled across the galaxy at many times faster than the speed of light. It killed on contact, no warning.

However, I examined Betty's evidence for myself. My nanites recognized the legitimacy of the information, and now it resided in my neurons and circuits just as naturally as if I'd personally witnessed the events. Some Ullinarians remained alive and were invading my friend's home planet, and I couldn't simply choose to deny it.

The gangway, meanwhile, was sparkling. At least one thing in the universe was. Fido had scrubbed every inch of the platform, the railings, and the walls. Leo trailed close behind, and we made our way to the airlock, catching sight of Fido overhead. He was clinging to bright silver girders with four of his feet while the other two polished the ceiling. His big orb-shaped head swung towards us when we passed beneath, his single eye bright with joy.

"Jason Miller!" a voice called from behind.

I turned to see Scheleene hobbling along the corridor as quickly as his tiny legs could carry him while his webbed hands waved frantically.

"Jason Miller, wait! I must speak with you!"

"Whatever it is, find someone else. I'm off the clock."

His tiny head bobbed from side to side. "No, I must speak with *you*."

I paused, reluctantly. I had enough on my mind, but figured I could spare a few minutes to hear whatever had the giant fish worked-up. He was so excited and short of breath that he never even noticed my Gorlack hanging from the ceiling.

"Yes?" I asked, disinterested.

"I just learned it was you. You launched the data bomb. We need your help."

My heart leapt into my throat. Actually, it leapt into my

throat, did a few summersaults, lit a roman candle, and dropped to my stomach and set itself on fire. Leo, being the smartest cat in the entire galaxy, hissed from the vicinity of my feet while his back arched threateningly. Fido was also on alert. His rags had gone still and his bulbous eye focused on the back of Scheleene's head.

"What are you talking about?" I bluffed, desperate to buy a few seconds, long enough to make-up an alibi, but Scheleene wasn't buying.

"One of the Cantreyssi over-heard you. I just reviewed his chip!"

Cantreyssi? Oh, those fucking, nosey-ass, ammonia breathers! It never occurred to me that those smelly bastards could have been upgrades, or were listening to my table. In fact, even if they hadn't been paying attention to us, their nanites were perfectly capable of gathering the information on their own, and uploading it to a card without their hosts even knowing what had transpired.

"Shit," I muttered, unable to find an extricating response. "I can't—I didn't—"

Then I noticed the little data card still clutched in Scheleene's flipper. Is it possible he hadn't shared the information with anyone else? Have I ever, in my whole life, been that lucky? My best hope was that Scheleene had come looking for me the second he made the discovery, but what was I going to do about him?

His face contorted in a desperate expression of... something I couldn't quite identify. It wasn't exactly accusatory, and why would it be? My actions set his people free as well as myself. Of course, there was that whole issue of a reward. My scalp was worth a lot to the right people. I knew the Rovalorians to be intelligent; I had no knowledge regarding their aptitude for greed. Regardless of what might be going through his long, sinewy brain, I couldn't take any more risks.

"Oh... fuck you!" I spat, just as my right hand balled into a weak fist, which I slammed against the fish's little head. He didn't see it coming, which is unremarkable considering the smallness of his eyes.

I wished Tony had been here; he was built for fighting while my body was better suited to check dates in the dairy cooler. But my attack sufficed; Scheleene reeled from the blow and staggered backwards. Fido dropped from the ceiling, landing on three feet in an acrobatic performance that would have made even Leo jealous, effectively barring his escape. Scheleene tried to call out, but Fido jammed one of his filthy rags into the poor fish's mouth and together, we wrestled him through the airlock.

"Seal the hatch, Leo!"

My cat interfaced with the door mechanism, and I left Fido to deal with our captive while I raced for the command deck, hoping Tony and Oola were present and had the ship ready for launch.

"What the hell is going on?" Tony demanded, looking behind me in an attempt to identify the source of commotion following close on my heels.

I ignored his question and struck back with one of my own. "Is the ship ready to depart?"

Oola, still practicing her haughty demeanor (and getting rather good at it), stepped in front of me as I approached the controls. "What have you done this time? Oh!"

My captive came squirming in at that very moment. Fido held him firmly under restraint, but Scheleene hadn't given up yet.

"He found out," I said, snatching the data card from Scheleene's flipper. "Someone overheard me talking to Betty."

"So you assaulted a local official? You wasted all that time and now—"

"Here," I shouted, shoving Betty's data card into Oola's hand, "read this and shut up."

"The ship is ready," Tony reported with an angry spray of spittle, "but we need clearance."

I could tell he was pissed, and anxious to explain that to me in profane detail, but I was preoccupied with more immediate concerns. I ignored both their disdain, plopped myself into the command chair, and interfaced. The mining facility was not on alert—that was the good news. Scheleene hadn't shared his revelation with anyone or, apparently, his intention to confront me. There was, however, a significant queue of ships waiting for permission to depart.

Space traffic outside the facility appeared nearly as heavy as it had been upon our arrival. With only a narrow path available through the dense asteroid field, keeping a well-organized flight plan was imperative to the safety of both the outpost, and travelers alike. Of course, I commanded the only ship with this level of firepower, and I could bloody well do as I pleased if I were to choose that particular route. And I considered powering weapons to that end, but refrained.

I remembered my escape from the K'Nostron mother ship several months ago. Many sentient creatures died, including an unknown number of Gorlack slaves. The varied persons aboard this facility were just as innocent as those Gorlacks, and considerably more innocent than the K'Nostrons.

I would not allow another act of desperation to cost lives, but I still needed to get the hell out of here.

The ship was still connected to the facilities mainframe. I pushed my mind into the host computer, and instantly felt contact with other minds, paid upgrades doing the job that once befell slaves. I couldn't bullshit them; they would surely see through any deception which would probably lead to suspicion, thus decreasing our chances of a clean getaway. I'd have to secure our escape with the truth.

"What the hell?"

I felt Tony join me inside the ship's circuitry. The runaway overload I started inside the engines was already beginning to signal warnings. I didn't bother to explain to my companion what was going on. I did, however, alert the station's controllers.

The upgrades on the other end quickly assessed the situation and all traffic outside came to a screeching halt. Station authorities cleared the moorings and depressurized the dock, ejecting us without a single word. I only needed a second to stabilize our position, but as I tried to engage thrusters, I discovered control had been wrested away from me. There were many upgrades directing traffic, and now all of them focused on my ship, maintaining contact through the communication system.

They plotted a course of their own, one taking us directly towards the proto-star at the center of the asteroid field.

"Where are you taking us?" demanded Tony, mind to mind.

If I'd been capable of shrugging from inside the computer, I would have done so. "I'm not in control; the station is piloting by remote. Fix the overload."

I heard the computerized voice of our ship summon Leo. In this weird state of cybernetic mélange, it was often difficult to identify who was doing what. Had my demand for repair been translated into calling our mechanic, or had Tony recognized the order as being over his head, thus leading him to make the request? No way of knowing.

Leo merged with us inside the computer, and I struggled against the foreign minds piloting the ship, fighting inertia, gravity and thrust all at once. Our overloading engines shuddered from my sabotage and the force of acceleration. I could see through the sensors a billion chunks of rock and dust hurtling towards our hull—or more accurately, we were hurtling towards them. I had barely enough control over thrusters to dodge the larger particles, but our speed was increasing.

I flailed my arms about the exterior of the ship, as if I was navigating inside some warped pinball machine, and swerving through the obstacle course. Bits of dust and ice were getting harder to avoid. Particles seemed to slam against my skin like tiny, burning missiles. I couldn't raise a stable shield around the ship, nor could I steer with any degree of accuracy. There were simply too many minds vying for control, some of which seemed nearly as experienced as me with such matters.

"Ullinarian Dreadnaught closing in," someone reported. "It's the same one that attacked us the other day. Weapons hot."

"Shit." That was definitely me swearing. The Dreadnaught fired. Fortunately, the obstacle course made targeting for them as hard as steering was for me. The first blasts came nowhere near our hull.

The distance between the outpost and ourselves increased quickly as we gained speed, but that did not diminish their overriding control. We veered close to one of the larger rocks, which I avoided by only a few inches. They were determined to destroy us, and seemed to be getting more direct in their efforts. I reminded myself it was merely an act of self-preservation on their part, but my own sense of the same was equally resolute. Perhaps too much. I dodged another giant boulder, overcompensated, and nearly crashed into another. This was also while trying to dodge multiple particle cannons from behind.

Tony, meanwhile, tried to change the encryption codes governing our ship. But with so many minds all connected, they could watch the changes in real time and adjust accordingly. Pangs of guilt distracted me and I realized this is exactly what the technicians on TBNL must have experienced when I wrecked their network.

No way was I going to let guilt get me, my cat, or my crew killed. But there must be some lesson to learn from my long history of sabotage. I'd turned a massive colony into a sprawling chain of turmoil with a mere sentence. Could I do the same thing again? I only needed a few seconds to complete my escape, and unlike the authorities on TBNL, their technicians could repair any damage I might cause.

The ship continued to buck while I tried pushing back into the facilities computer. So many minds in the way. So many. Like the crowds at fucking Disneyworld, everyone talking and moving in multiple directions... but with explosions. Every time I made a course correction, the minds pushed back and I lost ground.

I executed a sharp turn to avoid a catastrophic collision. The asteroid only skinned the ship, tearing away a brand new, and expensive, auxiliary thruster replaced less than an hour ago.

I didn't notice when someone else joined us inside the computer. I also didn't notice when that same someone shoved some unfriendly command into the mining facility's mainframe. Only when the drone of angry voices subsided did I realize I had control, and Leo had corrected the engines. With a single thought, someone opened a hyperspace window and our escape was complete.

Who did that? Who helped me fight them back? And where the hell were we going? I checked for a destination and sure enough, someone had plugged one in: Olemsi-Myucuc. Oola. She'd been the one who helped and who now operated the ship. No need for me to stick around inside the computer. I withdrew back into my own body and looked around from my position in the command chair. Oola leaned against the console, a stern, resolute expression frozen on her face. Tony had also left the computer and was waiting for me to finally explain.

"Here," I plucked the data card from Oola's statuesque fingers and tossed it to Tony. "This should explain everything."

"Not quite," Oola's voice sounded through the speakers. "It doesn't explain how you got caught by local authorities and why you abducted one of them."

"Sorry," I apologized, addressing Oola's body, even though I knew she wasn't exactly in there. "I got sloppy. It was worth the risk, don't you think?"

"That depends."

"On what?"

"On whether or not we can save my home world. I may have been happier not knowing about it."

Tony finished processing the information, looked at me, and clenched his jaw so tight I though his teeth might experience nuclear collapse. Yup, pissed off more than usual. I wasn't even sure that was a possibility until now.

"I would be happier not knowing. For fuck's sake, dude, what the hell can the three of us do against an empire? Last time we tricked the Kan Kan's into doing most of the fighting."

"It's my home," Oola pleaded from the computer. "I can't ignore them."

I held up my hands in a conciliatory gesture. There were certain traits about my friends that I could always count on. Oola was kind and compassionate, though lacking even the most rudimentary kind of street smarts. Whereas Tony on the other hand, bulldozed his way through life, perpetually jacked-up on his own testosterone, usually flushing away any common sense before it could manifest.

"How about this," I offered, "we jump out of hyperspace near Olemsi-Myucuc and assess the situation. We can decide how to proceed from there."

Tony's face was growing increasingly redder, but he didn't argue. Oola also remained silent; although I'm sure she was already developing her own arguments, should any be needed. As for me, I wasn't sure if any of this was a good idea, but I felt obligated to at least have a look.

The mood on the command deck had become terribly awkward. Even my prisoner had gone quiet, with his big fishy eyes bulging—more than usual. If he had been paying any attention to our conversation, he probably had a better idea than anyone did what we were facing.

CHAPTER 6

The nine-hour flight to Olemsi-Myucuc remained tense for many reasons. For one, the flight itself should have taken over twenty hours, but Oola drove like a mad woman. She stressed the engines so much the entire fuselage shuddered; even the seamless metal skin seemed to threaten collapse. Worse still was Tony's growing anxiety. Although he hadn't spoken a word in hours, he paced the flight deck, often slapping a fist into the palm of his other hand. In the time I'd known him, I had never seen this level of aggression. Yes, he had been upgraded to serve as a tactical weapon, but this visible anger was greater than when we had been under actual attack. Even his appearance changed; his already nanites-enhanced physique appeared to be growing before my eyes. That last part bothered me only because it was abnormal, if rather appealing.

At least Scheleene had surrendered. He slumped in the corner of the control deck, sniffling. His gag was gone; I felt bad enough for abducting him, I certainly didn't want his death on my hands—although that was still a looming possibility.

Leo was obviously the only member of our party not vexed by either the revelation provided by Captain Betty, Oola's sudden disregard for defensive driving, or Tony's impending hormonal overdose. Instead of worrying, as I was doing plenty for everyone, Leo sat in a corner grooming himself, paying absolutely no attention to the behavior of the stupid humans—and associated approximations thereof.

"We've arrived," Oola announced through the computer. "Transferring to normal space in five, four, three..."

Tony and I leapt towards the controls and interfaced, merging with the very fabric of our ship before she could complete the countdown. Oola was in control of the ship, so I devoted my attention to the sensors.

The distortions surrounding our vessel faded with our exit from Hyperspace, and I saw a green and brown orb before us.

My nanites recognized the image of Olemsi Myucuc, and the convoluted, paranoid coding of the Ullinarian Empire broke instantly and a flood of data surged through my head. So much data in a single, crashing wave, euphoric and overwhelming. I couldn't consciously process it all, even with the assistance of my nanites and the ship's computer. And I didn't have time to anyway; Tony was charging weapons.

"What are you doing?" someone demanded from within the computer.

We all seemed to answer in unison. "Taking out that fucking installation so we can be done with it!"

Well, fuck me sideways. I'd failed to notice the massive Ullinarian complex floating in high orbit above the planet. It was a structure common to the Empire during their expansive rivalry with the K'Nostrons. There were thousands of them across the Galaxy, most of which should now be defunct, their inhabitants dead from the data bomb. This complex, however, still functioned, the power signatures unmistakable.

Tony aimed all our weapons on the complex and... nothing. I pulled the plug, depriving the particle cannons the energy needed. I felt Tony's adrenalin surge through our cybernetic connection. I couldn't see his actual face, but I could imagine the implied scowl.

"Wait," I said, before he could protest. "That is an occupation platform; if you damage it in orbit, the fallout will poison the planet. We can't do that."

I think Oola might have said the last part, but it was so hard to be sure. Tony's killer instinct was boiling over but he allowed our weapons to stand down. He remained, however, on high alert and I felt our shields increase around the vessel.

Our shields didn't seem necessary for some reason, though. Although the installation appeared functional, something didn't seem quite right. No weapons pointed in our direction and no sensor waves touched my skin. Perhaps Betty had been wrong after all; this facility appeared to be of little threat.

"How shall we proceed?" someone asked.

I hated caucusing while merged, especially when that level of instant communication wasn't required, so I withdrew from the computer. Observing the planet and all sensor details with my own eyes—less efficient certainly, but the isolation helped me consider our position. The Olemsi home world appeared, at least on a technological level, even darker than the occupation platform. No advanced sensor waves, not even primitive radar, came from the surface. I could see concentrations of light from locations on the night side of the planet, typical of cities viewed from space. But again, it was otherwise silent, without any kind of broadcast signals, radio, television or microwave. The Ullinarian complex orbited the planet alone. No ships or artificial satellites circled the planet. This was like finding a Neanderthal hut with a Lexus parked out front.

"Let's take a look at the surface. The Ullinarians obviously occupied this planet, so let's see what the status of their presence is."

"Maybe our prisoner can tell us," Tony suggested, back in his own body and moving towards Scheleene. The poor fish moaned and tightened his flippers over his face.

"I already told you," he lamented. "Nothing. I know nothing. I'm just a technician."

Tony looked as if he were about to swing a boot at the poor land fish, but paused when Oola made an announcement.

"I'm going down."

"Adjust shields so we aren't visible," I instructed. She complied, but said nothing else.

The ship lurched violently as the local gravity expressed itself over our systems and we plunged through the upper atmosphere.

I wondered how our approach might appear from the surface. Oola often talked about her home world, at least how it was at the time of her abduction. They were far less advanced than the Earth as I remembered it, and their progress had been slow due mainly to a lack of necessity. The planet was rich in natural resources, abundant food, mild climate and few predators. She'd told me electricity was a very new development, and had failed to catch-on broadly. They had been, as far as I could tell, at a state of development approximating the late 18th century on Earth. However, as we descended from the night sky, I could see large cities ablaze with artificial light. Whether this was the result of Ullinarian occupation, or a sign that enough time had passed for the locals to develop this far, was unknown.

"Do you recognize anything?" I asked, keeping my eyes glued to the monitors, which Oola focused on one of the largest cities. Towers of brick and mortar reached above paved streets, lined with trees and electric lampposts. We glided over the surface and easily identified stores, schools, even parks and residential neighborhoods. The sprawling, urban landscape could have been Chicago in the 1940's, with one considerable exception; a total lack of the inhabitants or any kind of movement.

"No," Oola said through the ship's speakers. "If it weren't

for our two moons, I wouldn't even know this was my planet."

I scanned for life signs, and the results were resoundingly positive. In fact, there were so many life forms that I couldn't discern any individual species. But my sensors were a bit limited in this regard; our vessel was built for war, not scientific inquiry.

"I'm still not reading any kind of signal. On the upside, I'm also not detecting nanite carrier waves. Whatever the Ullinarians are doing here, it's not to upgrade the local population."

Tony made a grunt from behind and muttered, "If any of them are left."

A definite possibility we'd already considered. We learned from our experience on TBNL that it wasn't unusual for the Ullinarians to invade a suitable planet and wipe out the entire native population. They may have been here for centuries; upgraded all the Olemsi and colonized it for themselves. That could also explain the lack of any moving figures on the streets below; if everyone here had been Ullinarian, they would likely be dead now because of the data bomb. But Betty had evidence of recent activity, and I had already determined that there was still life. Moreover, nothing here looked even remotely Ullinarian.

Oola continued to drift through the night sky at an altitude and speed befitting a hot-air balloon. We saw movement for the first time just as we approached the local dawn. Motor cars began navigating through the streets. Although they looked nothing like what I would consider an automobile, their rate and style of motion was unmistakable. The roads were indistinguishable from paved roads on Earth, lacking only the yellow or white stripes. I focused my scan. The drivers? Olemsi.

I could almost feel Oola's relief, but it was probably more of a reflex than an actual rise in confidence. There was, after all, still a giant Ullinarian presence in orbit and this planet looked nothing like the culture she'd left behind.

Oola took us away from the city center and over the suburbs. A large landing port came into view, and with it, the first sign of an Ullinarian presence on the surface. Many ships, mostly shuttles and a few freighters, parked on the tarmac. A control tower sat at one end, encased in darkness, and beyond that was an empty parking lot. It was eerily Earth-like in so many ways, but every characteristic I recognized from home bore the unmistakable taint of the empire.

"There," Tony pointed at a monitor showing the deserted port. "No power sources, no Ullinarians moving around, no nanites... I think Betty got her facts wrong; these pricks are just as dead as the rest of 'em. Can we go now?"

Regardless of how settled Tony assumed the situation to be, I didn't feel the same, and I was certain Oola didn't either. However, I had to agree that things looked, so far anyway, positive, at least for the locals. I wondered if this meant Oola would soon be leaving us.

"What now?" she asked through the computer. "Tony may be correct; everything does seem rather peaceful. How do we find out for sure?"

"Well," I began. "In the absence of any kind of television or radio broadcast, I can only think of one way to get information. We're going to have to land and just ask someone."

"Bullshit! You wanna have an Oprah moment while there're wars to fight."

I looked at Tony, my mouth hanging open. He'd always been abrasive and bit obnoxious, but this level of hostility was something new. I could see the veins in his neck throbbing. Both his fists were clenched as if aching for a brawl.

"What is your problem?"

"We don't have time for this crap! Let's just blow the fuck out of that platform and move on. This is just stupid."

"Time?" I snorted. "We have time. We have lots of time. We don't age, remember?"

For a second, I thought Tony was going to slug me. Instead,

he grabbed his own scalp with both hands and, white knuckled, turned away. I considered pushing the subject; something was definitely going on with him, something that could potentially threaten us all if we didn't get whatever it was under control, but a more imminent risk captured my attention.

Oola plotted a course for the Ullinarian landing port. "What are you doing?" I cried and jumped back into the universe of wires and circuits. I wrested control away from my astonished friend and veered us away from the strip.

"You said 'land,' so I was going to land. Did I misunderstand?"

Not only are the Olemsi terminally naïve, they also seemed to have no small talent for understatement. "May I remind you that we're in a stolen ship in potentially hostile territory—hostile from the same people we stole this ship from, *after* killing most of them? I think a little discretion may be in order."

"The ship is still invisible."

Merged with the ship, I was unable to give her a sour look. "Yes, but *we* won't be as soon as we step outside."

"Oh yes," she agreed. "I hadn't considered that. Please proceed."

My current position also prevented me from doing a face palm.

I turned the ship towards the countryside surrounding the city. Like any metropolitan enclave, a substantial nest of suburban towns orbited the central hub. A little further out, the suburbs gave way to even smaller towns and farms. Naturally, this is where I was going. I've seen the *X-Files*; I know aliens never land in populated locations. If I'm going to be a little green man, dammit, I'm going to be a good one and plop my skinny ass down in the most deserted location I can find. And the approach does seem to have some actual merit since aliens abducted me in the middle of nowhere. Precedent. Take it seriously. Always.

Dawn crept in fast as I landed in what could have passed for a horse pasture—without the horses. Or deer ticks. Or even qweellie beetles, which, as I'm told, taste like chicken. I ran a check of the outside conditions and reported. "Looks like a nice day. Temperature is seventy-three degrees with a light breeze." I felt like a fucking flight attendant. I wonder if anyone needs direction to baggage claim. Nevertheless, I continued. "Seventeen percent oxygen—a bit low, but I think we'll be okay; nitrogen, argon, neon and a smattering of CO_2. Pressure and gravity are a little higher than what I'm used to, but again, I don't see any great risk."

"Really?" Tony barked. "You don't see 'any great risk'? Have you forgotten the several billion aliens who live here?"

"My people are not violent by nature."

I believed Oola's assessment to be true based on what I'd experienced from her, and from the few others of her species I'd encountered. However, even a non-violent individual is likely to react strongly when confronted with a perceived threat. And as far threats go, our little band would probably appear quite threatening. Imagine the Kardashians[5] meeting... well, poor people. Same thing.

"We'll try to keep out of sight," I said, trying to ease Tony's state of alert. "This is just a quick recon mission. Oola will make contact with a local, see if she can learn anything, and then we can reassess afterwards. Do we all agree?"

"Then she should go by herself."

That suggestion had already occurred to me. Oola was certainly the only inconspicuous member of our extremely conspicuous party. However, we also knew she'd been absent from her home world for a very long time; there was no knowing how customs, behavior and even speech may have

---

[5] Kardashians: An Earth family of tacky, useless, rich, arrogant, attention whores famous for being famous. In early 2012, the Ullinarian conscription service abducted several Kardashian family members, but promptly returned them. In the words of one Commander, "this shit's too weird, even for us."

changed in the potential centuries since she last spoke to a relative or neighbor. Fold into the mix the fact this planet is under alien occupation, either currently or at least recently, and the possibility for paranoia from the natives grows. One mistake and Oola could suddenly seem as foreign to her people as I would.

"No," I said, fearing Tony's reprisal. "We should go with her. We can watch from a distance. If it makes you feel better, we can bring guns."

Tony brightened at that suggestion, which scared me even more than his rage. Offering weapons is probably not the best way to deal with someone on the verge of manic overload. He was already trotting towards the hold to retrieve his little friends.

"Are you leaving me here? Alone?"

I turned to Scheleene, still balled in the corner, his latent gills turning distinctly pale. "You won't be alone. Fido will stay here and look after you, won't you, boy?"

Fido's orb-like head bobbed up and down, then swung on his long neck and repeated the gesture in Scheleene's direction. I don't think this made the giant fish feel any better, but I knew everyone left behind would be safe. Well, as safe as any of us.

Leo, immersed in typical feline indifference, looked up from his nap briefly, and settled back after I told him to remain with the others. He was the one thing I cared about the most, even more than soothing my own guilty conscience. I considered bringing him with me. At least I could keep a direct eye on him and know for certain he was safe. That idea was dismissed the moment Tony returned, carrying two massive Ullinarian riffles.

"Are we ready?" he asked, passing one of the guns to me. It felt even heavier than it looked. I had managed to survive the new reality so far without ever having fired a single weapon—actually in my entire life. I'm probably not even capable of shooting straight, especially with an object that weighs more than my old sofa. Its only purpose I could see was getting Tony to cooperate.

With growing apprehension, we exited the airlock. At this point, Oola looked absolutely petrified, which was an accomplishment in itself. Her tiny orange face and even tinier black eyes rarely showed any expression, but now her lips pressed together so firmly I thought she might be at risk of swallowing her own jaw. I sympathized. To her, this homecoming would be comparable to me returning to Earth and finding flying cars, jetpacks and robotic maids. She was about to step onto ground nearly as alien to her as it was to me.

As far as an alien ground goes, I found this to be quite pleasant. For the first time in an unknown number of years, I was standing under a clear blue sky—barely blue, almost white. The levels of atmospheric nitrogen were lower here than my home, so less blue light was being scattered by the yellow sun. But it was sky nonetheless, not rock or metal. The air tasted funny, but maybe because I had become so accustomed to artificial environments.

"You said the ship is invisible," Tony complained. "I can still see it."

"We're still in the shield envelope. Watch what happens." I started leading our group in the direction of the nearest dwelling, somewhere beyond a nearby grove of weedy trees. We walked and I kept looking over my shoulder. The sleek orange/white metal hull became fainter with each step of our progress until it vanished entirely. And yet, if one were to stare hard at the space, the ship's outline could just be detected, like heat distortion rising from a fire. To anyone who didn't already know it was there, though, they would never notice.

The scrubby woods were about a hundred feet deep and opened to a typical country scene. A rough gravel drive led from the main road to a small farmhouse. Wire fences cordoned off select patches of the yard where small animals grazed on the tall grass. Random outbuildings surrounded the property, most of them constructed from weathered boards. The architecture of the dwelling was really the only thing here that didn't look like a typical Illinois farm. It was a squared dome of brick and concrete, and had the effect of a sand castle or insect hive. The few windows were round openings backed by glass and a surprisingly detailed front door rested above a stoop of ordinary boulders.

"I grew-up in a house much like this," Oola said, seeming to relax a little. "Except for those wires."

How did I miss those? I squinted against the glare of the rising sun and finally noticed the large number of cables anchored to the house near the roofline. They extended across the field to poles that ran alongside the highway like a battalion of soldiers marching to war. Again, it was so twentieth century.

"Well?" Tony urged. "Are you going to do anything?"

Oola didn't move. "What should I say to them?"

"Tell them you were fucking abducted by fucking aliens and just got the fuck back," Tony snapped, "and ask what the fuck is going on."

The tranquility apparently granted Tony from packing heat had started to wear off. Worse still was the possibility Oola might regard that as a plausible suggestion. I interceded quickly.

"Say you're from out of town and are looking for the nearest person in authority. Ask *who* that person is. Just the name might give you an idea whether it's an Ullinarian, or one of your people."

Oola seemed to rehearse her speech in head before nodding. "You will be watching?"

"Right here."

"Very well," she said, brushing dead leaves and dirt off her clothes. "I'll do what I can…"

Brent D. Seth

Tony and I sank deeper into the underbrush and watched her amble up the country lane. She was stepping nervously, lightly, almost as if she were about to start dancing, except she held her arms rigidly against her side. From my point of view, it was as if Oola was trying to be as conspicuous as possible but, for all I knew, this might have been the polite pose for an Olemsi when approaching a neighbor. I could only hold my breath and watch.

Oola reached the entrance. She was now too far away for me to hear anything, but I plainly saw her knock on the door, which opened a few moments later. I could not see who was on the other side, but Oola was speaking, and listening to a response. She did not appear afraid. In fact, she seemed to relax; she even bent both elbows. I was starting to think this might actually work.

Is anything ever that simple? Absolutely not, otherwise Ann Landers wouldn't have kept a job. Something terrible happened, all right, something I should have predicted and warned against. All I could do was choke on my own terror as Oola followed the unseen person into the house, out of sight.

"Should we go in?" Tony asked, squeezing his riffle.

I shook my head. "Give her a few minutes."

"She could be dead in a few minutes."

"I don't think so," I countered, less confident than I tried to sound. "But if we force our way in, guns blazing, she's likely to end up that way. Just wait."

We remained crouched in the bushes for what felt like hours, but in truth, it was closer to thirty-six minutes. Time passed, and the farmhouse, dark and silent, started to feel like a tomb, a monument mocking the death of a dear friend. Of course, we didn't know whether Oola had been harmed, but our suspicion grew worse with every second.

"Okay," Tony announced, snuggling closer to his weapon. "We've waited long enough."

"Give her a full hour—a few more minutes probably won't

make any difference. We need to let this play out."

On this occasion, I have to blame myself. If there's one thing I've learned in the past few months, it's that when you tempt fate, she responds harshly, if not always quickly. That bitch knows how to play the long game.

As we remained hidden, we heard a low rumbling rising from the distance, the unmistakable sound of an approaching automobile. I prayed it was just some commuter, leaving his pastoral home for his mid-level accounting position under the scrutiny of some unappreciative douchebag in an expensive suit. Unfortunately, the rumble became the crunch of gravel as it pulled into the lane.

The automobile was just Earth-like enough to be recognizable, mainly a metal box with forward facing windows and four wheels, but that's where the similarities ended. The design was devoid of any style or appeal; the skin wasn't even painted. Every advertising expert in Detroit would be flummoxed on how to sell this totally utilitarian object. However, the appearance of the transport was much less perplexing as the place where it came to stop, directly in front of the farmhouse between our missing friend and us.

Things looked bleak, and were about to get a whole lot worse. I'd been so preoccupied with the ugliness of the vehicle, the significance of the strange proportions didn't even occur to me until two towering figures emerged. One was male, the other female—I knew this from the mountains of implanted data stored in my neurons and nanites. I also recognized them instantly as Ullinarians, but vastly different from the ones I'd previously encountered on TBNL. Their skin was smooth, the color of slightly weathered bronze, and each of them boasted a thick mane of platinum hair. They were fantastically slender, just like the ones I had seen before, but their arms and legs were proportionately much thinner. They lacked the lumps of artificially increased strength, making them much different from those people who fought for the empire.

Even with my expansive knowledge of their society, I had no information on any Ullinarian without enslaving nanites of their own. Not only was it a cultural norm, it was the driving principle of their entire system. It was also the means I used to kill them, and could possibly explain why these individuals were still alive.

"Dammit!" Tony howled softly, raising his weapon. "I fucking knew this would happen."

"Wait, you idiot!" I grabbed the barrel of his riffle and pressed it towards the ground. "They're already inside. Do you want Oola caught in cross fire? There's a lot more going on here than we can see. Wait, *please…*"

Tony was still quaking with adrenalin, his face so red I could almost feel heat radiating from his pores, but he submitted, glaring at me with unspoken, and unmistakable, recrimination.

I didn't bother to check his reaction when the farmhouse opened again and the male Ullinarian emerged, ducking under what must have been, to him, a very small doorway. Oola and the other female followed. I heard nothing, and could not see enough expression of any of their faces to indicate the nature of their meeting. They silently led Oola to the vehicle, and she climbed in quite casually, as if this was the most ordinary experience possible. The two Ullinarian agents followed, and the vehicle pulled away, again showing no sign of haste or urgency.

Tony and I dropped deeper into our cover as the automobile passed by, the driver obviously still unaware of our presence, making the situation that much more uncertain. Perhaps the owner of this farm simply regarded Oola as a trespasser, or perhaps a lunatic, and called the authorities to have her removed. I couldn't even be sure whether or not she had been arrested. The only thing I could conclude with any certainty was that, not only were there Ullinarians still alive, but they were likely in control of this planet.

"Get back to the ship," I ordered, knowing full well that Tony's current plan was to storm the house seeking revenge. Someone within that dwelling could answer some much-needed questions, only I'd just witnessed how quickly and easily the Ullinarians became involved. For all I knew, there might be surveillance in every home—the residents may not even have any part in it.

"We need to go after her."

"What, on foot?" I asked. Tony's eyes bore into mine. For a moment, I thought he might be about to strike me.

Reason replaced his anger and he backed down with a simple nod.

We backed slowly away from the house until the brush was tall enough for us to stand and remain hidden, then turned and bolted through the woods toward the field where we landed.

Our vessel was still invisible with only the slight distortion of its outline confirming its presence. Unfortunately, there was no chance of us reaching it. Vehicles filled the area, and uniformed Ullinarians surrounded the ship. More troops were moving towards the woodland framing the pasture—including our current position.

Fate was apparently not yet satisfied with her revenge, and she put the screw to me one more time. With a roar, and a brief wrinkle through its defense field, our ship rose quickly from its resting place and blasted skywards.

I think I peed myself a little.

No. I definitely peed myself a little... a lot.

"What the hell?" Tony demanded, to no one in particular. "Did they board? Who's flying the goddamn ship?"

Chapter 7

The Ullinarians closed on our position. I could tell they weren't specifically aware of us, but they were searching. They'd find us if we didn't do something soon. I considered surrender for a fraction of a second since it might be the quickest way to find Oola, who I now understood had definitely been arrested. They were on to us, probably had been since we entered the system.

This shit never happened on the X-Files!

Running probably wasn't going to work for us either, but with Tony's current state of mind, I figured surrender would more likely lead to a shoot-out and my subsequent death. Tony might be capable of surviving such an altercation, only I had little expectation of my own abilities. It was time to run, so I did, without consulting my companion.

Tony probably would have had much to say on my decision, but he kept that to himself while he followed me through the rapidly thinning forest. Our current path ran perpendicular to the imaginary line between our landing spot and the house where they apprehended Oola. It was an obvious choice, and if the Ullinarians had witnessed our flight, would already be in pursuit. I don't know if they saw us or not. I didn't look back to check. I just ran until the woods expired at the edge of an expansive field. Thousands of rows of cultivated seedlings stretched as far as we could see, and not a single form of cover anywhere.

We bolted through the field, trampling the crop with indifference. I heard nothing to indicate pursuit, but I continued with the same level of desperation, thankful my nanites supplemented my own lack of natural stamina. Tony, considerably more fit, quickly caught up with me.

"What now, genius? We lost Oola! We lost our ship! I told you coming here was a bad idea, and guess what, it's worse than I expected."

"Yes, yes, I know all that," I agreed between gasps. This pace was beginning to hurt even with my nanites. "You can cuss me out all you want later. Let's just try to survive long enough for you to get the chance."

"How about now? May I remind you that your precious cat was on that ship—does he know how to fly it?"

If it weren't for the heavy weapon in my arms, I would have shrugged. "Possibly. The ship knows how to fly the ship, it just needs an operator, and Leo's enhancements make it possible. Or it could have been the fish, if Fido and Leo allowed him to do it."

A distant structure was beginning to materialize from the morning haze. I altered my course slightly towards the unknown building. "As long as our ship isn't in Ullinarian hands, we have a chance. Leo and Fido won't abandon us. They have a much better chance of hiding if they keep moving. We just need to contact them."

"How?" From Tony, that sounded more like an accusation than a question.

"I don't know yet. Like I said, first we have to survive the here and now."

The building drew nearer. I could already tell it was the local version of a barn, but it appeared rickety in the extreme, or perhaps that was just an aspect of the design. The walls all tapered inwards as they rose like a giant trapezoid, the angles growing more severe on the second level, terminating under a flat roof. It had the overall appearance of a wooden pyramid, but something so primitive and ugly that the pharaohs of antiquity would never have sanctioned its construction.

I didn't care how ugly it was, or how potentially unstable, not when the familiar low drone of Ullinarian scout ships rumbled closer.

From what I'd already seen, both in orbit and on the surface, these particular Ullinarians didn't have full control of their technology. They certainly lacked the service of enhanced upgrades like me; my data bomb solved that permanently. The invasive program, unleashed months ago, would still be circulating through every piece of computerized equipment in the whole galaxy, spreading like a virus to anything new. Furthermore, I had produced a second program, which turned all nanites into killing machines, targeting the Ullinarians at a genetic level. A single nanite that penetrated the skin of an Ullinarian would attack the host like a cancer.

Oh, shit. I had not put that into context before. Not only I had committed genocide, I had done so by creating a new form of cancer. *I created cancer!* We reached the sprawling shanty of a barn and I vowed I would torture myself about that later.

We raced around the perimeter of the barn, searching for a way in. It was so similar to a rural scene on Earth; the presence of weeds, the smell of wild flowers and animal waste, and old pieces of abandoned machinery left to rust. The open doors, once we found them, looked even more Earthlike, with a mature farmer and his son working on what was clearly an old tractor.

The denim overalls were missing. So were shoes, socks, shirts and obligatory red paisley snot rag. In fact, father and son were both completely naked. I guess that's one way to keep your clothes from getting greasy. Personally, I would have felt very strange to work naked with my dad, or anyone else for that matter, but who am I to judge alien culture? What made this sudden encounter even less Earth-like was their reaction to our intrusion.

They jumped slightly from start, and then they recovered as if this kind of thing happened every day. We must be the first humans they'd ever seen, and the fact we were also heavily armed should have been a source of concern for these guys. Instead, they greeted us with a polite smile. Yup. *A polite smile!* Standing there, schlongs swinging in the open air, facing armed aliens, and smiling.

"Are you Guardians?" the father asked in his native language rather than Ullinarian standard. At least that was a good sign.

I still couldn't get over their lack of terror or even suspicion. Or modesty. Mostly the modesty. But the lack of terror and suspicion? I had come to expect a certain level of that from my long association with Oola, but... *really?* This would be like having Frankenstein's monster kick down my bathroom door during a shower and having nothing to say but *'How do you do?'* while staring at my kibbles and bits.

"What?" I asked, slightly dumbfounded.

The father pointed at my Ullinarian riffle. "Those are Guardian's tools. Are you Guardians?"

"Fine, yes, we're fucking Guardians," Tony bellowed, waving his *tool*. "Now keep quiet and stay put or I'll *Guard* your fucking asses into next Tuesday."

Ordering them to remain felt rather redundant, especially since neither of them seemed inclined to go anywhere. I half expected them to ignore us and continue changing spark plugs—or what-the-hell-ever they were doing before our arrival.

I gestured to Tony, hoping he could control his temper for at least a few minutes. The long, exhausting journey across the field seemed to have consumed some of his boiling hormones, but he was still holding the gun as if desperate for revenge against the first pretty girl who informed him he was as dumb as wet wool.

"How long have the Guardians been here?" I asked.

The boy answered, his face lighting up. "I know. I know. Um. Wait. On the eve of Pa Po Cleeja[6], no wait. I was in school the day after Pa Po Cleeja. Wait, wait—"

The boy rambled, providing information regarding certain religious ceremonies, the precise name given to that calendar day honoring Olemsi Myucuc's larger moon and something about a favorite school teacher. Between my implanted knowledge and that gained directly from Oola, I was able to translate his response to *approximately six years ago*.

"Why do you call them Guardians?" Tony demanded, sneering.

The father answered, his head cocked so far to the left that it appeared to be resting on his own shoulder. "Because they protect us."

"From what?"

"Threats."

"What threats?"

"Threats."

I've had conversations similar to this with Oola, so I could tell where it was going, and knew I had to intervene with more specific questions.

"What do you do for them? How do you reward their protection?"

The father stood a little taller. "We grow food."

---

[6] Pa Po Cleeja is the oldest holiday in Olemsi culture, but by this time no one really remembered who started it or why, but it provided everyone a day off work, and occasionally a discount on mattresses or small home appliances.

"What about the other Olemsi? Not everyone works on a farm, surely."

"True," the father agreed. "Some work in factories. Some dig in the ground for metal. Everyone has a way of paying tribute."

Tribute. That word likely carried more meaning than the Olemsi man could possibly comprehend.

"And you've paid tribute since they arrived?" *Dude*, I thought to myself, grow some fucking balls and defend yourselves. Olemsi men have schlongs as I indicated before, but their testicles aren't visible from the outside, a fact I was able to evaluate first hand from this unfortunate position.

"Yes," he answered casually, returning to his work. I was thankful the machine now blocked my view of his lower extremities. "But we thought we did wrong when they all died a few months ago. All of them at the same time. Some of us thought we offended their gods, but when the new Guardians came last month, they explained it wasn't us who caused offense. The new Guardians are better."

This came as a major surprise. I knew everything about the former Ullinarian Empire, all monsters, brutal killers and slavers. I found it impossible to believe that this group, although different in appearance, could be anything less horrific.

"How are they better?" Tony asked, probably thinking along the same lines as myself.

"They live among us," the father explained, "on the ground. They visit our homes. The old ones watched from the sky and visited only when they were displeased."

The farmer suddenly paused and looked up, a strange expression on his face, one I could not interpret. "Have they died too? Are you our new Guardians?"

What a question, especially the latter half. My success rate trying to help others was debatable in the extreme. I stared at the farmer's strange expression and remembered the old adage about the road to hell, a road I had traveled many times, and seemed to embark on once again.

I was *almost* thankful when Ullinarians appeared, sparing me the responsibility of an answer. Almost.

The quaint pastoral scene—father and son tinkering naked with machinery—the sun, the breeze, and the old barn, fell instantly to bedlam. Before I even knew what was happening, Tony was screaming and firing his weapon towards the sunshine. I turned and witnessed troops massing outside. I froze, clutching my own riffle.

Despite the considerable amount of galactic carnage I had caused, I've still never discharged an actual weapon. That should almost be brag-worthy, right? Hell, I wasn't even sure who the enemy was, or if there was one at all. The farmers certainly didn't seem afraid of these particular Ullinarians, although thanks to Tony's violent outbreak, they'd both taken cover behind the tractor.

My lack of confidence and the hesitation it caused would be my undoing. Tony struck down a number of Ullinarians before any of them raised their own weapons. The ambient temperature seemed to drop fifty degrees, and a low hum throbbed through the barn.

This was the second time in my life I experienced an Ullinarian sedation field, the first being the moment of my abduction. That was before my nanites, which now tried their damndest to resist the effects, but both were the products of the same source, now in competition. The result was confusion. I dropped my riffle—it was useless anyway—and stumbled backwards onto the tractor. Everything spun around me, my legs went limp, and my vision blurred. I could just make out the farmer and his son through the apparent distortion; they'd instantly collapsed, but would probably be fine after this was all over, and that would be very soon.

Nausea began to settle over me, and I felt hands around my arms and shoulders. Something pushed against my neck, followed by a sharp sting. An injection of some kind? I felt a brief moment of terror, and then the sunny world around me turned black.

*

Just like that first morning of my new life aboard the wrecked Ullinarian scout ship, I woke up groggy and confused. I remembered the injection and, for a moment, I worried my nanites might have been somehow deactivated. That fear passed quickly. I felt just as comfortable and rested as I had every day since my initial abduction, meaning my body was still in perfect health—except for a banging in my ears.

Well, a buzzing in my ears—the banging was something else entirely. While the former cleared, the latter increased. Tony was already awake, and pounding on the door with bloody fists, the thumping reverberating around the tiny room. We must still be on Olemsi Myucuc, I reasoned; the walls were simple clay brick masonry, rising from a concrete floor. There were no windows, the only source of light being a single incandescent light bulb dangling from a timber ceiling. Only the orange-white metal door suggested any kind of Ullinarian technology.

"How long were we out?" I asked, not expecting Tony to respond, but rather as a prompt for my nanites to open the necessary file; twenty-seven minutes, three seconds. "And would you please stop making that noise?"

Tony did respond to that.

"Fuck you!" he screamed, pounding the wall one last time before turning on me. "I told you not to bring us to this planet! I told you not to land. We should just mind our own goddamn business. Does any of this sound familiar, asshole?"

Tony and I had had our problems since the day we met. He was often angry with me, and we disagreed in general, but this level of hostility was unprecedented. Not only were his hands still balled into tight, bright red fists, but every square inch of skin was the color of fire. Sweat poured from his chiseled face and his breathing sounded erratic.

"We can't change that now, but—"

"—Shut up!" A strange mix of fury and something else not quite so easy to define imprinted on his exaggerated features.

He dropped me from his crosshairs long enough to bellow a few more obscenities towards the ceiling, phrased in perfect Ullinarian dialect; courtesy of his recently acquired upgrade.

Dawn came suddenly—well, not all that sudden since Tony's behavior had been escalating for some time. But my understanding of the underlying situation came with the same abruptness, and shock, of a virgin experiencing the first pangs of giving birth. Or suffering from a kidney stone—I've heard both experiences are very much alike, except no one has to put a kidney stone through college.

"What did you do?" I demanded. "What other *apps* did you buy besides the translator program?"

I could almost see the adrenalin surging through his body, his hormones racing as if the entire breadth of his adolescence had been compressed and concentrated into a single moment, replaying now.

"You think you're so smart, don't you," he sneered. "Well, I've had enough of your fucking wisdom. You're a fucking box boy. Who the hell are you to tell me what to do? You and your damn mouth, running all the fucking time…"

I was shocked, genuinely shocked, by Tony's outburst; I didn't know how to react when he lunged towards me, grabbed me by a handful of my own hair and pinned me to the wall of our cell with his body and wrapping his other hand around my neck. His eyes bored into me, his nose only inches from mine. I half expected him to use his enhanced strength to break my spine; the fire in those eyes was like nothing I had ever seen before.

"You just talk and talk and talk," he hissed, pressing his face closer. "Talk. Your damn mouth, always talking…"

And then he pressed his lips to mine.

I never expected this. I tried so hard for so long to deny my attraction to this man that I was totally unprepared for such a move. My body went limp as his right hand went from my scalp to the back of my neck, pulling my head closer. I thought my skull might collapse between these two extensions of his body. Tony jammed his tongue forward; I didn't resist. My hands, which had been captured by his armpits, relaxed and moved to his back. I pulled him closer as his left hand found the LaGrange point between my shoulder blades. We fell into a perfect orbit, squeezed together; I wanted us to press until the thin membrane that separated us broke and we could merge into a single entity. I could smell his sweat; feel the heat of his skin and the emotion boiling just beneath the surface.

Even through the Kevlar and denim of our respective clothes, I could feel his rising erection pressing against my own. Our hips began to thrust in rhythm, the feeling of it terrifying and intoxicating. I didn't even notice when Tony released my neck and pulled down the zipper of his jumpsuit. I don't know when my hands moved from his back to the bare skin of his hard chest—his sweat-drenched hair felt to my fingers like fine silk. I reached for his shoulders and with a single move, drew away his clothes to free his naked body.

He continued to press forward, his lips and tongue working my face with the same expertise as a concert pianist performing an aria with a bizarre, yet exquisitely balanced, mix of passion and fury. I'd lusted for this man since the first time I saw him unconscious on that Ullinarian scout ship. But he had become a friend, or at least an ally, so I knew to keep a certain distance. Yet he was the one making advances now, giving me license to drop my guard, to take advantage of this opportunity. Hell, we would likely both be dead before the next sunset, so what harm, or long-term discomfort could possibly come from this enormous breech in personal boundaries?

I don't know what happened to my shirt, or even who had

removed it, but I was glad to feel its absence, allowing Tony's bare skin to grind against my own. The heat of his body felt like an oasis in the desert, a shelter against the cold, damp, sterile environment of our cell. I was conscious of the fact that our captors were probably watching, possibly confused, even disturbed by our behavior. This would have been a serious impediment to... *performance*... in my old life back on Earth, but here and now? It didn't matter. I wanted this: the passion, the intensity, the ferocity...

I grabbed Tony's hips and pulled him towards me. My nanites served for data processing, not strength or aggression, but my grip was so strong I thought I might tear the skin from his bones. He groaned and pressed harder. He and I had often merged, mentally, within the confines of cyberspace; we'd already shared a level of intimacy far beyond the understanding of purely organic life forms. This was just a completion of the journey, the removal of the last, but least significant, barrier.

With the rising heat of our cold cell, I forgot about Oola, Scheleene and Fido. I even forgot about my beloved Leo, the center of my universe. All of them were out there somewhere in the dark, suffering, calling for me. But, for now, there was nothing I could do for them, so I surrendered to the situation.

I released my tension and apprehension, grateful when Tony placed his massive hands on my shoulders and pushed me to my knees. I began to honor his request, and vowed to make amends to my compatriots at the first opportunity. For now, however, I was satisfied with this moment.

Chapter 8

Usually, after a physical encounter like the one I had just experienced, I would have fallen asleep and stayed that way for hours. My nanites, however, did not see any reason for the rest, and prevented that particular route of escape. We, Tony and I, had to endure a fully conscious, awkward silence.

We got dressed and withdrew to separate corners of the cell, splattered with sweat, semen and a fair amount of blood. My nanites were busy repairing the injuries, yet seemed incapable of balancing my hormones. I now felt embarrassment, like getting caught with a boner in Junior High gym class, and a massive level of euphoria, like popping a boner in gym class without anyone noticing. I figured my own internal conflict must pale in comparison to whatever Tony was feeling.

He sat in his corner, arms around his knees, cradling his face. At least the exertion had dampened whatever had been going on in his body. Perhaps this would be a good time to ask again what kind of upgrade he had given himself at the Rovalorian outpost, and if he knew how we could fix it. He was calm, for the first time in quite a while, but I could tell it was still not wise to broach that subject, or any other.

We wouldn't have been able to discuss it anyway. The door opened with a judgmental squeal—at least that's how it seemed. I felt just like a teenager getting caught with a dirty movie and used tissue, but the terror was much worse than the fear of being grounded.

Two Olemsi males entered. They weren't Ullinarian, that was comforting, but their austere, gray uniforms, complete with swaying billy clubs quickly reminded me I was still in custody—and that my predicament continued to escalate.

"Greetings," one the Olemsi said, with surprising cheer. "If you are rested, the Prefect would like to meet you."

"Huh?" was the only response I could muster. What were the clubs for, I wondered, rolling-out cookie dough?

The speaker continued to surprise me by apologizing before he asked, "Do you understand our language?"

"Uh... uh... y... yeah. Yeah, I do."

These guys seemed as inoffensive as every other Olemsi I'd ever met. If this race was actually in charge of their own planet, I wouldn't have been remotely concerned. However, I felt confident this was not the case, and I strongly doubted the Prefect, whomever he might be, was almost certainly not Olemsi, and if he was Olemsi, certainly not the one really in charge.

I rose to my feet, realizing this might be my only chance to really learn something useful, not to mention the fact that I really didn't have any choice. Tony continued to cower in his corner, apparently oblivious to the new arrivals. "Are you coming?"

"Why should I?"

His self-pity was worse than his anger, and a lot harder to get around.

"Oh, c'mon now," I said in my most patronizing tone, hoping to piss him off enough to make him move. "The Prefect wants to meet us. Now, doesn't that sound exciting?"

He glanced at me with a masterful mix of contempt, resentment and otherwise utter loathing. I smiled nonetheless and motioned for Tony to follow as I bounded towards the guards, grinning. I might as well enjoy what little time I had left since I'd probably be executed before long.

Tony did follow, slowly, sulking the entire way. I wondered if perhaps he was putting together an escape route, but if that were the case, he wasn't going to make much progress. The path the guards led us along allowed few choices. There was a short hall outside our cell with three other doors, probably all leading to other cells. At the end of the corridor, a wide staircase ascended into filtered sunlight.

I learned several things during the climb. First, my earlier assessment of Olemsi Myucuc's stage of development had been correct. Second, their development was obviously quite slow. This building was just as primitive as the ones I had seen from above, and it was old; it smelled old and as we finally exited the stairwell, I could see the age and wear in the finely carved woodwork and chipped plaster walls. The electricity, such as it was, had been added after the building's initial erection. And, just like old buildings on Earth, the wiring was contained in conduits located on the surface, weaving from switches to light fixtures, to receptacles.

One thing I hadn't divined yet was the overall purpose of this building, except that it was definitely more than a prison. The hallway was wide and well lit, with many fancy doors, all closed, with sunlight streaming through the tiny gaps. The room ahead, however, was open, and apparently, our destination. My pace increased, for reason beyond my conscious grasp, and I even overtook the guards to reach what turned out to be a grand chamber.

There were no obvious answers in this room, but plenty of possibilities since it contained half a dozen Olemsi, mostly males and only two females. Each of them sat dressed in what

I could only classify as business attire, and they all rose from their chairs as I entered. No sign of Ullinarian presence was visible so far, which I found both comforting and suspicious. Very suspicious.

"Welcome to our chamber," beamed one of the males as he strode across the room. He appeared to be the youngest member of the party due to the green veins on his orange head looking so much brighter than the others. I have no idea if that actually meant anything in practice, but to my eyes, he looked very young. He also looked creepy; that bright smile and warm voice did nothing but convey threat, and his sterling while suit seemed pretentious. However, please note, cheery people always have that effect on me.

"I am Eureets Temoosh, Prefect for all the people, lands and territories of Olemsi Myucuc. It is so kind of you to join us."

I had a choice?

"Thanks," I said, looking around the room for anything familiar. A computer would have been fantastic, or at least something to indicate the location of Oola, Leo, Fido, or our ship. But there was nothing in here but peeling paint, a faint skim of dust on the marble floor and the overwhelming stench of bullshit.

I did not return the polite greeting, but instead launched into the real questions I needed to ask. "Where are your masters?"

Temoosh looked at me with a black expression, one similar to Oola's general responses to my behavior. His head even tilted hard to one side.

"Your superiors?" I clarified. "Your bosses? Overlords, chiefs, priests, dogcatchers…?"

Still no response from the Prefect other than his display of confusion—but I wasn't buying his act. I realize that not a single Olemsi I met ever showed any comprehension of deceit or subterfuge, but this is a fucking politician. My experience on TBNL taught me certain universal standards exist, and one of them is that politicians always lie. Another rule is that you must jiggle the handle of every toilet in the galaxy before the water stops running.

"The Guardians," I said, finally resorting to the established terminology.

This time, Temoosh perked up, showing his understanding, which I still believed was only an act. "Yes, of course. Their representatives will be with us shortly."

Temoosh moved closer, his demeanor changing dramatically. Sounding less jocular, but still cordial and yet very somber, he said, "But you have the wrong idea about them. They are not the same Ullinarians you have met before."

"Well, they certainly look different," I agreed, partially. "But they're still from the same race that waged war across the whole galaxy."

"That is a matter of perspective, of course."

The response came not from Temoosh, but from a towering figure that entered the chamber from a rear doorway. I turned to face the Ullinarian, or rather two of them, escorting a third figure between them. Oola wore a broad smile, or as broad as her tiny mouth would allow, and there might have been tears forming around those beady black eyes. She appeared in good physical shape, as well as good spirits as she cried out, "Jason! Tony! I'm so pleased to see you both. Everything is fine; you mustn't be alarmed."

My suspicions were compounding by the moment, even after her warm greeting.

"Ambassador Helmemminon," said the Prefect over my shoulder. "Please come in."

Ambassador? That's one term I wouldn't have expected.

The male Ullinarian continued. "Although we share common ancestors with the individuals you recognize as the Ullinarian Empire, our families broke away from the body politic generations ago. Our forbearers recognized, as your recent actions have proven, that the rise of micro/cellular enhancement technology would lead not to the transcendence of our species, but rather, the deconstruction of our inherent character and, ultimately, our destruction."

"I have no knowledge of any break-away groups," I countered. "My database is rather thorough."

"Indeed," he agreed. "But also incomplete. The Empire disavowed our existence. As you well know, theirs was an authoritarian regime, dependent on conformity and obedience from the populace. They would not allow anyone to know some had chosen a different course. We were relegated to a penal colony on Pollaxus, near the K'Nostron border."

That sounded as convincing as a community theater production of King Lear. "Why are you here?"

"We sent for them to meet with you."

Everyone, Ullinarian and human alike, ignored the Prefect. Instead, the bronze female addressed the actual question.

"Because of your actions—"

"—The data bomb," chirped Oola, obviously having already spilled everything.

"Yes, the data bomb," the female agreed and continued. "The security procedures that kept up prisoners failed, and we were finally allowed to leave. Pollaxus is a barren world orbiting a dying star. We require a new home."

My digitalized memories processed the information and I *remembered* something about a mining colony called Pollaxus, but the file indicated they abandoned it a long time ago. Perhaps she was telling the truth, on some level, but it still didn't explain their presence on Olemsi Myucuc. Wouldn't they prefer to return to their ancestral home, especially since they seemed concerned with biological integrity? I didn't hesitate to ask the question.

"Our home world?" the female was obviously appalled. "There are fourteen billion dead bodies littering the surface. The power facilities have overloaded, the air and water is contaminated, the—"

Helmemminon interrupted her, possibly concerned with her rising temper. "Yes, Kressada, that's enough." He turned back to me before continuing. "All the worlds inhabited by the former Empire are no longer viable. And, as I have indicated, we had already rejected their society. We have no wish to go back. However, we do need a place to live, and so we have chosen Olemsi Myucuc. Theirs is a more simplistic lifestyle, one that we find appealing. We have offered to help them advance, with caution of course, to avoid the disaster that befell our own people and in return, they have the shared the bounty of their beautiful planet.

"You see, we owe you a debt," he mused, moving about the spacious room, smiling at the local authorities as he swayed passed. Less community theater and more Roger Corman[7]. If these Olemsi recognized themselves as some kind of ruling body, they were certainly showing considerable deference to the Ullinarian. I was correct before: The Prefect was *not* the leader here.

"Had you not interceded, we would still be cowering in the abandoned mines of Pollaxus, waiting for the scant shipments of food and supplies provided by the Empire. You freed us from that, just as you freed the others like yourself."

The *ambassador* sounded warm enough, but a glance toward Kressada implied something else. She had a rather haughty expression, and a bold stature. I couldn't picture her cowering in a mineshaft or squabbling over scraps. At least, they didn't seem like they wanted to kill me. Yet.

I glanced over at Tony, wondering why he had totally failed to participate in this confrontation—I mean conversation. He'd brightened for a moment when Oola arrived, and then returned to brooding. He was beginning to quiver, as if

---

[7] Roger Corman: Filmmaker on the planet Earth, responsible for some of the worst movies ever made, exemplified by terrible acting and lame special effects. Movies so bad, they're actually kinda good.

struck by a sudden chill. I still didn't know for sure what he had done to himself, or what effect it was having on his body and mind, but it was serious, and probably getting worse. However, it did bring something to mind.

"You say you owe us a debt?" I asked. Ambassador Helmemminon nodded. "Even after that shoot-out in the barn? I know Tony got several good shots off."

Kressada answered. "No one was hurt. They were all wearing protection."

Again, I looked to Tony for a response. His modification made him an expert with weapons so he would be the best person to evaluate that response. I saw no reaction from him, which was quite a disappointment, because as far as I was aware, the Ullinarians did not have any kind of protection against their own weapons. At least, not something they might carry on their personage. There is no such thing as a tachyon-proof vest, or charged plasma condom.

"We understand why you were afraid," one of the Olemsi Councilwomen added. "The attitude of the previous Empire was explained to us in detail. And your role in that Empire."

"My role? I was a *slave*."

The Councilwoman's trunk-like nose twitched slightly as her head tipped. I know I was speaking a language she understood; everyone in this room appeared to understand one another. I discovered weeks ago all I had to do was look at an individual, and as long as that race was known to me and their language programmed into my nanites, their translation matrix did the rest. At the same time, I shouldn't have been surprised that a translation for *slave* was missing from common Olemsi vernacular.

"Compelled to perform duties against my will," I clarified.

Her head righted and she nodded, comprehending at last. That did not, however, seem to initiate any doubt about her new allies. The council apparently bought every single line they had been told.

"There is no way we can ever make amends for what was done to you," Helmemminon stated, taking a seat directly on the council's conference table. "We can only move forward, and strive to create a beneficial situation for all concerned. Please give us the opportunity to prove our good faith and, perhaps, you will choose to assist us. If not, you will be free to leave, as long as you do not disrupt our relationship with the Olemsi."

"We cannot allow disruption," another council member piped up, earnestly, and the Prefect was quick to elaborate.

"The sudden absence of the previous Guardians caused considerable unrest. Now that stability has been restored, it must be maintained."

Perhaps that was the first sincere thing I had heard since entering the room. Stability over actual freedom; many humans have made that same choice in our history, like the battered wife who stays with her husband because the bills are paid and the children are fed. Such a choice is always a mistake.

"What do they want from us?" I asked, directing my question at Oola. I spoke in English, knowing full well that her translation matrix would compensate. Forcing my nanites to operate outside their inherent program was difficult, but over time, I gained a greater sense of control. Hopefully, she would recognize my effort and take the question seriously.

She responded only with silence.

Helmemminon inhaled a giant breath and held it through his entire response. "We have been attempting to restore the orbiting space platform to full operation, but have met considerable set-backs. We require the assistance of an integrated data base."

This caused major concern, firstly, because it sounded quite likely true. Worse still, it implied something a little too permanent. I hadn't fought too long to willingly give myself to slavery once again.

Dread must have been visible of my face because Kressada interceded quickly. "Oola Oola described a similar exchange between yourselves and the Rovalorians. We will compensate you for your time."

"Please," Temoosh urged. "The Ambassador has explained that you have no reason to trust them, but consider this for our benefit. If the deuterium reactors fail..."

It was clear to me by the way he delivered his lines that the Prefect did not understand a word of what he'd just said. These people barely have a handle on electric lights; they certainly didn't know anything about deuterium. It had been rehearsed; he had gotten all the words right, but completely failed to give the speech the level of sincerity that comes only with knowledge. Scratch Corman; this is elementary school Christmas Pageant territory.

"The platform's condition *is* deteriorating," Kressada reiterated, shooting the Prefect with a subdued, but clearly disgusted, look. "But we also need its resources. I doubt the K'Nostrons will distinguish any difference between us and the former Empire."

Not sure I do, either, I thought. "The K'Nostron Empire is in shambles. Most of their navy is so much firewood, and the Gorlack revolution is spreading fast. You're welcome."

"They've been knocked down before," Kressada sneered. "They always come back."

There was obviously more going on here than anyone wanted to reveal, and the attempted snow job wasn't fooling anyone. I didn't believe or trust these Ullinarians, and they knew it. But they maintained their act, perhaps to gage my reaction, or because they still had more cards to play, but hoped to save those for later. Either way, despite my concern, I also saw an opportunity—or at least the chance for an opportunity.

"You don't have to do this, Jason." Oola held out her flipper-like hands palms up. "I am perfectly capable of doing it myself. But it would be easier with your help."

I would have to remember to give Oola a big kiss later. Either through collusion or blatant ignorance, she had just given me the perfect opening."

"Very well." I fought to hold back a smirk. "I'll give it some thought."

Chapter 9

After my false capitulation, came the council's false congratulations and the Ambassador's false commendation. Just like a row of dominoes. There had been more lying in that meeting room than the 1968 Republican National Convention... well, any Republican Convention. The only thing I had yet to ascertain was how much the Olemsi, Oola in particular, knew about what was really going on. For that matter, *I* still needed to know what was really going on; sure, I knew something was up, but no details and no idea of the Ullinarian's long-term goal.

I had a goal, however, short-term. By allowing them to pressure me into restoring the orbiting platform, I might gain access to scanners and a communication system. With that, I could hopefully track down our ship and my two best friends.

Unfortunately, I had no idea when I was going to have such an opportunity. When our meeting with the Council ended, Olemsi guards escorted us, kindly, to permanent quarters more appropriate than the basement cell.

Our babysitters led us from the meeting room, through the building, and surprisingly, out the front door to a deserted city street. Local authorities may have cleared the population for our benefit, or to hide us from the public. Or maybe the cold, pounding rain that had started a short time earlier kept the locals indoors. None of it mattered anyway; I wasn't looking for an escape since I had nowhere to go, or any way to get there.

We only traveled a few blocks from what I assumed was the capitol to an old, slightly dilapidated, brick building, closely approximating a turn-of-the-century New York brownstone. My hair and clothes were completely soaked by the time we entered our temporary home, and all I wanted to do was dry off and clear my head. It was early evening, the end of my first day on an alien planet, but sadly, rest was not on the agenda.

As soon as our escort departed, Tony began ransacking the apartment, which I expected, and would even have encouraged if my opinion meant jackshit to him. It didn't take him long to wreck the entire apartment; it was very nearly empty other than a table and a few chairs in the main room, all illuminated by a single electric lamp. Two other rooms contained a pair of bunks in each, and the last was a charming combination of lavatory and kitchen. Where's Martha Stewart when you need her?

"I meant what I told you earlier." Oola spoke softly, watching the falling rain outside. "I can take care of this myself. Both of you can go if you want."

Before I could respond, Tony's dopamine levels crested. He stormed back into the room, having fully dissected both bunks. "Go? How the hell do expect us to go anywhere, you stupid bitch; our ship is gone!"

Oola flinched from Tony's attack, but ignored the insult and focused on the more salient parts. "Gone? What happened to it?"

"It left," Tony raged. "It just took off, leaving us stranded on this stinking rock. Stranded! Do you understand that, Oola

Oola? You're home now, you got what you wanted, so to hell with the rest of us, right?"

Small trails of spittle were running down Tony's face. He was quaking, and for a moment, I thought he might have a seizure. Oola turned to me, her head resting on one shoulder, silently asking for an explanation.

I complied. "Remember that translator upgrade he bought at the mining outpost?" She nodded. "Well, that wasn't the only upgrade he gave himself."

He swung around, about to tear into me. I already figured out a way to diffuse his rage, but this didn't seem to be the time or place. However, if I could just push the right button...

"Oh," I added casually, "and we fucked."

Tony's face remained red as his anger quickly turned to shame. He fell silent and dropped into one of the plain wooden chairs.

"Who took the ship?" Oola asked, her eyes darting between Tony and myself, as if trying to complete a picture. I understood why the sudden revelation didn't make sense to her—I would have never seen that coming. "Of everyone we left behind, only Leo is capable of interfacing with the controls. Why would he..."

"That's right," Tony confirmed, calmer, but still distinctly bitter. "Jason's housecat stole our only transport off this planet. A cat." He started laughing and leaned forward, burying his face in his palms. "I've been screwed over by a pussy!"

"The Ullinarians had already found the ship," I explained, calmly. "Taking off was the only way to prevent its capture. I'm sure they're in orbit, waiting for us to make contact."

Oola's posture stiffened. "That's why you allowed the Prefect to convince you to stay; you need to access the platform in order to contact our vessel. You have no interest in aiding my people."

I thought, erroneously it seems, Oola had understood my intentions during the meeting. Her recrimination surprised me, and it hurt. "I will do anything I can to help your people, but cooperating with the Ullinarians is not going to help anyone."

"They lied to us at least three times in that meeting. Tony shot and definitely killed several Ullinarians. I saw it happen. If they had been using a force field, I would have noticed. Did you look closely at Kressada? That Barbie doll has never done manual labor in her life; she certainly was not a prisoner on Pollaxus, or anywhere else. And we have proof from Captain Betty there have been convoys between here and the Ullinarian home world for weeks. Their home world, not Pollaxus."

"Yes, Jason, I know all that. But you saw the orbital platform. It is capable of annihilating all life on my planet. I cannot remove that threat without getting aboard."

This was my turn to look dumb, and rather surprised. For all the time I spent with Oola, I knew her to be, like the rest of her species, one without suspicion, or cynicism, or any awareness at all of subterfuge. I guess she had learned a few things from me; she was now lying to the people in power, all to advance her own terrorist plot to save her home. My heart swelled with pride—maybe it was a perverse sense of pride, but pride nonetheless.

"Well then," I said, smiling. "I guess we need to cooperate."

"We don't have any other choice, do we, *Jason*?" I could feel Tony's thermostat soar, and he was probably about to explode yet again, but he stopped abruptly when someone knocked on the apartment door.

"Do you think they were listening?" Oola whispered, terrified.

Tony shook his head. "I searched everywhere; there aren't any bugs."

Tony moved for the door, either out of a sense of protection for the group, or a bold eagerness for another fight. But there was no fight coming, only two Olemsi males, each carrying a cardboard box.

"Councilor... Orlaan..." one of them stammered. "Councilor Orlaan ordered this meal for you..."

The two Olemsi nervously entered the apartment and set their boxes on one of the chairs. Under normal circumstances, as if that's still possible in my life, I would understand their apprehension. However, they seemed twice as jittery as those two naked farmers I ambushed a few hours ago. I caught those farmers totally by surprise. These guys must have been forewarned about the strange aliens. So what could explain the abject terror in their behavior? Perhaps it was the Ullinarian lingering in the hallway who made them so nervous.

"Please convey our gratitude to Councilor Orlaan for this generous gift." Oola extended her empty hands while offering a tiny nod to her countrymen. The two Olemsi returned the gesture and then hauled-ass out of our apartment.

"What is this crap?" Tony demanded after opening the first box.

"Seed cakes," Oola answered, a little offended. "In my culture, there is no higher kindness than giving food. I don't think such a kindness deserves a derogatory—*don't eat that!*"

I jumped, and so did Tony as he was just about to bite down on one of the cakes. It was a thin disk of bread, sprinkled with small black seeds, similar in size to a cookie or even a communion wafer. Nothing outwardly suggested danger.

"What? You criticize me for calling it crap, and then you say I can't eat it?"

"No, look!" Oola snatched the cookie from Tony and pointed at its surface. He shrugged, not seeing anything of interest. However, my translation matrix was much more sophisticated than the hack-job program Tony purchased on the outpost. I recognized the pattern of the seeds; it was an Olemsi character indicating plurality, equivalent in function, if not sound, to the letter "S" added at the end of English words.

"It's a message," I explained as Oola began lifting the

cookies one by one from the box and placing them on the floor. After all sixteen disks had been laid-out; I saw only a stream of gibberish, until I realized it was simply backwards. Now, the message was perfectly clear.

Clear to everyone but Tony, that is. "Well? What does it say?"

Oola read aloud in her native tongue. "*Three Rivers.*"

"What the hell does that mean?"

No one had an answer, not even Oola.

"Something just occurred to me," I said, staring at the baked message on the floor. "Everyone in that meeting was speaking Ullinarian, even your people. These guys don't have nanites—at least not like what we've seen before. They don't have a built-in translator. I doubt they can even speak Olemsi, let alone read it. And the men who delivered it were being watched. Sneaky way to deliver a message."

Tony was on the verge of another attack. "But what does it mean? Why not say something useful?"

"If they had tried to spell-out the Articles of Confederation, someone might have gotten suspicious," I snapped. "Maybe there's more in the other box."

The other box contained a loaf of bread, some raw vegetables, and a container of juice. We ate these items while contemplating the wafers. I questioned Oola about the cakes, making certain there was no cultural reason why letters may have been included if not as a message. Although Oola admitted many things had changed on Olemsi Myucuc during her absence, she didn't see any possible intention other than to communicate. She even described, in nauseating detail, the traditional preparation for the cakes, which, in itself, was good reason to leave them on the floor.

I didn't say anything, but I did agree with Tony. Whoever sent us this message could have been more specific. My best guess was this referenced a specific location, probably not a small city in southwest Michigan. Even if my assumption proved correct and this indicated a place, the reference still didn't mean much. Is it dangerous? Should we avoid going there? Or is it the location of something crucial, or a meeting and we should head there as quickly as possible? And who the hell is Councilor Orlaan? He or she must have been someone at the meeting, but is this person trying to help us? The Councilor may not even have had anything to do with the message, but simply ordered food, and someone else took advantage of the situation.

The cryptic message confirmed one thing; the true situation on Olemsi Myucuc was considerably more complicated than appearance suggested.

Worse still, I was already deeply involved.

Chapter 10

Two things regarding the local Ullinarians and their feelings towards me became quickly evident the following morning; the Ullinarians *really* needed me, and they *really* did not trust me. Fair enough on both counts. Actually, it was somewhat liberating having all these cards on the table. This was a game, and we all played on a somewhat-level field. At least for the moment. Sure, there were an unknown number of them against my friends and me, but since I had already committed a nearly comprehensive act of genocide against their entire society—all from the comfort of one of *their* ships—I felt certain I still had more points in my column.

Their need and lack of trust were both revealed in the manner they wanted me to fix their orbiting platform. I was hoping, indeed counting-on, being transported to the facility so I could access the data modules and a transmitter. However, they so wisely saw through that strategy and instead of allowing me aboard, simply brought various components to our apartment. The task was much like what we had done on the fish outpost; Oola and I would interface with the various pieces of equipment and make slight adjustments to the programming as directed.

Although disappointed my grand scheme went to shit before it had a chance, I played forward anyway. I still needed to access the platform at some point, and as long as I was alive and valuable, that remained possible. Also, I managed to get a few inches of new ground on them. I implanted a few tiny lines of invisible programming in several of the modules I repaired. Not much, just a few simple instructions that, as soon as someone returned the component to the platform mainframe, would propagate throughout the system like a virus until it could ultimately fulfill its purpose; a short message to our ship. It was a simple message, instructing them we were safe, and that they should remain in orbit until they hear otherwise.

There was nothing for Tony to do, a mixed blessing to be sure. First, it suggested weapons were not currently a priority. But that also meant he had nothing to do but pace our quarters, constantly agitated. I really needed to check his… *software*, as it were, only I was having difficulty finding any pretense to get him involved in our work. Several Ullinarians supervised every piece of equipment and its adjustment, so I had nothing to do but press on.

The greatest disappointment, however, remained the absence of additional messages from a potential ally. I realized right away how unlikely it would be with guards standing over us all day, but I still hoped for something. Perhaps this mysterious Orlaan person might show; if indeed, he or she had arranged for the message in the first place.

Someone did show up late in the day, only it was not the enigmatic Councilor Orlaan. Instead, Prefect Temoosh and the Ullinarian Ambassador Helmemminon graced us with their bureaucratic stench. The striking contrast between them spoke volumes just watching them enter our apartment together. The short, orange-skinned Olemsi followed the towering, lanky Ambassador. It was like a visit from Princess Toadstool and

Bowser, but only after Peach sold out the entire mushroom kingdom and ordered Mario's execution. That impression might have only been an illusion created by my point of view from the floor, but I was quite sure which of them carried the real power.

"All goes well?"

I wasn't sure if this was a question from the Ambassador or an analysis, or for that matter, to whom it was even directed. It appeared for a moment that one of our supervisors was about to respond. He opened his mouth, a sound was surely about to escape into the air. But then...

"Why the hell are you holding us captive?" Tony erupted, classic timing as always. Annoying, really, but classic in the sense that he sometimes opened avenues of opportunity not easily seen. "We said we would help you, and we are. Why lock us up?"

"You are not captives," Temoosh answered, only slightly patronizing. "You are our guests."

"There are guards outside the goddamn door!"

"Not guards. They are there in case you need anything. I can't expect you to know your way around our city."

Tony's aggression clearly disturbed both men, and I saw that Tony-classic avenue of possible opportunity. I rose from my workstation on the floor and approached, cautiously, puppet and master alike.

"Ambassador," I whispered, "may I have a word?"

The Ullinarian seemed surprised, even amused, by my request, but he consented nonetheless. He gestured toward the hallway outside, and we withdrew.

"When we were aboard that Rovalorian outpost," I explained, "Tony did something, some alteration to his nanites' original programming. It's having... unpleasant side effects."

Helmemminon nodded, understanding. "I don't see how we can help you. As I've already said, we rejected that technology long ago—"

"I think I can fix this, but I need access to the right equipment. Your orbital platform must have a medical bay." The Ambassador's expression quickly changed from one of bemusement to suspicion. He was smarter than he looked. "I'm sorry Jason, but we can't allow you on board the platform. Not yet, anyway. You must understand, we don't completely trust you, and you don't trust us. If there is another way..."

"Fair enough." I struggled to sift through the mountains of artificial memories in my head. The piles of data stored by my nanites were quite thorough, but difficult to translate without the aid of a digital, virtual environment. But by concentrating on Tony's predicament and what I might want to do to correct it, I started envisioning what a Ullinarian medical facility might look like, and what kind of equipment might be lying about. Then I imaged what I wanted and made a list for the Ambassador.

"I need a type four micro-scanner, equipped with a turogenic probe, and a standard medical monitor—for the processor."

The Ambassador didn't even flinch. He removed a small, transparent object from his pocket, similar in size to a pack of cigarettes, and tapped the surface. I couldn't see anything happening on the device; it just looked like a block of clear acrylic. However, I easily recognized the motion of his fingers and the blank look on his face from my previous life experiences; it was essentially a cell phone and he was either issuing orders or playing Candy Crush.

He paused, reading a response visible only to his eyes (or collecting game tokens), tapped another series of invisible keys, and then replaced the communicator. "The equipment you need will be brought down on the next transfer. Tomorrow morning."

"Thank you!"

My response startled me. I realized that for a moment, just

a small moment, I questioned my earlier suspicion. The Ambassador hopefully sensed the sudden shift and it would help me get closer to my ultimate goal—which itself was still a bit hazy.

I hurried back into the apartment, fearing I might betray my reversal of that sudden aforementioned shift. Tony silently glared at me from across the room, knowing full well what I had been up to. But he didn't say anything, so it was possible that somewhere in that beefy, hormone-blender of a brain he knew I was right.

Meanwhile, Prefect Temoosh and Oola appeared to bond. They chatted on about the city, its history, and Oola's home district, which apparently, was somewhere very far away.

"I would really like to know how long I've been gone," Oola lamented, continuing their conversation.

Temoosh nodded. "You say you never heard of the first World Unity Conference, which means you left over two hundred years ago. Records from that far back are rare, and hard to trace, but I have already sent a request to Longlaria—which is now a large city, by the way. There are thousands of people named Eenepret there, but hopefully, one of your relatives made a record of your disappearance. That is the best I can do."

Their use of euphemisms was fascinating. *Been gone*, *left*, *disappearance*... but not *abducted*, *imprisoned*, or *enslaved*, all of which would be far more accurate.

Oola flapped her hands by her sides, exhibiting obvious excitement. "That is enough, sir, thank you."

"What about a library?" I asked, getting an idea of my own. "Perhaps if Oola could look around and find something familiar. A point of reference..."

"That is an excellent idea. I will have you shown to our central library when you are finished for the day."

I gave the Prefect a momentary cold stare, which he completely failed to interpret correctly. "It's been a long day already. I think we are finished."

Temoosh didn't respond. He just stood there, obviously waiting for something... something quite obvious: permission. The Ambassador, listening all along, spared the Prefect from his awkward predicament. "The library is across town. I will arrange a vehicle to take you."

Tony grunted and left the main room. I heard him flop down on one of the bunks. Probably for the best.

Helmemminon tapped away at his alien smart phone. Forty thousand light years away from Earth and I still can't get away from fucking Twitter. And he's not even driving! This did, however, bring an important issue to mind: that device must work by transmitting signals, yet we detected nothing of the kind when we arrived in orbit. Also, I did not recognize the device by name or function in Ullinarian terms. I only recognized it by its obvious similarity to its Earthly counterpart.

The absence of knowledge regarding Helmemminon's device, like a kind of digital *color-blindness*, perplexed me the entire time we waited for our ride, and even during the ride itself.

I was no closer to answers by the time our transport stopped at a large, classical-looking building. Not that I know what passes as *classical* on Olemsi Myucuc, but the grand colonnade surrounding the first floor seemed to qualify. A small, tasteful sign mounted above the main entrance read Capitol City Library.

Inside, the resemblance to every library I had ever visited was unmistakable; it felt, sounded, and even smelled as expected. Olemsi citizens quietly shuffled around between the shelves or sat in comfortable chairs reading. A slight twinge of mildew and old paper perfumed the air. There was even a large desk at the center, staffed with individuals, presumably to answer questions. Yet, there were no actual books. *No books!*

Instead of traditional shelves, these racks were a series of cubes, open on one side, filled with scrolls, or long sheets folded accordion-style. A quick inspection of the nearest selection suggested the scrolls were much older. Unfortunately, my quick survey also revealed a total lack of labeling, or any visible system of organization.

Oola appeared right at home. She marched into the building as if she'd been coming here every day since childhood. I trusted she knew what she was doing; perhaps all libraries on Olemsi Myucuc were arranged the same, and had not changed since her abduction.

I felt fantastically awkward, and conspicuous.

Every melon-colored head in the room turned in my direction, their tiny black eyes fixed and glazed. The whispered voices increased in both rate and volume. Some of them pointed, while others moved either closer for a better look, or backed shyly away.

Hey, a captive audience. I felt like I should start singing the National Anthem or a selection of power ballads from late 80's hair bands. My digitalized memory could provide me with all the words, but fortunately, it also contained the knowledge that I lack anything even approaching musical talent. Instead, I hurried to the nearest rack, removed a scroll and hid my face behind the title.

Observations on Malgagron Rahorahaz
The Devoted and Beloved Service of Shashanee[8]
By *Professor Porlinorea Porlatta Koricorba Yaks.*

Well, this certainly wasn't going to help. If alcohol had been available to me at this time, my liver would definitely be

---

[8] Shashanee: The Shashanee tradition began after Malgagron Rahorahaz said good night to a neighbor and watched as a golden arrow descended from the sky and carry her away in a blur of red and green light. Incidentally, the neighbor in question was a young woman named Oola Oola, whose name, unfortunately, was forgotten over time and replaced with the title *Shashanee* by Professor Yaks herself, as it was the easiest way to deal with a missing typewriter key.

in for a fight. A colligate examination of some local religion would probably put me over the edge. Cue a nasty flash back to Sunday Schools past, I replaced the scroll.

The library patrons, and their previous fascination, began to wane. *Shashanee* be praised! I was the third (or at least second, depending on how thickly you draw the line between first and second crops of Ullinarians) alien race to visit their planet. The population, apparently, had adapted to the whole thing, a development that might serve me well.

I had not come here to study the behavior of the natives, nor did I care too much about how long ago Oola was abducted. What I really needed were answers regarding that damn enigmatic clue left in last night's dinner. *Three Rivers*. This had to be a location of some importance for someone to take the time to spell it out in garnish. Either that or we were being punked by the only asshole who understood sadistic humor on the entire goddamn planet.

Having no idea where to begin my search, I did what every lazy high-school student would do. I went to the librarian. "Excuse me…"

Her tiny black eyes became momentarily enormous when she looked up from her desk. I don't know if it was my sudden appearance that surprised her, or my perfect use of her own language. Or perhaps I had just completely misinterpreted the reason for this desk and her presence behind it. She quickly resumed her composure and turned into a block of disapproving ice.

"Is there something you need?"

Oh, this does feel like high school. "Do you have maps?"

"Yes. In the map room."

We stared at each other for what seemed like an obnoxious amount of time. I was fully aware that the Olemsi tended to be fiercely literal people, and not sensitive to nuance. Asking about the map room would have expedited the process, but I was more in the mood to be difficult, again, just like high school.

She eventually figured out what I was waiting for and pointed to a distant corner of the building. "Are you looking for something in particular?"

I hesitated asking for more, specific information; after all, it had come to me as a rather cryptic message. But the phrase *Three Rivers* seemed perfectly innocuous to me, and searching through maps could take hours, if not days.

I decided to take the risk. "Three Rivers."

Had the librarian possessed anything approximating a sense of humor, she would have asked which three I had in mind. She was, however, clearly not amused, and even more interestingly, she suddenly tensed. Her brow narrowed, and her hands even began to shake.

"I don't know what you mean," she replied, crisply. Her tubular nose crinkled as if I just dumped a pile of shit in her lap. "The maps are in there."

Her gaze quickly returned to her desk, where she began randomly straightening objects with trembling flippers. I started to move away, heard her shift, and glanced back as discreetly as possible—which wasn't very discreet at all. This was one occasion where the native's lack of street savvy proved useful. She her back to me, but made no attempt to hide the object she lifted to her ear. It was unmistakably a telephone receiver—low technology that I already suspected was present on Olemsi-Myucuc because of the wires seen outside the farmhouse, and how the Ullinarians had somehow known to come and apprehend Oola.

Of course, the presence or absence of a telephone was hardly of any real consequence. What did matter was the reaction garnered by my use of the phrase *Three Rivers*. Not only had these words shaken the dust off the librarian's rafters but had also motivated her to make a quick phone call. But to whom?

I remembered watching Ullinarians march Oola from that farmhouse. Despite having ample opportunity, I never bothered asking my friend exactly what transpired *in* the aforementioned farmhouse. We reunited not too long after, so the event completely fell off my radar. How long did Oola speak with the farmer's wife before making a phone call? And how long after did it take for the cops to arrive?

An unpleasant feeling began to seep under my skin, like that feeling when, as a child, you know your report card has been mailed, but you don't know if your father has seen your chemistry grade yet. It wasn't panic, or even dread, but that miserable period of waiting for the unknown.

I considered making a run back to the apartment, but where would that get me? There was a grand total of two human males on the planet. One couldn't be persuaded to leave the house, and the other, me, was an idiot who went to the library with an Ullinarian escort. If that librarian was narking on me, I'd be toast wherever I went. Maybe my best bet was to what I came for before an almost certain, and unquantifiable amount, of shit hit the nearest fan[9]—kinda like my chemistry grade.

I shuffled towards the map room, trying to look as casual as any alien can in a library full of educated locals. The patrons had mostly lost interest in me, but when I walked by, some would look up, observe, and go back to their reading. A few even smiled or nodded in some kind of gesture I couldn't easily identify.

Only a few casual steps before the map room, one foot in front of the other. Just a guy browsing. I could handle this. I had truly become the master of my own domain, the master of my own destiny, the master of many destinies if I'm honest, and—

"Finding anything useful?"

---

[9] Olemsi are biological organisms, therefore they eat and produce solid waste material. Olemsi also have electricity and motorized vehicles, therefore, they also have fans. It is a galactic constant that when a society produces both shit and fans, invariably, these two disparate objects eventually come into contact. Another constant is this event always permeates the common vernacular of the species in question, resulting in phraseology with exactly the same meaning for every species on every planet across the entire universe.

Shit.

I stopped in my tracks. My blood went cold, and I wondered how the librarian had known to call this particular individual.

I turned to face the speaker. Kressada had crept up from behind, wearing a smirk perfectly suitable for any spring Formal or public execution. Whatever was going on at this point, it was pretty clear who was winning and who was losing.

"No," I offered, carefully. "None of this makes much sense to me."

The Ullinarian seemed content with that response. She even nodded and surveyed the room. "Yes. The Olemsi are very... simple."

The contempt in her voice was unmistakable. Her eyes swept the room full of people and paper, and her delicate features seemed to turn in on themselves as if trying to shield her senses from so much unpleasantness. Those same features came to bear on me after a few seconds, and she leaned forward, her lips coming close to my ear.

"Your message was successful," she said with an audible sneer.

I tried to play it cool, but since I was nervous even before she arrived, I'm sure I failed miserably. "What message?"

She scoffed. "The one you hid in those components. Your ship—the assault vessel—is now in geo-synchronous orbit opposite our platform."

"Uh..." I had no idea how to respond, or how to proceed. My legs turned to lead, and my brains to mush.

Kressada could read my reaction, and knew she had her fingers on all the right buttons. *My* buttons. I could see her feeding on my terror, making her taller and stronger. She continued, "I... *we* allowed the message to transmit because there was no reason to stop it. I have no desire to harm your colleagues. They mean nothing to me. But if you try anything like that again, I will call in every ship under our control and burn them out of the sky. We're trying to help you."

Her smile blossomed, as menacing as it was bright. We both knew her threat was real and we both understood there were deeper implications. My friends in orbit were now essentially hostages.

"I had to let them know I was safe," I admitted, subtly acknowledging the threat, and conceding. "As long as they're safe too, I see no reason to try anything like that again."

"Good. I'm glad we understand each other." Kressada's business-like demeanor returned; she seemed satisfied. She started to move away, then stopped suddenly and turned back. A look of delight came over her haughty face, an expression I'd seen on certain regular clientele walking into the Peking Steakhouse on all-you-can-eat-crab-legs night.

"One more thing... I've gone through our records and found the location of your home planet. I believe you call it *Earth*?"

A chill gripped my chest. *So that's how it's going to be?* Was she now to use my entire planet as a hostage? On the bright side, I suspected these particular Ullinarians didn't have the manpower to launch a planetary onslaught, especially without the use of upgrades. They could always invade the Peking Steakhouse, though—much like the County Health Department on numerous occasions.

Still gloating, Kressada must have surmised what was going on in my head, and clarified, "I'm telling you this so you know what we have to offer. When our platform is fully functional, and we are safely established on this planet, I'll give you the coordinates. You can go home."

I forgot myself for a moment, along with my suspicion, and my fear. I started asking questions about Earth. "Is it safe? Are there still people there?"

Kressada played the situation like a master card shark, and refused to say anymore on the subject. She didn't even twitch an eyelash. The perfect poker face.

"When you're finished," she insisted, politely, "I'll tell you everything you want to know. Enjoy your reading."

I remained like a statue as the Ullinarian finally left me. She accomplished her mission with considerable finesse, placing me in a position of even greater bondage. But she'd made one critical mistake. For the first time since landing on Olemsi-Myucuc, I was now absolutely certain who was in charge around here. It was not the Olemsi Prefect, or even Ambassador Helmemminon. Kressada, young and beautiful by Ullinarian standards, was my greatest enemy.

CHAPTER 11

The map room was small and completely deserted when I arrived. In fact, the layers of dust and insect webs suggested it tended to be deserted on a regular basis. Kressada's surprise attack, and resulting victory, still had me shaking, but at least she never mentioned anything about *Three Rivers*. Whomever the librarian called, it clearly wasn't that horrible woman.

Just like the main part of the library, this small annex displayed no recognizable system of organization. The phrase *half-assed* came to mind with a single wall of cubes, all stuffed with oversized paper sheets. I grabbed one at random and unfolded the awkward map, wondering if this was what my mother had to do on road trips when I was a child. A table would have been nice. So would better lighting. And a pizza from Grady's[10]. I strained to read the labels on the finely, hand-painted landscape, and realized neither of those would be

---

[10] Grady's: A mom and pop pizzeria in Bloomington, Illinois on the planet Earth. Easily the best food on the entire planet. Not you-didn't-kill-me-even-though-you-had-the-chance good, but rather please-take-what-little-functioning-lung-tissue-I-have-left-for-another-piece good.

of much help. The script was light, delicate, aesthetic, and completely illegible. Calligraphy impersonating cartography. Lovely to look at, but useless for navigation. I tried another and found the same thing. One apparently can't travel to anywhere on Olemsi-Myucuc without already knowing how to get there.

I was flummoxed. Libraries are repositories of knowledge, and this one might serve that very purpose in some respect, but with no visible system of organization, I required more than translator nanites to make any use of it. Oola seemed to know where she was going; perhaps they taught schoolchildren how to navigate the unmarked shelves.

I decided to track her down and enlist her guidance, but when I turned, I found the doorway barred by a young Olemsi male. He was tall for his species, nearly matching my stature, but he also had wide shoulders, thick arms and a chest that made him more closely resemble Tony. That resemblance increased markedly by his attitude.

"Are you trying to get us all killed?"

The question surprised me even more than his sudden appearance. I'd never seen any Olemsi display hostility or recrimination, and this guy radiated both. He waited for a response, his beefy arms on each side of the doorframe, quite successfully preventing any chance for me to escape.

"I, uh, um… huh?" Even with a half-computerized brain, I had no idea how to process this encounter. I almost wanted Kressada back because I understood her.

Those tiny black eyes made it hard to tell if he actually rolled them or not, but I'm pretty damn sure he did before continuing. "You asked the hostess about *Three Rivers*. Could you be any more reckless? You're just lucky she's a sympathizer or you would be dead already."

Well, at least I'd identified whom the librarian had phoned. Now, I just needed to figure out why. I'd have to proceed with caution, however; this man obviously had little patience with my naivety—, which I could certainly understand. I generally had the same feeling towards his entire species, possibly incorrectly.

"I just want to know what it means."

"Why?" he demanded. "So you can use the information to bargain with the Guardians? We know they hate you, and we know why. Somehow, you're still alive and freely roaming the city. What have they offered you?"

I was reluctant to reveal anything since this man was obviously very angry and suspicious of my intentions. He also seemed to know considerably more about what was going on here than I did. Perhaps my own fears were simply an aftereffect of my recent conversation with Kressada, I reasoned, and so I considered trying to get more information out of him than I imparted to him. Usually, such an effort with an Olemsi would be easy, but I didn't think my usual manipulation would work. Not this time. I would have to offer him something before I could expect anything back.

"I agreed to help them restore the orbiting platform before its stabilizer's fail; if we don't, everyone on this planet will die."

His tiny black eyes widened. My guess was that he had not been aware of this particular danger. Or, once again, maybe he just knew a hell of a lot more about it than I did—which was looking more likely.

If he were going to offer me anything, I would never know. A voice came from outside the map room, a familiar female voice calling my name.

"Jason, are you in here?" Oola appeared behind the imposing male figure and her eyes met mine. She ducked under one of his massive arms, and even bade he excuse her as she passed.

"I found something," she said. "Sorry to interrupt—oh. Where did your friend go?"

I watched, helpless, as the man turned and hurried away

through the library, but I couldn't follow him without shoving Oola from my path. That would do little to endear me to the local population, so I just watched him retreat. *Shit.*

"Doesn't matter now," I said, resisting the urge to castigate. "What'd you find?"

Oola held up a folded ream of heavy paper and waved it excitedly. "When I was a little girl, my parents told me about a massive fire that consumed the forest near our home a few years before I was born. Even though we didn't have any kind of official calendar back in those days, I thought maybe I could use that event as a reference, as you suggested, because it is easy to establish the age of trees. So I looked-up the Tandarish Forest, which, sadly, burned again about twelve years ago on the current State Calendar."

Her voice rose in both pitch and speed. "I found this account, written after the last fire, which describes 'the extensive damage to Tandarish included the loss of over a hundred Parpara trees, many of which were nearly a thousand years old.' Since Parpara trees can live for several thousand years, I think it is reasonable to assume all those trees began to grow sometime after the fire my parents witnessed. That means I was abducted and in the Ullinarian's possession for a thousand years."

Okay, I had to admit that was a big deal. I'd been wondering how long since my abduction after awakening months ago on the Ullinarian scout ship. My nanites were wonderful little machines, capable of so much, including a meticulous record of passing time—beginning at the point of awakening. For some reason, no records were kept as to how long I served as the core of a central processing unit. But Oola's discovery didn't answer any questions about the Ullinarian's plans or the meaning of the culinary message, so I didn't really give a damn. I had much bigger fish in the oven.

"That's good to know," I patronized, "but I was trying to find out something about that whole *Three Rivers* message.

Got anything on that?

"Of course," she said evenly. "Isn't that why we came here?"

I may have to reconsider my attitude towards both Oola and her entire species. Perhaps, all along, I have been mistaking simple politeness for naivety. On the other hand, she really probably should have opened with that.

"Well? What does it mean?"

"It's a name, just like we thought, for the city—this city. It was changed to *the Capitol* when the Ullinarians first invaded six years ago."

For several minutes, actually one hundred and forty seven point three seconds, I stood still, staring at Oola, expecting more information. None came. "*And?* Is that all?"

"Yes."

I reconsidered my reconsideration. Maybe her entire species was just one giant whoopee cushion; loud, full of air, and, ultimately, empty. "What the hell does that have to do with anything?"

"You still don't understand?" Oola asked, her eyes bulging out in shock—which produced very little effect. "Names are very important to my people; they can't just be changed."

"It's not a message, it's a signal," I whispered, mainly to myself. This was one of those rare moments in life when something that should have been obvious from the beginning, yet wasn't, suddenly became clear. I'd regarded Oola as childish every time she corrected me for misusing her name. Indeed, I typically regarded her entire species as childish, but I was looking through the lens of my own bigotry. I was the whoopee cushion.

I quickly recapped my recent encounters, particularly the angry young man, and assessed what it could all mean.

"That man who was just here," I pointed at the empty space where he previously stood, "said something about the hostess being a *sympathizer*. Do you think there could be some kind of underground resistance among your people?"

"I'm certain of it."

I agreed. It made sense, but I had no idea what it might mean for us. Any organized group would recognize my potential as both ally *and* threat, which made the initial message even more ambiguous. Why provide me with the password, only to confront me about using it? Maybe they weren't as organized as I hoped.

Another possibility was that the resistance didn't send us the message in the first place. It could have come from the Ullinarians to smoke-out the rebels. No. Kressada wouldn't have challenged me here if using me in that function. Instead, she'd be the first one offering me greater freedom; enough rope to hang myself and anyone else she regarded as her enemy.

My head started to ache. If I'd learned anything from my experience on TBNL, and the disastrous uprising I launched there, it was that politics is well outside my capabilities, even with my enhanced brainpower and memory. I needed to avoid assumptions and stay the current course.

"Let's get out of here," I suggested. "Maybe they'll try to make contact again."

Oola started to protest, but I dismissed her. After two unfriendly exchanges in such a short time, I just wanted to get out before another one could begin. Besides, the librarian had mysteriously disappeared from her desk, and the stares from the locals seemed even more menacing than before.

Chapter 12

Sleeping that night was impossible. True, I didn't really need sleep, not with my nanites constantly repairing my cells at a molecular level. However, just as with my normal life before abduction, sleep remained the best and most efficient way to pass time, which dragged on long and slow without it, especially when I wasn't plotting, sightseeing, or committing genocide on a scale that would make Pol Pot[11] salivate.

Tony flew into a rage almost as soon as we got back to the apartment. Apparently, I should have "kicked the dude's head in" for not giving me the right answers, and I should have gotten the same for asking the *wrong* questions. He resumed his usual task of stomping around the various rooms after his little rant, sweating and swearing. I think he also ate some of the cutlery[12] in the kitchen/lavatory, but I'm not sure; I didn't check.

---

[11] Pol Pot: Former Prime Minister of Cambodia, and mass-murdering fuckhead.

[12] Nanites require certain base materials for self-replication, so upgrades occasionally consume metal. For what it's worth, copper pennies are particularly nutritious.

Morning finally came and our first load of Ullinarian system components arrived. I was quite grateful because Helmemminon carried through on his offer and provided my requested medical equipment. Unfortunately, he remained to supervise the procedure.

Tony watched while I prepped the equipment. Anger poured from him like pepper fumes rising from a fajita prepared by a particularly vindictive sous-chef at Benningan's circa 1987, but he remained stationary nonetheless. Somewhere under all that muscle and surging hormones, he must have known I was right; I had to correct whatever was going on in his body. If that knowledge did exist in his thick, sinewy head, it clearly wasn't strong enough to penetrate his outward resistance.

"You understand this technology," Helmemminon asked, hovering over me as I wired the micro scanner into the medical monitor. "Even without being interfaced? Can you recall all knowledge from your nanites?"

"Yes." Although the Ambassador acted genuinely interested, I could smell a fishing expedition from three blocks away. I could have explained the need for certain prompts, or how information occasionally blossomed randomly for no apparent reason, but I kept that to myself. I was now completely convinced, after my latest encounter with Kressada, that this crop of Ullinarians represented danger. I still couldn't wrap my head around how, or for that matter, who they could possibly be. Worse was the growing certainty that I should understand why they appear so different from what I remember about them, but for some reason, that knowledge escaped my conscious mind.

"I'm ready to begin."

Under Tony's burning glare, I raised the micro scanner with one hand towards his face, while my other hand remained on the processor. The name of the device was misleading. It scanned on a microscopic level, but was itself rather large, and

I had difficulty keeping balanced with one hand.

"May I assist you?" the Ambassador offered, already leaning forward and taking the probe in both his clamp-like hands.

"Thank you. The tip has to touch his skin. That's fine." I interfaced with the device the moment everything was in place.

I'd performed this kind of activity so many times that it was no more effort than tying my own shoes. The scanner instantly became part of my body, like my eyes or nose. I could see into Tony's body as easily as looking out the window—actually better. Like looking out the window onto a detailed schematic of the very fabric of reality with everything mapped, charted, measured, illustrated, indexed, color-coded and labeled—all with the complexity of a child's coloring book.

I followed the street signs, examining every block of data along each path with a care that would have touched Tony if he didn't turn so damn red at the thought of being touched by me, especially after what happened. Prude. *Here we go.* I came to the spot where someone had colored outside the lines. Rather than the ordered series of neurons and digital links, this was a jumble of alien code, almost indecipherable. *Almost.* I peeled through the program, layer by layer, and determined its purpose, if not its function. As expected, this *app* did increase the strength and stamina of the user. Unfortunately, it didn't contain a clear expectation of whom that user might be, or the targeted physiology.

There's no way it could never operate properly with these gaps in its program, and because of the carelessness of its insertion, it wasn't removable. Tony's integral nanites had already adopted the foreign instructions and now overwhelmed by the implied urgency of the foreign directions. And from my perspective, these instructions were in ink, not pencil. My only option was to adjust those instructions, reduce the urgency for more strength, more anger, and more aggression. I could not remove the blot, but I could darken the surrounding lines.

I decided to try something risky before withdrawing from this cyber reality. Helmemminon held the scanner, and aimed the tip at Tony. But, with my mind in direct control, I knew I could expand the sensor, and direct the data collection in any manner I chose. I turned my scrutiny towards the Ambassador and saw... nothing.

What the shit pickles—or whatever passes for shit pickles in this corner of the galaxy—? I couldn't even detect his presence, only the memory of him holding the device as seen from my natural eyes before interfacing. It was as if my nanites were blind to his very existence.

Great, I thought to myself. Every step I took to get a handle on this situation was a step backward. I might be the only person in the whole galaxy who got dumber after visiting a library, and now a highly sensitive scientific instrument provided more questions, and no answers.

I disengaged from the device and indicated that we were finished. Helmemminon lowered the probe, apprehensively, probably because Tony continued to glare at us both with a clear desire to kill.

"Was the procedure successful?"

Tony scoffed in disgust and rose from the chair. "Fuck off," he growled, and stormed into the bedroom. Had there been a door present, he would have slammed it.

"As successful as possible," I explained. "I don't know how that program was supposed to work, or who designed it, but it was quite a hack job."

"You deleted it, I assume?"

"No. I couldn't. But I think I neutralized its effect. It'll take time for his body to normalize."

The Ambassador appeared strangely curious; I could see it on his face. He examined the probe and the processor, as if formulating a rationale to take the pieces away. I knew what he wanted, a detail of my activities inside Tony's brain, and anything else they might gain from my operation. They were bound for disappointment, though, since I deliberately, and thoroughly, deleted all records.

"If you don't require this equipment further," Helmemminon spoke diplomatically, casting his line again. "I will return it to the medical bay, where it may be required."

"Fine with me." I knew that was bullshit. Any Ullinarian medical bay would have micro scanning probes lying about as commonly as used condoms in a low-rent frat house along with instruction on how to use them and phone numbers suggesting who to use them with—the condoms, not the probes. Well, maybe the probes too.

Helmemminon gathered the equipment and offered a cordial goodbye. I still wasn't sure what to think of him. Unlike Kressada, who I understood perfectly, the Ambassador seemed to have a glimmer of... I couldn't think of a better word... *humanity?* I wasn't willing to hedge any bets on his better angels, however.

Only one guard, an older Ullinarian female who looked intensely bored, focusing more on the hemline of her tunic than her alien charges, remained. Oola had already started work on the pile of components when I joined her. I picked up the nearest piece of technology and instantly recognized it as a control circuit for radiation shields. Actually, there were two dozen of these waiting for me. I made the first adjustment and moved to the next.

The work was not physically demanding in any way, but it was still drudgery, almost as bad as stocking baby food. The only good thing was that all the technology I examined and corrected contained the invasive programs I'd unleashed upon the galaxy, now ubiquitously referred to as the data bomb, still infected each circuit.

We worked for several hours, paused for a meal—again without any messages, and continued. By this point, I was barely paying attention to the items before me until something caught my attention. It was part of a life support system, specifically, a carbon dioxide scrubber. Perfectly innocent; the Ullinarians, just like humans, breathed oxygen and exhaled CO_2. This was exactly the kind of thing you would find on a space installation, except... Something strange caught my eye as soon as I interfaced with the circuitry.

My upgrading wasn't for mechanical skill—that honor befell my cat Leo—but, as a database, I had sufficient knowledge to recognize something missing. If what I was looking at was part of the platforms environmental control, there should have been a safeguard against depressurization, only nothing of the kind was present. The Ullinarians weren't sloppy, nor were they negligent. This couldn't be a design flaw or an oversight. This was not part of the space platform, but rather something terrestrial.

I started paying closer attention after this, and worked more quickly. The projects began to flow in and out of the apartment like a springtime flood. Most of it was from the platform, but every once in a while, something else was slipped in, stabilizers from a shuttle, circuits for ore processing, and so on. None of it was particularly threatening on its surface, but none of it was useful to me either.

I couldn't keep doing this indefinitely. Oola correctly pointed out two days ago that the orbital platform, in its current condition, was a threat to the planet. However, getting the thing fully operational without me personally having direct access was potentially more threatening. I had to find a way out this apartment—or rather cell—and find out what exactly the Ullinarians are doing, and how to stop them.

An opportunity finally presented itself late in the afternoon. Another device, absolutely not part of the orbital platform, came to us for modification. It was a crudely fashioned power converter created to translate a simple electric current, like that generated here by the natives, into a frequency compatible with Ullinarian technology.

It was the *crude* part I found most promising. No advanced engineering degree was required to see the error or predict the likely outcome from its operation. I recognized the potential immediately. All I had to do was make my required adjustment and let the converter pass. Even if my scheme didn't work, if someone found the error before installation, I had deniability. I sat back for a moment when the faulty component was carried away some time later, and wondered how long before I saw the result.

It certainly didn't come soon. Oola and I continued working long into the evening. The Ullinarians continued to bring us materials at a brisk rate. Either this was because of my zeal earlier today when I realized the mix of sources, or because they were pushing hard for a particular objective. The components became increasingly ground-based as time went by, so I was leaning to the latter.

I really wanted to communicate this to Oola, but a guard always stood present. Now it was a young man; at least I think he was young. Hard to tell really, these creatures were just so hideous. But his expression was one of apprehension rather than the disinterest shown by the previous guard. I doubt this Ullinarian male could change his own clothing without help. He nearly jumped out of his own skin every time Oola or I moved, finished a piece of equipment, or farted.

The stress became visibly worse for him when Tony fell out of bed and wandered into the main room. He swaggered in casually, wearing the most placated grin I'd ever seen.

"Still playing with your toys?" he asked. Something closely resembling a giggle passed his lips as he dropped into a chair.

Oola peered at me, concerned. "We are working, yes."

"Oh. Working," he mumbled, fidgeting with the zipper on his jumpsuit. "Working. Work. To work... You work, Jason works, I work—no, I haven't been working. Sleeping. That's a good idea, I think I'll go back to sleep."

Tony curled-up in the chair and I realized I must have made

Loose Cannon

an error in his adjustments. Not only did his sense of aggression appear completely absent, so too was his sense of, well, everything. He seemed intoxicated.

I visually scanned the equipment in front of me, searching for anything with a processor powerful enough to get me inside his head. Of course, I would have to convince him to interface with the same piece of equipment I would be using, and in his current state, I figured he would be willing but probably not capable, of cooperating. I had to do something, however, since he was not only useless right now, but also a liability.

I never got the chance to finish my survey. A loud boom sounded from outside, a substantial distance away, but still loud enough to shake the building. The electric lights brightened for a second, then went dark. I glanced through the windows. No light came from the street or any neighboring buildings. Just a faint glow from one of the moons above trickled in.

Timing had never been my strongest ally—indeed it was probably my greatest weakness—at least in this life. In my old life, my greatest weaknesses were cigarettes, alcohol and guys with really hard pecs. I'd been counting on an incident like this happening, but couldn't it have waited another nine minutes? Too bad life doesn't come with a snooze button.

My nanites responded to the sudden darkness, and I could see the Ullinarian guard scrambling for his clear block, the same kind of mystery device used by the Ambassador. If my assumptions were correct, and that object was some kind of communicator, I had to stop him. This was our chance, and I wasn't about to let it slip by.

"Get him!" I screamed. Tony only raised a hand to dismiss my order, and resumed cuddling his own arm on the back of the chair.

Fucking useless.

I launched myself at the guard without a second thought.

Hell, without much of a first thought either. My enhancements, never geared towards strength or even agility in general, provided no help, but the Ullinarian was so terrified and unprepared, none of that mattered. My weight collided with him before he could respond, and both of us were on the floor. I pounded my fist against his face. Not only did these creatures look as if constructed from telephone poles, they felt like it as well. His flesh was as hard as sun-dried leather, but I continued the assault, tearing bloody gashes in my knuckles. I didn't relax until the guard had fallen completely silent.

"What is happening?" Oola demanded. "Did you cause this?"

I stood and allowed my nanites to normalize my breathing and begin repairing my broken skin. "Only partially..."

Finally free to explain about the power converter, I brought Oola up to date. I expected a better response.

"Are you serious? Sabotage? Didn't that event in the Library last night teach you anything?"

"Yes," I insisted. "It taught me that we can't keep playing along. Have you noticed the stuff we've been working on today? None of it has pertained to the orbital platform for hours. They are on a push for some ground-based operation—which cannot possibly be good for your people. We have to find out what it is, and stop it."

"But they will be coming for us."

The sound of sirens and general disorder rose from the city outside. It was nowhere near the scale of chaos I had deliberately unleashed aboard TBNL, for which I was grateful. However, the present civil unrest, of which I expected none, would do little to slow the Ullinarians who, as Oola just mentioned, were definitely coming for us.

"You're right. That's why we need to get out of here. Fast."

"And go where?"

"We'll start with the Capitol Building. There has to be information there, maybe even a command center."

Oola composed herself, apparently agreeing or at least complying. "What about him? Is he dead?"

I looked at the guard; my nanites had completely compensated for the darkness, and I could see him as vividly as if in full sunlight. "I don't think... wow." The Ullinarian's face looked much different now than before I started pummeling him. It looked different even than it had when I finished pummeling him. My blood splatters on his skin were beginning to eat the tissue like an acid. A terrible smell wafted up to my nose.

"The data bomb," I said, both awed and disgusted. "I programmed all nanites—including ours, to attack Ullinarians at a cellular level. The nanites in my blood are attacking him."

"That might be useful," Oola still managed to sound somewhat indifferent. "Let's go."

It took us several minutes to convince Tony to wake up. He continued to act drunk, and extremely disoriented. We finally helped him stand up, and when he saw the guard's body on the floor; very little of the face remained.

"Cool," he said. "Did you do that?"

"Yeah, let's go."

Another siren sounded outside, only this one was much, much closer. I hoped the darkness and lack of preparedness on the side of the locals would give us enough cover while we made our way down the street.

Chapter 13

The Capitol building reminded me of the Victorian architecture smattered around the small town where I grew up. And just like that abandoned house I broke into when I was twelve, every inch of the exterior woodwork reeked of age and neglect. We had gone to the backside of the building, where only a few windows faced the blackened alley. Although the main street showed little evidence of patrols, this still seemed the safest location to engineer an intrusion.

"How do we get in?" Oola asked, scanning the mostly blank wall. Her wide, flat hands were flapping at her sides as they always did when she was either nervous or excited. "Someone might hear us if we break the glass."

I pressed my face against the nearest pane, essentially ignoring her very legitimate concern. It was high off the ground, and I had to stand on my tiptoes just for a peek. There was nothing to see but more blackness and my own reflection in the moonlight. I don't know what I was expecting; maybe the swipe of a flashlight beam as a security guard patrolled the hallway. Seeing someone pass would at least provide evidence someone *had* passed, and thus reveal an opportunity. For that matter, I wasn't even sure if the current state of Olemsi technology even included flashlights. I certainly had not seen anything along those lines during our trek through the city.

"We don't have much of a choice," I said, moving to the next window and repeating my futile examination to the same result. "Unless you have a better idea, Tony?"

I had been trying to get Tony interested in this mission since before we left the apartment—hell, for that matter, just keeping him awake remained a struggle. He didn't offer any suggestion, even now, or display any desires, except to sleep.

"Help us get inside, and you can nap while we search," I offered. Bribery often works, and this was no exception. Tony heaved himself onto the narrow window ledge and pushed gently against the glass. The pane swung open with only the faintest protest from rusty hinges.

"It wasn't locked."

Once again, my Earthly bias nearly betrayed me. Tony lifted Oola and me through the open window, and I reminded myself yet again I had to stop thinking like a human. The Olemsi were trusting. Humans were not.

My eyes soon adjusted to the room, and I found nothing of particular interest: two desks containing stacks of paper, dark lamps, and silent telephones. A rack of shelves, all crammed with folded papers, much like what I had seen in the library, occupied one entire wall. There might be something useful in what I assumed was the Olemsi version of a file cabinet, only with the typical lack of discernible organization, it would take us far too long to sift through so many documents.

Oola crept to the door and inspected the corridor, then turned back to Tony and me. "Helmemminon and Kressada questioned me in her office when I was first brought here. There was a computer on her desk…"

"Lead the way," I bade, and dragged Tony, protesting, behind me.

"You said I could take a nap."

"I lied."

We moved down the deserted hallway and up to the top floor. Everything here was just as dark and deserted as the rest of the building, except this door was locked. Fortunately, it was made of old wood, not updated like the cell where Tony and I spent a few hours. All I needed were two good kicks to break the jam.

We entered the office, and it immediately struck me as unlike anything I would expect from an Ullinarian presence. There was a computer on the desk, just as Oola said, and a metal cabinet in one corner. Otherwise, the few pieces of furniture, a desk and two chairs were of Olemsi design, and I had to assume they would be uncomfortably small for such large assholes—most of it was too small even for my completely average height. Evaluating the immediate décor wasn't really the point of my musings, but rather the basis of a salient conclusion; Kressada did not spend much time here. We weren't going to accomplish anything unless we could extract something of use from the computer.

I placed my hand on the part of the computer that my digitally enhanced memory identified as the processor, and found the machine completely dead. The device, for reasons unknown to me, had been adapted to run off the local power grid rather than the typical Ullinarian source, vibrating fibers keyed to the frequency of universal dark energy. The interior power cells should function indefinitely, but as I had previously suspected, these Ullinarians lacked proficiency with their own technology.

"No luck?" Oola asked.

"No power. What about the cabinet?"

"Locked."

"Tony, could you...? Tony!"

In the few seconds I'd turned from the desk to the cabinet,

Tony slipped onto the old wooden surface right in front of me and was already sawing lumber. I had no idea which was worse at this point: a raging lunatic or narcoleptic baby. The sound of my cry merely prompted Tony to roll over and cover his face with one beefy arm.

"Maybe if we both try," I suggested.

Oola and I tugged at the single handle together until the bolts snapped and we both fell backwards to the floor. The door remained obstinately closed. The handle, however, made for an adequate pry bar. The cabinet was a local product, just like all the other furnishings, and probably never designed for too much security. I worked the handle into the narrow gap between the door and frame until it was large enough for us to get our fingers wedged inside. Again, we pulled together. The whole thing snapped open while Tony snored.

"Just weapons," said Oola, showing her disappointment. "But we may need them, I suppose."

Oola was right about the weapons, but she gave up on the cabinet too soon. Something else promising appeared inside, although I understood her failure to recognize the significance of those objects considering the state of Olemsi technology today—not to mention how primitive it must have been before her abduction. I reached past her while she examined a Charged Particle Gun, and grabbed one of several clear blocks. This was same as the device I'd seen Helmemminon use only the day before.

I knew it was a communication device; I had directly observed its use. If it were anything like the cell phones available on my last days on Earth, I knew it could conceivably contain mountains of information. It certainly contained some kind of processor. What if I interfaced? Would all that information be open to me, or would I inadvertently broadcast my location and thus condemn myself to a speedy death? I rolled it around in my hand, staring into what seemed a transparent hunk of plastic. I sensed nothing. My nanites existed to interface with technology; it was almost compulsory. But this object felt as technologically active as a rotten potato.

Perhaps Tony had been correct from the start; we had been in over our heads before we even arrived. I quite likely was not going to save this planet despite my best intentions, but in the attempt, would likely lose my own life, and that of my friends, and who knows how many others...

I wondered if I'd ever see Leo or Fido again. The thought even brought me close to tears. I held the fucking block of plastic, staring through it, and glanced at the *CPG* Oola was using to practice her aim. My eyes darted between the two: transparent block to *CPG*.

"Something's missing," I announced, barely registering it was me who's spoken the words. I gestured with the block and looked at Oola, hoping for some kind of help. "I can't put my finger on it, but something is missing. Something right in front of me, and I can't see it..."

Oola let her gun arm go limp. "Something to do with that?"

"I think so... what is it?"

"It's... It's..." Oola inspected the object I held aloft, her head slowly dropping to the left. "You *are* holding something..."

That last statement sounded odd. I couldn't tell whether it was a statement or a question. Based on her posture, I assumed Oola didn't know either. She was clearly struggling. Her tiny black eyes narrowed. I could tell she was as close to the same conclusion I was. One of us had to get through this.

"What are you holding?" I asked.

"This?" she asked, waving the *CPG*. "Don't you—?"

"—Just tell me."

Dumbfounded by my question, but fully versed in the answer, she recited from implanted memory, "It's a Charged Particle Gun. It draws electrons from the surrounding environment, energizes them through a magnetic sequencer, and propels them forward at the speed of light."

"That's right," I said. My digital memory provided me with every detail on the weapon she was holding. I knew how to use it, who manufactured it, and I could take it apart and rebuild it with perfect confidence. "So what is this?"

Her tiny black eyes grew large. "I don't know."

If a soundtrack accompanied this point in our respective lives, the noise made by a 1990's dialup modem should be playing in the background. Oola had no data on this device, I wasn't sure if she could even see it. For that matter, perhaps I couldn't either. I saw only a clear block, but possibly, there was more to see, but for some reason, I was blind to it.

"This is a communication device. I'm sure of it. I saw Helmemminon use one when I asked him for the medical equipment. We had something similar back on Earth, so I know what it is. But I have no *knowledge* of this."

"But we know everything the Ullinarians know. *We are databases*. How can we not remember, especially while looking at it?"

"Exactly. What does it mean?"

I paced the small office—I always paced when thinking. Part of my brain, a very quiet part, was close to connecting the dots. I could feel it. Unfortunately, I could also feel the fourteen quadrillion nanites in the same region, idling. The little bastards could probably decipher the key, but they didn't function reliably outside the embrace of a computer. Again, I considered interfacing with the communicator despite the risk. If I interfaced and it transmitted a signal…

"Signals!" I cried, my organic brain finally making the connection without the help of nanites. "When we arrived in orbit, we detected no signals of any kind, on any frequency."

"Yes," Oola agreed. "My people still haven't developed that kind of technology. The current communication system is an electronic pulse carried through wires."

I nodded, fully aware of how old-timey telephones function. "That's how my people began. But these," I indicated the block, "must transmit and receive signals—which we *did not* detect. Why not? We were in orbit for a while, scanning the whole time. Certainly, someone must have made a call during all that."

"Are you suggesting our ship's scanner could not detect those signals? But why, if it's all Ullinarian technology?"

"I know, I don't get it either," I said, growing more frustrated. The answer must be close, something so relevant it might change the world, and as invisible as it was crucial.

My frustration might actually have been my greatest weakness. And time. And a few other things like... Well, fuck it. I have weaknesses. Oola watched me pace, considering the questions I'd posed. She looked very calm, at ease, even wise...

"What if the sensors did detect the signals," she postulated, "but we couldn't access the data?"

That struck a chord, and I felt something deep inside my head squirming under the weight of my own stupidity. A revelation lurked somewhere amid my neurons and nanites, but it needed coaxing. She had to keep this going. "What do you mean?"

"Our nanites might be set to block certain information. We know they can implant knowledge." Oola glowed; her organic brain had locked on to the missing details still evading me, and she was running with it, full of confidence. "Perhaps they can implant ignorance as well."

That was it; the one key detail I was missing, and now a multitude of ideas were beginning to crystallize in my conscious mind. "Yes! That explains why we don't know the location of our home planets. We only found Olemsi Myucuc because Betty told me. She only knew because she witnessed the transports and from what she learned from the Rovalorians. It would make sense to block that kind of knowledge from the upgrades."

Something else rose to the surface along with the flood of

new insight, a small seed of wisdom, sprouting under a rising sun.

"Before our interference—okay, *my interference*, who ran the Empire?"

Oola answered quickly, automatically. "High Command; the government."

"Yes, but who was the government? Who made the decisions?"

"... I... I don't know..."

"Neither do I." The small office did not afford much space for pacing, but I took full advantage of what there was. "I never even thought to wonder before. It never occurred to me that someone needs to call the shots. We know that the Empire functioned as a police state, a totalitarian dictatorship, but we never questioned who the actual dictator was. Their own nanites drove the Ullinarian population; maybe they didn't know either. Maybe they were also programmed with this ignorance and lack of curiosity."

Oola's head went more horizontal than I had ever seen it go; her neck even seemed longer. I was certain she had just reached the same conclusion I had, but there was still reluctance in her voice, perhaps from shock. "So these people are..."

"We aren't dealing with a group of outcasts, but we already know that. And they're not just random survivors. The word *Empire* suggests an Emperor. What we have here is... Royalty."

Chapter 14

Voicing my epiphany aloud sent a chill through the room—along with a high-pitched whine that made the wooden chairs bounce up and down. Metal fragments of the cabinets danced across the floor, carried on the faint gravitational waves of an approaching vessel.

I ran to the small window, Oola beside me. We saw a number of orange-yellow darts moving slowly above the city. Even without the benefit of a computer processor or electronic sensors, I knew these patrol craft were scanning the streets, looking for the three of us.

"Oola, you have to get out of here. Quick!"

I could see horror in her tiny black eyes. "You want me to leave you? I can't do that."

"You have to. There are only two humans on the planet, which means they'll be able to find us easily. You can blend in. I've made a mess of this, and it's up to you to save your people. Go!"

"I can't do this alone," she insisted, even as I started dragging her towards the corridor. She struggled, and although I certainly appreciated her loyalty, neither of us really had a choice.

I could never make a run with Tony in his current condition—another result of my disastrous choices. Someone had to continue the fight, and Oola was the only one who could do it.

The patrol craft reached the Capitol building... and continued. Already the sound of their engines was fading, and the surrounding city returned to the dark, calm of night.

"Huh... What the hell?" I asked, mainly to myself. Pressing my face against the glass, I searched for cars racing down the street, shock troops storming the building or at least a single Olemsi peace officer, with a flashlight, donut, and truncheon, checking the front door. There was nothing. The search moved on.

"I know these Ullinarians haven't mastered their own technology, but they should still be able to detect me and Tony."

"Maybe they sent for help?"

"I don't think so," I guessed. "The patrol would have remained, keeping us in their scans. No, they didn't see us."

"Because I have already taken care of that."

Oola and I both spun around to face the speaker, a diminutive Olemsi male who had hobbled into the room, completely without our notice. He was fantastically old; the orange had faded from his face and seemed to blend seamlessly into his gray Councilor's robe. The bulk of his minimal weight rested on a wooden cane. Behind him was another figure, but a far more impressive brute, lingering just outside the door. I instantly recognized him as the same Olemsi who had accosted me in the library.

"Who are you?" I demanded, wishing that I had taken one of the weapons from the cabinet.

"Do not fear me," said the old man soothingly. "My son and I are alone. But we need to leave. Although the Ullinarian sensors are not an issue, they will soon come to make a physical search of the Capitol. Temoosh is certainly on his way, and I doubt Kressada is far behind."

The demeanor of the old man confounded me. Despite looking as frail as tissue paper in high wind, he emoted confidence, and a sense of subdued authority. "You must be Councilor Orlaan."

The old man made a gesture with his free hand, which I interpreted as confirmation.

"Father, we don't have time for this. If they find you here…"

The young Olemsi had moved into the room, his face illuminated by the faint moonlight from outside. I could see the contempt on his face. Whatever he thought of me, his opinion had not improved since our last encounter.

"What do you mean the sensors are not an issue? How can you be sure?"

"Father."

"Just a moment, Tragito," Orlaan dismissed his son and addressed my question. "We implanted a self-perpetuating program into the Ullinarian network, much like your data bomb, ordering their sensors to ignore you. More specifically, they ignore the signal from your tracking devices."

"What tracking devices?" Oola asked before I had the chance.

Orlaan balanced himself carefully and pointed to Oola's collarbone with his cane. "There. You all have them."

"I don't know what you're talking about—"

I was not going to get an answer, at least not at this time. Orlaan had already turned and was shuffling back into the dark corridor, Oola close behind.

"Wait!" I yelled. "We can't go anywhere. Something is wrong with Tony; I can't get him to move."

The young man, Tragito, grunted in obvious disgust and moved to the desk. Even though he was a good ten inches shorter than Tony, the young man scooped my friend off the desk and threw him across his shoulder, fireman style. Tony roused enough to yawn, and then settled back to sleep.

I sighed and finally admitted to myself I'd lost control of the situation and followed Tony's bobbing head from the office. Lost control? Hell, I never had any control in the first place; I had been in over my head before landing on this rock. Really, I should have been pleased that someone else was showing some leadership, regardless of whether or not he could be trusted.

Orlaan, despite his considerable age, got up to speed and moved quickly through the building. He led us to a back staircase, nearly concealed behind a rack of cleaning products, and up to the roof. The sky wore a thin sliver of salmon-colored light. Dawn approached, and with it, we saw the glow of headlights moving about the city, many of them in our direction. Patrol craft still scanned the streets from above, but none of them was in our immediate vicinity—except for one.

The small ship rested on a makeshift pad not far from the exterior door. It looked more like something you'd find in a hillbilly's front yard than on a government building or alien planet. One of the three landing feet was missing, substituted by a pile of lumber. The hull was marred with rust and numerous dents, blanketed by a thick layer of dirt. The forward view port was cracked. The most surprising thing about this vessel, however, was that it was our destination.

"Are you fucking serious?"

Orlaan shuffled past me. "It is perfectly safe," he assured. "We made it appear damaged so no one would think to use it. Come, quickly."

Tragito, still carrying Tony as if he weighed nothing at all, raced across the rooftop to the vehicle. I doubted the thing was capable of flight considering its appearance, but if so, I'd certainly be able to pilot the thing. Ullinarian vessels were pretty much all the same, and my experience more than adequate, despite never having operated this model before.

"I assume you want me to fly this pile of crap?"

No one answered my question. I climbed through the hatch and it became clear my skills were not in demand. Tragito had already dumped Tony on the floor and positioned himself behind the controls. My confidence in this new confederation, which was never very high to begin with, deteriorated at light speed. I doubted the Ullinarians, no matter how shorthanded they might be, would ever train locals to pilot their ships, and it was even more unlikely one could learn on his own. Again, I didn't really have a say in this, so I squeezed into the small area behind Tragito with Oola and the old man.

"Sealing hatch. Brace yourselves," a voice announced through the ship's speakers. It was a familiar voice, but in a most unexpected context. I turned to the front of the small craft and saw Tragito perched absolutely motionless over the control panel. *Holy shit.* Although I couldn't see his face from the backseat, I knew his eyes were blank.

"Your son is an upgrade?" I asked the Councilor, gasping. No wonder the young man reminded me of Tony the first time I saw him. He was far more muscular—and aggressive—than any other Olemsi I'd ever laid eyes on, and now it made sense. Tragito was a military upgrade, just like Tony.

Councilor Orlaan ignored my question, which to be fair, was more of a statement. I felt a slight lurch as the ship rose from its long rest and began moving slowly over the city. Although I could not see out from my position, I assumed Tragito was trying to mimic the behavior of the other patrol craft. I hoped Tragito was at least a better pilot than Tony, especially if their upgrades mirrored each other.

This could be an excellent opportunity. With the young, hostile man interfaced with the ship, I could easily join him inside the computer and take any information I wanted directly from his brain. I could wrest control away from him—I was confident my knowledge of both this technology and experience with it would be enough to give me any easy edge. Eluding the Ullinarian search was more important at this point, however.

I still needed answers, and there was another, possibly even better, potential source sitting right next to me.

"I said *your son is an upgrade.* Explain!"

The old man stared at me with graying eyes for a moment, saying nothing. I'd already accepted the fact that my interpretation of the Olemsi was often flawed, so I tried hard not to make assumptions as to what he was thinking. Fortunately, I was not alone in my needs.

"Yes, please explain," Oola cooed, taking the old man's hand and offering a sincere smile.

Feminine wiles; I never would have considered that one.

"When the Ullinarians arrived seven years ago," he began, giving in to the gentle persuasion of a pretty, I suppose, young woman. "They took family members from several of us on the Council, as hostages to ensure our cooperation. Tragito was such a hostage—or so I was led to believe. In fact, he was upgraded and used aboard the platform.

"He awoke after the data bomb along with six others. It took him a few weeks to figure out where he was and how he had come to be there, but once he did understand, he used an escape pod to return to the surface. The others were afraid to follow. We don't know what happened to them.

"After Tragito came home, he and I were preparing to make a public statement, to inform my people of the true nature of the Guardians, but this new group of Ullinarians arrived before we had the chance. I convinced Helmemminon and Kressada that I believed my son was still a hostage. Because of that, they think they still control me, and my influence with the people."

"Giving you the chance to work against them, right under their nose?" I suggested, filling in any gaps on my own. Once again, I had failed to give the Olemsi their due credit. "So, if you have established some kind of resistance, what the hell was with that cryptic message you sent? If you wanted our help, you could have been more direct!"

Orlaan's head dropped to one shoulder. "The message was for Oola Oola, not you. I do not trust you, or this unconscious creature on the floor. I have been working against the Ullinarians for seven years, and now, because of your interference, their plans with Olemsi Myucuc have accelerated."

"You can trust Jason," Oola urged, still stroking the old man's hand. "And you can trust Tony as well, even though he is a bit of a... well, he's not particularly bright. But he means well.

"Furthermore," she continued, "you should be grateful. If not for the actions of Jason, Tony, and *me*, your son would still be enslaved to these monsters."

The Councilor continued to gaze at me from a right angle, but said nothing more. I figured it would be best to let him mull over everything Oola had said. Pushing him might strengthen his resolve against me, and if I were to get out of this, I needed allies. I also needed to survive, which was looking and feeling shakier.

Speaking of shaky... The ship rocked violently and the force of an impact knocked me forward. The ride had not been terribly smooth to begin with. Tragito, as expected, was not much of a driver, but that ruckus was not the result of hitting the curb, or sideswiping a parked car; we were taking fire.

"They see us," Tragito announced over the ship's speakers.

No shit, you melon-headed gym rat.

"I will have to make a run," Tragito continued.

This didn't seem like a good idea, so I suggested Oola merge and assist. She was a competent pilot, and likely to be trusted by our Olemsi hosts. Orlaan did not object as Oola maneuvered herself to join Tragito at the controls.

The ship leveled and roared into high speed. From my position in the back of the craft, I couldn't see much of what was going on outside, except for rapidly moving patches of sky, and the occasional glimpse of a tall building. What I *heard* was far more revealing. Our rear pulse cannons fired and sounds of near-by explosions followed. A severe lurch suggested we were evading enemy fire. I assumed Oola must be solely behind the wheel while her partner worked the weapons; she wasn't keen with weapons.

We made a sharp turn to the left, followed by a steep bank and roll. I tumbled around the small compartment and caught a brief view of the planet's surface dead ahead. We leveled and accelerated. Cannons flared but nothing hit us. Oola had become quite skilled at piloting in the last few months, and that skill paid off big time. I worried about the old man next to me, though. He was sure to break a hip, his neck, or something.

Councilor Orlaan appeared to handle it well, however. If anything, I needed to worry about Tony. He bounced around like a wet sock in the dryer like the rest of us, but, nearly unconscious, he was in no condition to brace himself. I'm pretty sure I heard a snap when one nasty turn sent my head directly into his ribcage. His nanites would repair any damage.

The broken rib did rouse Tony, finally. With one big, meaty hand, he pulled me away by my own hair. "Dude, should you be doing that in front of people?"

The ship lurched again, this time throwing me backwards, dragging Tony along with my scalp. His head rammed my collarbone and he released his grasp—and a number of detached follicles.

"What the hell is going on here?"

"Oh, *now* you notice? Don't worry about it, we're in good hands," I assured him, unconvincingly, especially as we took a further hit, causing an electrical fault that blew out the interior lights and filled the compartment with smoke.

Tragito returned fire, and thunder from another kill rumbled the cabin.

"Are those pulse cannons?" Tony asked through a yawn. "And where did grandpa come from?"

"This isn't a good time to explain," I said as the ceiling whacked my chin during another steep dive. "But you've been nagging at me to do something, so, well, I've really fucking done it."

"Great," he moaned. "And get this fossil off me."

I tried to help Orlaan find a more dignified place than Tony's lap, but we all went to the floor face down anyway as our stolen ship banked yet again.

"Only three targets left."

The report gave me a boost of confidence, briefly. With such a limited idea of what was going on outside, the sound of a particularly vulgar expletive over the ship's speaker quashed my optimism.

"What is it?"

Tragito answered. At least I think it was Tragito. Hell, who can tell? "Arrow class assault vessel approaching to intercept. We can't repel that kind of firepower. We're already losing shields…"

Assault vessel, I asked myself. Could I be that lucky?

"Don't shoot it," I cried, climbing over Tony and the old man to get a better view. The ship in question screamed towards us from high altitude. It was already in the perfect position to destroy us, but when they fired, the blasts passed safely overhead. We reeled under the shockwave of three explosions some distance behind, and then silence. The assault vessel continued forward and, I assume, took flanking position.

We made one last violent turn and raced away from the Capitol towards the low mountains beyond the city. The landscape before us, bathed in a beautiful dawn, suggested for the first time since landing here, that a bright new day might actually be possible.

"So, Jason," Tony grumbled, rubbing his ribcage. "I take it your cat came back?"

"Yes!" I was certain I had a massive grin plastered on my face. "Unlike me, he has a great sense of timing!"

Chapter 15

The combined efforts of Tragito and Oola piloted our group to a location in the hills just north of the Capitol. Frankly, at this point I didn't give a shit about where we were going, I was just anxious—screw that, I was beside myself with joy, waiting to reunite with my friends in the ship behind us. The rather high speed at which we traveled, high enough it would be banned over any residential neighborhood on Earth, seemed to me inconsolably slow. Eventually—two point twelve minutes after defeating the last patrol craft—we set down inside a gaping hole in the side of a low mountain.

As soon as the hatch opened, I leapt out and waited for my own vessel to land. The cave was dry and dusty, and reeked of sulfur, but I ignored all that. I was also oblivious to the mountains of Ullinarian technology that littered the cave, or the chunks of rock raining from an unstable roof. My Olemsi companions gathered around me, and even Tony was on the move again, yawning and stretching, but awake.

The giant, sleek arrow of orange-white metal eased silently

into the cave. It was so large compared to the opening, I doubted whether it could fit through the wide, but low, opening. There must have been no more than half a micron of free space. Piloting skill like this was the result of more than just nanites; I always knew Leo was a smart cat, even smarter now with the aid of an expanded, digitalized brain, but still... Either the big fish had helped him guide the craft, or there was someone else in the ship.

My anticipation turned to dread. What if angry Ullinarians filled that ship and this was a trick to reveal our base? They certainly were the kind of people who would sacrifice their own to pursue a goal, even for basic revenge. Or it could be another group of liberated upgrades, possibly even Captain Betty, and my beloved cat still somewhere far away.

All of these ideas were nonsense, of course, but acknowledging that wasn't enough to dispel my fear. I held my breath. The hatch opened slowly. A sweet cry of feline bliss sounded even before the ramp began to lower, followed by a flurry of yellow fur. Leo jumped in my arms, and purred—almost as much as I did.

Fido followed close behind. Although he lacked *some* of the grace indicative of a cat, he lacked none of the affection. He bounded towards me like that cartoon dog that dwarfed his human owners. But, unlike any mystery-solving Great Dane, Fido had six legs for balance. He skidded to a halt, reared on his hind legs, and threw the other four around my beautiful cat and me. His big, pink eye was damp as he wrapped his long neck around mine. If Gorlacks had the capacity to pant, or the inclination to lick faces, he would certainly have done so.

I was still hugging my closest friends when Scheleene waddled up to us. His flippers flailed like one of those ridiculous inflatable men advertising over-priced used cars. His lips trembled.

"Oh, I am so grateful you all are safe. We've been waiting for the chance to collect you—"

Fido swung his enormous head towards the walking fish and unleashed an angry "gloop!"

"Oh really?" I asked. "Fido seems to think otherwise. You took the ship up yourself, didn't you? Going to make a run for it?"

"No! I would never—"

Fido released me and turned on the Rovalorian in a flash, using two of his appendages to restrain the fish, and give him more than a gentle shake.

"Fido seems to think you're lying," I pressed. "Tell me the truth…"

"Yes!" Scheleene cried, his fishy eyes looking down in either shame or surrender. "When I saw those Imperials, I wanted to go home and tell my people what I'd seen. But the furry beast interfaced and locked me out."

Fido indicated with a bob of his orb-like head that I had heard the truth, and ceased his throttling. My loyal Gorlack, however, did not relinquish his hold on Scheleene, so there might be more to the story.

"And then what?"

"They wanted to come right back for you three. I talked them out of it. I insisted that if we were shot down, you would die too, so we should wait." Scheleene squirmed and continued. "To convince them, I taught them how to track you all through the implants I gave you when you boarded our colony."

"So, it was *you* who gave us these tracking devices?"

"Yes," Scheleene confirmed. "We do that to everyone who enters our territory. That's how we keep records, to determine who can be trusted, or identify troublemakers. I even have one myself."

"Does that mean your people know where you are?" This could be a serious problem. It never occurred to me that his people might have been tracking us this whole time. If they know what's going on here, and Captain Betty indicated as much, they might just choose to sanitize the whole planet. By sanitize, of course, I mean annihilate. The Ullinarians would most certainly be aware of this likely contingency, which was probably why they were willing to risk my involvement to get the orbital platform operational. They may need its defensive capability.

I ended one war only to start another? Damn.

"No," Scheleene admitted, sadly. "Short range. Quarter light-year only."

Oola chimed in, sounding more aggressive than I was accustomed to, "Why don't we remember it?"

Scheleene fidgeted with his tunic before removing something from one of the pockets. I recognized it instantly as one of the data cards we used at the outpost. "The first command on these is to forget the implant. Your Gorlack is the only one who would remember."

For a second, I thought Oola was going to bitchslap the craven land fish. Honestly, at another time and place, I would pay good money to watch something like that. "I was right, then. What else have you kept from us?"

The fish never had the chance to answer, if indeed an answer was even forthcoming, when Tragito inserted himself into the group, and nearly scolded Oola. "You should be grateful to the Rovalorian." This also cemented my notion that he was an upgrade—not that I needed confirmation. Only an upgraded Olemsi would have recognized the species by name.

"Is there any possibility the ship was tracked?" I asked, wanting to get back to business. "Either while you were in orbit, or when you followed us here?"

Scheleene's lower lip quivered, and nostril flaps pulsated with rapid breathing. "Not accurately. Their reactors are still out of faze, so—"

I silenced him with a dismissive wave. My brain contained an ample amount of technical knowledge, although not nearly as much as did Leo's, so I didn't need further explanation.

Most of the work Oola and I had performed centered around life support and basic functions, before they started coyly inserting more terrestrial matters.

Wait. Nanites were fickle little beasts, full of useful information, but surprisingly stingy in their willingness to give it up. Without the use of a computer processor, or any digital, cybernetic environment in which to expand, these semi-living techno bastards revealed knowledge only with the right combination of thought and stimulus, two sides of a coin that almost never coincided. They did, however, at this particular moment.

"The reactors need to be calibrated with the gamma collectors," I said, to no specific listener. "This is usually done routinely by an integrated component—an upgrade—or it can be done manually. Obviously, none of these Ullinarians know how to do that. I'm not surprised. I doubt Kressada could find the front end of an uncut coc—"

"—Kressada?" Scheleene gasped. He recoiled into Fido's grasp, as if seeking protection. "That monster is here?"

The Rovalorian race had collaborated with the Ullinarians for more than millennia. I was neither surprised that the fish recognized the name, nor by his reaction.

"So, you've heard of her?"

"Heard of her?" It was now impossible to tell if Fido was holding the fish, or if Scheleene was clinging to the Gorlack for protection. "She is the Emperor's daughter and twice the tyrant he was."

Tragito listened with interest. "Father suspected she was the one in control rather than Ambassador Helmemminon."

I'd honestly stopped trying to figure out who the hell was in charge. My batting average for solving that question was, as in baseball back in high school, crap.

"Her uncle!" Scheleene began to hyperventilate; his latent gill slits were throbbing and his coppery face started turning blue. He began to pull away from the Gorlack, who successfully retained his grip.

"We have to get out of here. We have to go back and tell my people, so they can act."

I tried to calm Scheleene by placing a hand on his diminutive shoulder and making shushing noises—which likely meant nothing to him. Certainly, neither effort had any effect. I felt badly for him; after all, it was entirely my fault he was in this position. However, guilt needn't lead to stupidity. I couldn't allow him to contact the outpost, Rovaloria Prime, my great Aunt Hilda, or anyone else.

"You don't understand," he continued, "how dangerous these people are. We knew the Emperor was dead; he was in space when you launched the data bomb. We never thought the rest of his family, and the other powerful families could survive on their own. But they are alive, and trying to restore their empire. We have to stop them!"

"I agree we do have to stop them. Why haven't your people done anything already? Captain Betty told us about this," I said, trying to fill in the gaps. "You must have been aware of everything she discovered."

Scheleene began to calm a little, or perhaps he was just getting weak from the struggle. "Yes, we saw her reports. We were hoping the traffic between the home world and here were liberated upgrades, but we have been preparing a defense if needed. If I can let my people know, they can come in force and wipeout the Imperials. We will all be safe."

"*We* will be safe," Oola barked, stepping forward and shoving her trunk right in the fish's face. "But my people will be caught in the middle."

This prompted a sudden change in Tragito, who had so recently defended the Rovalorian. "We will handle this ourselves. If we fail, then you may do as you see fit."

Turning to me, Tragito continued. "I learned much about you when Oola Oola and I shared the computer. You have made plenty of mistakes—some of which are substantial.

However, I understand you did what you had to do, and that your intentions are honorable. I am willing to trust you."

The elder Olemsi had been following the discussion closely. I assumed his silence was strategic. The surprise endorsement from his son must have tipped the scales in my favor—at least I rose to a position of slightly less animosity. In truth, I probably would have been better off if he continued to freeze me out. The stress of responsibility became heavier every passing minute, and to be perfectly frank, it sucks.

"If we are to resolve this matter on our own," Orlaan began, "all of you must be informed."

About motherfucking time, I thought to myself, and almost screamed it aloud. I had been bumbling in the dark since..., well, since I awoke on that first Ullinarian ship so many months ago, but in recent days, that darkness had measurably increased.

Orlaan didn't say anything further, but instead began hobbling deeper into the cavern. The farther we advanced, the more clear it became that this was not a natural feature, but rather the remains of an abandoned mine. Not that I hadn't seen enough mines or ore processing facilities already. I realized this is a modern galaxy, and raw materials are always in demand, but for fuck's sake, why do I always end up either stranded in space, or struggling for breath underground? Okay, I wasn't actually struggling for breath. The tunnel was quite large, and the air flow more than satisfactory. Even if oxygen was a little scarce, my nanites would be perfectly capable of compensating. I just didn't like it here.

Fortunately, *here* didn't last long. All light seemed to fade away and a new, bright pinprick appeared ahead, growing larger as we approached. The tunnel burrowed straight through the low mountain and opened up above a valley, completely hidden from the Capitol city. From this vantage point, among blooming wild flowers and chirping birds, I could clearly see a sun-lit hellscape.

Dozens, possibly hundreds, of Olemsi toiled in the open air. Many of them constructed, or reconstructed, equipment and small transports. Others carried baskets of raw ore from a mineshaft lower down the slope; huge, overflowing baskets, many times heavier than the Olemsi frame should be able to shoulder. They all appeared to be of the exact same age, same perfect health, and same blank expression, but differed only in clothing. Some were fully dressed in business attire, some more casually, and many were completely naked. The only consistency in their dress was a band around the forehead, holding a small black disk tight against their scalp.

"Upgrades?" I asked, not really requiring a response. "How is that possible? And how can they be moving freely?"

Scheleene shuffled to the edge of the overlook on his webbed feet. "That's old technology," he said, "from the earliest soldier program. They stopped using those centuries ago in favor of a more reliable design."

His explanation only scratched the surface of the questions forming in my head.

I looked around, and besides a number of small Quonset-like huts, where native upgrades worked on ships and equipment, a huge, windowless building dominated most of the valley. Even from this distance, the sound of machinery was as distinct as it was chilling.

"They still have power," I observed. "Or they've recovered from my sabotage. How big is that facility?"

Orlaan's head dropped to one shoulder. "It is much larger than it appears, much of it underground. The first Ullinarian invaders built it and used it to process my people—I only know that from Tragito, because that's where he was taken. From the few reports I've managed to acquire, the harvest has continued. People from all over the province, entire villages, have been taken."

"Are you fucking serious?" The scale of what I saw before me was staggering. So many individuals, all removed from their homes and lives, and seemingly, unmissed by anyone. Certainly, that farmer I met a few days ago seemed totally unconcerned about the presence of the *Guardians*. "How can this be going on right here, a few miles from the Capitol city, and no one know anything about it?"

"Some people do know about it. In the city, rumors abound, many of them true. In the countryside, however, and across the planet, the people suspect nothing. The Ullinarians, through the Council, control the news too well."

Oola's tiny black eyes nearly popped out of her head. "The Council is complicit?"

"Completely. Some, like me for so long, out of fear or coercion. Others because collaboration increases their wealth and power. Temoosh is the worst of them. He sees this as an opportunity for Olemsi Myucuc to become a galactic power, with him at the center. He is greedy and foolish and believes every lie Kressada and Helmemminon tell him. Already, Temoosh has placed many of the more affluent Olemsi families into positions of power, essentially reconstructing our world to conform to Ullinarian standards.

"They keep me around because I'm respected by the citizens. I pretend to cooperate because it allows me some insight into their activities."

This sounded all too familiar. It happened on Earth more than once, and if my home world still existed, it probably happened again. But the sight before me still boggled my mind, the willful ignorance and indolence of the people—although, that wasn't too far from Earthly either.

"If all of them have been upgraded," I said, trying to work all this out in my head, "why haven't they been freed by the data bomb? It's still out there, constantly being retransmitted by every functioning computer in the galaxy..."

My voice trailed off, and everyone turned away from the horrors before us and waited for me to share my revelation. Nodding, mainly to myself, I explained. "That's why they came to Olemsi Myucuc. Your people haven't developed that kind of technology; no broadcast signals of any kind, and no receivers. All they had to do was deactivate their own communication equipment, and the planet would be inoculated."

"What about their personal communication devices?"

Oola's question was valid, and I didn't have a definite answer, but a good guess. "Perhaps the same program that keeps us blind to their existence is enough to filter my program."

I could see the skepticism, not only in her face and in her words, but also by the fact that her head remained fully upright.

"That would mean they have the ability to manufacture new nanites, operating on a new carrier frequency, manufactured with new, uninfected equipment," Oola said. "We already determined they lack a complete understanding of their own technology; most of it, certainly in recent years, developed by either the Rovalorians or the Pardeks."

"Good point," I agreed. "Scheleene, any ideas?"

The fish squirmed. "We analyzed the data bomb right away—just to understand what had happened. Believe me, my people are grateful, and only wanted to make certain how effective it had been. But…yes, if they isolated their systems, they could have purged the program. Your composition was self-replicating, but not immune to removal. As you said before, with its lack of computer technology, this planet would be the perfect place to do that."

Oola took his dismissal of her concerns in stride. In fact, she seemed charged by it. I could see her tiny black eyes grow large; she seemed to rise three feet in stature. There was almost a glow about her.

"Councilor Orlaan, is this the only facility of its kind?" Her voice was bold, and yet respectful.

He nodded.

"Good. Then this is the seat of their power, and their only chance of resurgence. Our efforts must be focused on destroying this facility."

"Use the ship!" Tony cried, his voice echoing slightly off the distant hills. Everyone immediately shushed him! "We have an assault vessel with plenty of missiles. This could be finished in twenty minutes."

Oola turned to him and stabbed a long finger at his face. "No. That would kill too many innocent people. We will do that if we have no other choice, but first we explore other options."

"What options?"

She almost growled. "What is wrong with you humans? You want to shoot everything while Jason manipulates others to do the fighting."

Her accusation stung, mainly because it was entirely true.

"This is my planet. These are my people. From now on, you will all follow my instructions. If I fail, then, and only then, you can proceed with force."

I was both humiliated and exhilarated. In one respect, I had known this woman for only a short time, a few months. Simultaneously, I had known her almost from the beginning of this new life. She had been like a child when we met, naïve and complacent. Oola had grown up right before my eyes, and I couldn't help but feel impressed.

"I'm with you, Oola," I pledged, sincerely. "I'm sorry. Oola Oola. What's your plan?"

Her face twitched in a manner I had never seen before. I suspect it was satisfaction.

"First, we need to see inside that facility."

"I agree." Turning to the Councilor, I asked, "What's the best way in?"

Leo pushed his body hard against my shin and growled. Everyone else in the group responded similarly; well, they didn't rub against my shin, but they made it clear that my intention to go in was foolish, and had no support.

Oola was the most direct at shooting me down. "Not you.

Really? A human. You would be spotted before you even made it inside. *I* will go myself."

Chapter 16

The thought of Oola undertaking this mission on her own ate at my core like the morning after too many chilidogs. Chilidogs with raw onion and half a gallon of warm beer. Tragito volunteered to go along—with Oola, not to the sports bar—, which eased my apprehension only slightly. I wasn't entirely sure why I was so concerned. Was it because I still regarded her and her people as children, foolish and incompetent? Or was it a matter of my own need to be in control? I hated leadership, hated responsibility, and yet, time and again, I'd forced everyone to acquiesce to my will. Perhaps it was just the possibility of these two conducting this mission while I remained ignorant to its progress, or lack thereof.

Back at the cave where our ships landed, we discovered there might be a way to keep the rest of us informed. Orlaan and his son had collected a surprising amount of Ullinarian technology over the past few months, some of it discarded, some of it stolen. Because Tragito's upgrading had been for defense, just like Tony, he lacked knowledge regarding most of this stuff, and so grabbed anything and everything he could. As a former database, I recognized almost everything by name and function, but didn't really know what to do with it either. Only Leo, redesigned for maintenance, repair and operation, and who now stood watch with Fido at the cave opening, would be capable of that. Unfortunately, his skills outside a cybernetic environment weren't of much use due to a lack of opposable thumbs and a language anyone could understand.

One member of our party, however, was capable, despite his own lack of upgrading. Scheleene's people had been responsible for the original design of most of these components, and he possessed the technical skills to build exactly what we needed.

Leaning over a makeshift table consisting of a sheet of deck-plate spread across several ore baskets, Scheleene constructed three small, identical devices. They looked like a cobbled mess of leftover parts from antique transistor radios and children's toys, with bits of quartz and chalk thrown in just for fun. These pieces were, however, complicated circuits and artificial, power-generating crystals that had allowed the Ullinarians to conquer half the galaxy. Not bad, huh?

"Don't I get one?" Tony asked, sounding like a disappointed child on Christmas morning. He was continuing to recover from my adjustments, his nanites and hormones finally near balance. Even so, he still wasn't looking me in the eyes. He turned slightly pink and quickly looked away on those rare occasions when our gaze met.

"We only have enough parts for three units," Scheleene mumbled. Watching the giant fish work was a strange experience. For one thing, the cloudy eyes set on either side of his head appeared incapable of seeing the fine wires and circuitry he handled and, secondly, his hands. Long fingers, developed over countless millions of years, still had the shape and texture of fins, only subdivided and enhanced with strong, but slight, muscles. He worked with exquisite precision and speed, enough to make any Swiss watchmaker, or the ghost of Karl Fabergé[13], sick with envy.

I was more concerned with how my friends were going to get in than how many of us would be monitoring their progress. Councilor Orlaan described where his son had been to the mines several times, which is where most of this material came from originally, and how none of the enslaved upgrades even noticed him. However, that was just the mines, with no Ullinarian supervisors. We all saw Ullinarians in the yard, and certainly more of them were inside that complex, especially if Oola had been correct—and I feel she was—that it was the base of their operations here. More importantly, at least as far as my doubts were concerned, Tragito was an Olemsi. I already accepted that my original assessment of their species was flawed, but I still wasn't sure they had the same capacity for subterfuge as an Earth-born human. Hell, we were *the* masters of subterfuge. We frequently lied to ourselves, so doing so to a neighbor or an enemy was as easy as killing a spider—except the spider always deserved it.

While I stressed, Tony pouted and Scheleene worked. I didn't have the skills to do what the Rovalorian was doing, but my nanites did have the data for me to recognize *what* he was doing. I didn't entirely trust him—actually, the only thing I really trusted about him and his entire species at this point was their desire to survive, and a willingness to do almost anything to guarantee that desire. I watched carefully and knew he was doing exactly as promised.

"You're adjusting the processor to the carrier frequency of our nanites," I observed aloud. "Is that necessary?"

Scheleene used a molecular resonance capacitor—which looked a lot like a blow dryer—on the crystal chunks. "Necessary? No. But it will increase efficiency, and help establish a strong connection with less power. I don't know how long the

---

[13] Karl Gustavovich Fabergé: Jeweler for the Russian Royal family, best known for eggs as seen in the documentary *Octopussy* 1983.

cells will last; they are old."

My nanites processed his response and confirmed the statement. I remained silent after that, content to observe, even though it was obvious the fish did not appreciate me leaning over his shoulder. That I understood; no one likes someone else hovering this close but, fuck him. As I said before, I didn't quite trust the cold-blooded, scaly bastard.

I didn't take my eyes off Scheleene or his work until Oola and Tragito returned from their supply run. They had acquired new clothing—*new* being a rather relative term in this instance. More accurately, they were wearing different clothes than before they left. These latest threads were far from new; torn, dusty rags stained with sweat, grease, and had a charming stench of Olemsi feces. In short, a perfect match for the workers we had seen from the hilltop.

Another portion of their haul was a pair of those disk-shaped devices, complete with elastic headbands. Part of me wondered about the design; the Ullinarians were not exactly kind people. In fact, they were fucking monsters: cruel, brutal slavers, murderers, and conquerors. The headbands seemed strangely humane and radically out of character. The Ullinarian controlled soldiers who invaded TBNL had control devices attached to their skulls, permanently attached. When I transmitted the data bomb, all of them died. I carried many of their faces in my digital memory.

"Oh, yes," Scheleene exclaimed, examining one of the disks. "Just as I thought. Early control devices. The Pardeks created these centuries ago. They tried to cooperate with the Empire... for a while."

The Rovalorian didn't continue with that discussion, but rather went back to his work. I wasn't entirely sure, but I think his gills had turned bluer.

"I've worn one of these every time I've gone in," Tragito explained. "It's like being invisible."

This brought to mind another possibility, one I hadn't considered until now. "Have you tried to interface with that? If one of us can merge with their new network—if there is one—the data bomb should infect that network. We could end this right now."

Tragito made a flapping gesture with both hands. "I've tried. Nothing happened."

Damn. "There must be a block; either in the device, or in us." We were back to the previous, possibly ill-conceived plan.

Most of us waited for the next few hours while Scheleene continued to work on his communication devices. I signaled for Tony to take over when I got tired of watching him. On one occasion, Leo and I ventured out the cave opening and climbed a near-by hillock to observe the city. From this distance, I couldn't see what was going on, but the distinct sounds of occasional gunfire and the faint traces of rising smoke promised things there were not going well. My guess, and it was only a guess, was that the Ullinarians were tearing the city apart looking for my companions and me. Once again, I caused pain and suffering among a civilian population. I felt better about letting Oola take the lead.

It was early evening when Scheleene finished the makeshift communicators. They appeared large and bulky, and seemed very fragile. Placed next to our skin, however, and secured with strips of fabric stretched over the top like bandages, they were secure enough. Once everyone was properly equipped, we tested the connection.

I was still concerned with Scheleene while I prepared to interface. He could have been lying, could have tricked me, and this could be a trap, something to get me and my friends out of his way so he could contact home and have this whole area sterilized. But I was too far into this to back out now. I felt the device strapped firmly to my left arm, and allowed my mind to reach out, expecting the warm, loving, intoxicating embrace of a digital paradise…

Nothing. I continued to see through my own eyes, could feel my own lungs swelling and contracting, move my head and arms, and my thoughts seemed to be entirely my own.

Jason, can you hear me?

The voice did not come from a living mouth, but sounded in my head as if I had thought them myself, but with a difference, a distinct tone and quality, unmistakably Oola.

Yes, I hear you, I thought in response, and I saw a smile cross her face. Tragito chimed in as well, and we all knew we were connected.

Scheleene watched carefully during the test. "Perfect," he said. "You should all have direct communication and autonomy. I told you this would be efficient."

Efficient? Quite an understatement. "How can I see?" I asked. That was the most important part of this endeavor, that and hearing.

"Concentrate on whose senses you need to share. It may help if you close your eyes."

I did so and concentrated on Oola. I don't know if she was aware of my efforts more than just from overhearing the instruction, or if her assistance was even required. But after a second, I could see through her eyes, looking back at my body. I mentally requested Tragito say something, and I heard his response through her ears. Oh yes, this was just as the fish said, *perfect*.

I made myself comfortable on the rocky ground and watched through Oola's eyes as she and Tragito attached the control bands to each other. This was a new experience for me, especially in this semi-artificial reality. Previously, whenever I shared a space with another mind, including Oola, there was little sense of individuality; part of the insidious design of our nanites to keep our personal identity suppressed by Ullinarian processors. This was so different. Although I could see through Oola's eyes as if they were my own, and I could see her hands moving before my eyes, I could not feel the elastic band between her fingers, and I had no control over her motion. Equally, I could still feel my own hands clasped together on my lap.

"Are we convincing?" Oola asked aloud, as she moved and twisted to get a feel for the thing strapped across her melon.

I shifted my point of view to Tragito to get a better look and caught a quick glimpse of Oola's backside. Well, it wasn't really all that quick. More of a linger. I was glad I couldn't hear his thoughts.

Jumping out of the link, I helped them each gather a basket of ore. Overall, their disguise was flawless, and after I spent a few minutes working with them on acting like a zombie—and explaining what *zombie* meant—they were ready. I felt rather confident they could pull this off, especially with me watching and able to advise.

They departed and I settled back to monitor. I followed through Oola's eyes as they made good time through the mines, Tragito leading the way. Obviously, he had indeed explored these tunnels, it was even more maze-like than I would have imagined; if I had undertaken this mission on my own, I'd likely spend hours or even days wandering aimlessly... much like I did in life if I was honest.

I also got an occasional assessment of Tragito's hindquarters.

They did not slow down until they neared the working portion of the mines. They only paused long enough to check their headgear, link, and baskets, then continued.

"They are entering the work zone," I reported to those around me. "No guards yet, but none of the upgrades seem to notice us."

As they progressed, I witnessed a scene even more disturbing than my previous view from above. The Olemsi slaves worked like machines, but without the luxury of using actual machines. Men and women swung pieces of metal against the rock walls using nothing but brute force to splinter stone into dust. Others scooped up the material with bare hands. All of them appeared the same age, so I knew their nanites, even if newly developed, must function largely the same as my own, maintaining ideal physical health and condition. There were remnants of heavy excavating equipment and electric tools, lying abandoned in numerous places, all infected with the data bomb, and thus, presumably, quarantined.

We didn't see any guards until the tunnel opened up into a large cavern. Two male Ullinarians stood in the tunnel exit, one of them leaning casually against a support column. They chatted with each other like executives waiting to board a jet for Vegas, ignoring the upgrades. This was a good omen, but still, I tensed.

Leo, who had been watching our own entrance, must have sensed my anxiety, because I felt him climb into my lap. I could still hear Tony and Orlaan nearby, so I knew nothing had gone wrong. Fido was perfectly capable of sentry duty.

We neared the Ullinarians, and I focused on Oola's hearing, but it was difficult to filter out the local sounds of shuffling feet and nervous breathing.

Slow down a little, I thought. *I want to hear.*

To my surprise, the surrounds passed slightly faster. The Ullinarians neared, never turning in our direction. Their voices became more distinct. "...said I could have the Laralia system." One of them boasted, and the conversation faded back to noise.

I'm trying to be discreet, Oola thought, rather angrily after safely passing the two. *If I can find a computer, we'll get much more of that than listening to two minor royals nattering.*

Fair enough. I remained silent and observed as we continued through the cavern. This was not a natural formation, but rather hewn from the living bedrock of the planet, dark orange and brown, and damp with seepage from above. Giant metal footings for the complex were numerous, placed at even intervals, giving it the impression of a forest of steel and concrete. Electric lights hung from above, mounted to the base of the structure.

My friends fell into line with their enslaved fellow citizens, slowly approaching a conglomeration of machinery. Each Olemsi deposited their basket of ore onto a massive conveyer system, conducting the material into the facility itself. The machinery was a strange mix of old and new. Some of it rusted, driven by gears and belts, with the occasional bit of sleek, orange-white shine of Ullinarian technology.

No guards were present in the cavern, which I found both relieving and perplexing, but there was a single Ullinarian technician, watching both a monitor, and the Olemsi workers. His workstation didn't appear original to the facility, but an improvised supplement to an empty alcove, once reserved for an integrated upgrade. Some of the visible components were those recently modified by either Oola or me the previous day.

Watching the technician through Oola's eyes, I mentally instructed Tragito to scan the room. A single staircase led from the rocky floor upwards into the facility. The line of workers obstructed their access, so they had to proceed forward with the others.

I held my breath as we neared the belt. The Ullinarian technician gave us only the most cursory glance as Tragito, then Oola, tipped their baskets onto the conveyor. They mimicked the others, turned away and started walking back to the mines. As they neared the stairs, I watched Tragito look back over his shoulder, gave us a quick nod, and both Olemsi broke from the line and rushed to the stairs.

The deafening sound of machinery both in the cavern and from above was more than enough to mask their steps. The other Olemsi, following only their programmed instructions, did not interfere, or even seem to notice.

"We're in," I reported aloud to my partners who couldn't watch.

I relaxed a little with this part of the mission having gone so well. But it was far from over. Indeed, it was only the first step.

They climbed and peeked around the first level. It was an ore processing plant, nearly entirely automated. A few upgrades worked, and a few more Ullinarians watched. Just like before, no one paid any attention to my group. They continued up several more levels, all with the same mix of native and alien equipment.

The surroundings began to change when they finally neared the upper most floors. The presence of Olemsi technology was almost completely absent in this area, devoted to a production line manufacturing what looked like tiny coils of ultra-fine copper. I recognized the product instantly as master nanites, the device that, once implanted, was responsible for the replication and programming of system nanites. We had already concluded this was going on, so the only real surprise was the sight of the line workers.

Presumably, in the days before the data bomb, Ullinarian workers would be doing this. Now, it was non-upgraded Olemsi children, dressed in rags, and obviously on the brink of starvation. The children removed the coils from the belt using forceps, and loaded them into large, ugly injectors. Several Ullinarians watched over the children, all of them armed with the technological equivalent of a whip.

Tragito looked into Oola's eyes, and mine by extension. No one thought any messages, it wasn't necessary. This was the epitome of slavery, the lowest act a sentient being could impose on another… though I'm certain Apple and Nike would not only approve, but also adopt a similar strategy and have a proposal ready for the next investors meeting.

Don't do it, I warned. *You'll be spotted.*

If we can infect that machine with the data bomb, we could end this. Oola replied, mentally.

I could feel her desire, and I sympathized. Her suggestion

had some merit; indeed, these new nanites, insulated from the effects of the data bomb, were at the core of the new Ullinarian initiative. One touch from her or Tragito could conceivably release all the new upgrades in service.

There was, however, a problem with that idea, one that I was trying to articulate in my head before voicing—or rather broadcasting—as thought. Fortunately, Tragito was ahead of me. *That would not eliminate the two hundred Ullinarians on our planet. If you want to save these children, we have to continue.*

Oola didn't respond, either verbally or cyber-telepathically, but as my worldview turned sideways, I knew she was considering it. When the image before me jogged up and down, I assumed either my vertical hold needed adjustment, or she had submitted. The latter must have been true, because the image rotated a full one hundred and eighty degrees and began to move quite quickly. Either angry or more determined than ever, I couldn't be sure, but Oola had taken the lead and was marching up the stairs like an atomic-powered slinky. Through her ears, I could hear the slamming sound of her footsteps, but I was afraid to offer a warning.

I jumped to Tragito, making sure he was keeping up, and more importantly, prepared to calm her if necessary. Instead of getting reassurance, I got another eyeful of Oola's ass. Tragito was obviously a butt man.

For fuck's sake people, just get a roo…

My Olemsi friends reached the top of the complex, and my gentle stroking of Leo turned into a fearful embrace. Tragito scanned the immense chamber.

Everything changed.

Chapter 17

My Olemsi friends, through whose eyes I could see the scene before them, entered what seemed to be the ground-level floor of the facility. A number of sealed sliding doors ran along one side of the chamber, with sunlight streaming through gaps in the metal. Wire grated floors separated two upper levels, visible through the dim light. Otherwise, it was obviously a warehouse, but not one used to store supplies, or material ready for transport. The use here presented itself as far more disturbing.

Hundreds of Olemsi stood in this place, like statues created by some demented artist, or perhaps the work of an alien version of Medusa. My hosts stepped carefully into the chamber, breathless. The scene felt creepier than anything ever envisioned by Madame Tussaudes or even the most deranged Hollywood directors. All of these people, men and women, were examples of Olemsi physical perfection; young, healthy and strong, forged into war machines by the same tiny mechanisms that flowed through my own blood.

I'd seen this kind of thing before, when the Ullinarian Empire invaded TBNL. Warriors like this stormed the station. Something even more sinister about this scene stood out. Perhaps it was just the humiliating sight of slaves arranged and stored like cans of generic cat food. Or maybe it was the list of atrocities for which they were destined. No, it was worse than that. I possessed digital memories similar to this, always barbaric, but the difference here lies in the details.

The soldiers in my experience were equipped with control devices, which looked much like silly hats or headbands from the disco era, physically grafted into the victims' skull. This rig was a single, small cube, sporting a few projections I recognized as hyperspace transmitters. Light and efficient for sure, and probably no more brutish than before, but this seemed somehow much worse. These soldiers all had rivers of dried blood caked around the implant, and the metal forks that pierced their skin. Surely, nanites sealed the wounds, only no one cared to afford the victims the dignity of a wet cloth.

This warehouse was clearly a staging ground for plans yet unrecognized, with a whole legion of soldiers on ice, already equipped with weapons and armor. Only thing missing: their marching orders. But what could those orders be? No one in my trinity really needed to ask.

"They have an entire army here," Oola gasped. "With a force this size, they could take the Capitol in a day."

They continued to scan the warehouse, and I saw something in the distance, a pocket of light in the dim glow of horror. *What is that?* I thought. *Take a look. To your right.*

My friends crept in the direction indicated without discussion. There was no sign of Ullinarian guards or working upgrades. Everything remained silent except for the three of us—two of them—moving through the barrack.

The source of brighter light came into view, an antechamber separated from the rest of the room by clear, plastic curtains. I watched through Tragito's eyes as Oola carefully pulled it back. I half-expected alarms to sound, or at least a battle cry from the motionless army, but nothing happened.

No one was in the room, but distant voices trickled through an open doorway. The partitioned room contained only two tables, piled with neatly arranged crates. I anticipated something akin to a medieval torture device, like a rack or an iron maiden.

What's in the boxes? I transmitted. They would probably have checked without my input, but then again, Tragito was fixated on Oola's rear, and Oola was probably still thinking about the unfortunate children on the lower level. In any case, Oola reached for the nearest crate without commentary.

She lifted the lid, and no one was particularly surprised. The same control devices we'd seen on the waiting soldiers, although the anchoring mechanism was now visible. It was much in line with what I expected, but the sight was still disturbing. Three long, razor sharp, prongs with numerous barbs adorned the backside of the block. Here, in Oola's hand, was the iron maiden. I could only assume application was accomplished manually. Based on the sharpness of the prongs and the overall mass of the average Ullinarian, even a prissy bitch like Kressada could force this into the skull of an Olemsi, Cantreyssi, Human, or so many others. Kressada and her kind probably enjoyed the personal touch.

Crates on the next table contained injector devices equipped with master nanites.

We could interface with this, Tragito thought, sounding excited. *We could free this army. Set them on the Guardians...*

"No!" Oola whispered, frantically. "No. When we re-leased the data bomb, all soldier units died at once."

Perhaps it was the sudden sound of a living voice, or the fact that Tragito obviously trusted Oola, but he backed down.

I'd been worried ever since these two first set off on the mission, and now my feelings intensified. I certainly had a habit of blundering into destructive situations, but their emotional investment in this may be just as dangerous, perhaps even more so.

I shifted back to Oola to make certain he was listening. Tragito's face was a redder shade of orange than usual, and his tiny black eyes appeared wet. He bit his lower lip, blinked a few times, and inhaled deeply.

The distant voices grew louder. I didn't have to instruct my friends. They hurried back into the dimly lit storeroom, took position near frozen soldiers, and watched through the curtain. We were very nearly invisible in the gloom.

Unfortunately, or perhaps very fortunately, we could see little through the curtain, only silhouettes. Several Olemsi entered; a few of them walked like zombies, indicating upgrades. The other three were more like rabbits, jumpy and huddled together. One Ullinarian followed along with two other shapes that I couldn't identify. They were larger than the Olemsi, and bulkier, but still far shorter than the towering Ullinarian.

"What is this place?" the mother rabbit asked, her head resting on one shoulder.

They were unable to see the horror from where we watched. I suspected what was coming, and although it was something I absolutely never wanted to witness and would have preferred to prevent if it all possible, I was, at this moment, much more concerned with my friends getting captured.

Don't do anything, I warned. *We can't help them now.*

"Hold them," commanded the Ullinarian as he moved towards the crates.

The mysterious shapes obeyed. The trio, which I now assumed was a family, squirmed, but still failing to recognize the extent of their peril.

"I don't understand," the father said. "We just came to inquire about my mother. She was invited here last week, and we have not heard from her. We didn't intend to cause offense…"

"Yes," the Ullinarian patronized, obviously enjoying himself. "You mentioned that. We don't keep records on our slaves, but since you're here, you might as well be of service." He approached the family with one of the application devices. I could not see him clearly enough through the plastic to know if the monster was smiling, but I would be surprised if wasn't. He pressed the end directly against the father's chest, and injected the master nanite. Everyone in the family screamed as he went from one to another.

The nanites immediately began to populate and the family's cries grew weak. I personally had no memory of this event in my own life, but could only assume it had been much the same. What followed, however, was not in my own experience.

The family remained free in their own thoughts while the upgrading proceeded. Not until they interfaced with technology would their own identity succumb to the will of their nanites programming. Those disks we'd seen would do the job, obviously, but these bastards had something more insidious in mind. The Ullinarian retrieved objects from another crate and retrieved a spiked cube. The family continued to suffer from their first taste of true fear, and he slammed one of the cubes against the smallest member.

The spikes tore into the grey-green flesh of the teen's head, burrowing through the bone. His screams sounded weak, but agonized. Blood splattered on his family's faces and they watched, aghast. The cube quickly drew itself tight to his skull and both the bleeding, and his struggles, ceased instantly. He settled into an upright, impassive, stature.

I was as horrified by this as the other witnesses. I was also keenly aware of a certain disconnect with my own presence. At the same time I watched this barbaric demonstration, I also experienced the tranquility of Leo's warm, soft presence on my lap. I unconsciously stroked his fur for comfort.

The Ullinarian conscripted the entire family one by one, and then applied the armor and weapons. The image through Oola's eyes blurred with tears, and shook under her muffled sobs.

The Ullinarian wiped his bloody fingers on what remained of a family member's clothing, and one of the unidentified shadows gave an order to the less recent upgrades. "Put them with the others and return to your duties."

The Olemsi escorts led the statuesque family into the warehouse as the others left by the same route they'd entered. Oola and Tragito pulled themselves together while the drones, ignoring us completely, placed the family in stasis.

The four escorts finished their work, turned, and lumbered back towards the antechamber.

Follow them, I ordered.

What? Oola thought. I could almost hear her sniffles through the link. *Won't they notice two more?*

I shook my head, which was entirely redundant since no one in my scouting party could see me. *Trust me. They see you all as tools. I'm sure no one will take the time to count.*

I switched between my two carriers, equally concerned with their acting abilities as I was with their destination. However, from what I could see, they had perfected their walking dead act. They proceeded down a hall and into a large laboratory and, as I hoped, we were invisible.

I imagined Oola and Tragito holding their breath, stealing themselves to deal with this new horror. And it was definitely a horror. The entire length of the room, which was considerable, was a series of, for lack of a better term, hospital beds, each containing a comatose Olemsi. Life support, medication, and feeding apparatuses shrouded every victim, along with a full contingent of computers. Some of the computers had leads running directly into the Olemsi hearts—or rather the master nanite therein and others leads grafted onto brains. Surgical instruments gleamed at other stations, along with the bloody remnants of experimental prosthetics.

This was the nerve center of current Ullinarian research, and a stark reminder of how sadistic these people were.

Olemsi upgrades performed various duties, ranging from cleaning dried blood to removing corpses. A line of three others stood against a wall, awaiting assignment. From my distant point of view, I could tell we joined them, which gave us a good opportunity to examine the space.

Look over there, Tragito thought, just as I was about to issue instructions regarding the newer-looking computers. Oola's attention remained glued to the tortured bodies, and so I didn't know what Tragito had seen until I shifted my perspective.

"Jackpot!" I couldn't see Tony, Orlaan or Scheleene while my eyes were closed, but I imagine my exclamation made at least one of them jump. Leo twitched, and possibly even hissed, then settled back quickly.

I stared through Tragito's eyes at an area adjacent to the torture chamber. I'm sure it was the centerpiece of the Ullinarian presence on this planet, and their campaign to reclaim their lost empire. It was also reasonable to assume that this was their command center based on the number of Ullinarian workers, computer banks, charts, graphs and schedules on display. Even more than that, the presence of Kressada implied it might also be something akin to a throne room.

A transparent wall separated Kressada and her minions from the lab. We could not hear her ranting voice—which was a guarantee, based on her emphatic arm swings, and rapidly moving lips. Even some of the researchers, all of whom would make Josef Mengele[14] look like a rank amateur, kept turning their heads uneasily towards the partition.

Tragito, go to the window and pretend to wipe the glass or something. Try to hear what she is saying. Oola Oola, keep out of sight. She might recognize you.

---

[14] Josef Mengele: German SS officer and physician during WWII, and barbaric, blood thirsty, mass murdering fuckhead. He escaped justice at the end of the war, and died from a stroke in 1979 in Brazil. If anyone deserved immortality, it was this asshole, just so he could be imprisoned and tortured until the universe itself collapses.

No one responded directly, either in gesture or thought, but through Tragito's eyes, I saw Oola slink up next to the other waiting Olemsi and take position; her eyes glued to the floor. Tragito, however, took the initiative I'd requested. He went considerably farther than I had asked, and actually entered the control room. The Ullinarians here, just like everywhere else, only gave him the briefest glance, if at all, and continued without pause.

I, however, nearly lost my shit.

A brief scan as soon as Tragito entered the room provided the answer to that mysterious, bulky shape I saw moments ago. I recognized the sandy skin and ugly gray hair instantly. Several Benzonites, in full armor, stood there, including the same menacing asshole from the Rovalorian outpost.

"—the whole damn power grid, and still got away," Kressada ranted. "Does anyone have a clue where his ship is now? I need a target, people."

One of the Ullinarians, a male who appeared twice Kressada's size, and half her stature, answered. "Excellency, we know they are still on the surface somewhere. If they had broken orbit, we could detect their hyperspace wake. They are still here."

The man gulped as the Emperor's daughter swung on him. "Should that make me feel better? This weak, primitive human has already collapsed my empire, killed most of our service units, and in two days, wrecked our current plan. And he's still here."

My nanites informed me that the Ullinarian species never developed sweat glands, but this young man was about to evolve right before my eyes. "Yes, that's...yes."

"Do we know where?"

"Uh. No, Excellency. We are sweeping the surface with all our operational ships we have left, but can't find any alien life."

Kressada's eyes bored into the man. It was obvious to me

she wanted to strike him, probably even kill him. She refrained, almost certainly because of her own needs, rather than any sense of mercy.

"What do you suggest," she asked, almost gagging on the question.

The Benzonite Commander watched silently during the whole exchange. He now stepped into the circle of Ullinarians, who dwarfed him in height, but certainly not in overall mass. His gray hairs puffed when he spoke, exaggerating his mass further.

"If you could get the space platform operational, scans would be much more effective than ship to surface."

The presumed Empress nodded to the Benzonite, showing him a shocking amount of deference. Whatever they were doing with the Ullinarians was still unknown, but it was clear he was helping of his own accord.

Kressada pressed closer to the young Ullinarian and spoke slowly, with grossly exaggerated enunciation. "But we have been unable to get the platform operational, have we not? You told me two days ago that we only needed to modify a portion of the stations components to have it running, did you not?"

"Yes, Excellency, that is correct."

"That filthy human and his Olemsi whore completed all the parts you requested, did they not?"

"Yes," he gulped.

"Have those components been checked out—better than the rigged power-converter?" Kressada stood so close to the young man that he could probably count her eyelashes.

Another Ullinarian in the room, a young female, entered the exchange. "Forgive me, Excellency, but if we could only access our database, we could have the platform on line in a few minutes."

Again, Kressada appeared to resist murder only for the sake of expediency. "We can't access our database without an upgrade. You fools, who have been feeding at my family's tits for a thousand years, can't seem to complete the filters. Any upgrade that contacts our systems will contract the data bomb. Does this sound familiar?"

"Filters," I said aloud to those near my physical body. "Kressada said something about filters and upgrades, what can that mean?" I spoke quickly, trying to gain information from both ends at the same time.

I continued to watch the scene and listen to Scheleene hypothesize. "They may be trying to create their own program to nullify the data bomb."

"Is that possible?"

"Certainly," Scheleene said, sounding strangely optimistic. "But I doubt any of *them* could do it. It would take time, even for my people."

That explained the house of horrors in the next room. I turned my attention back to Kressada, who was still grilling the female member of her staff.

"What exactly are you suggesting?"

"We could upgrade one of the local collaborators; we can trust their compliance. They would willingly do the work, even with the data bomb. Temoosh, perhaps?"

Kressada appeared to consider for a moment, and that filled me with terror. If Temoosh were to acquire all the knowledge I possessed, and the technological, strategic potential of the space platform, what damage could he do? Fortunately, Kressada arrived at the same conclusion.

"No. We can't trust any of these savages with that kind of power."

The Benzonite grunted. Perhaps he was trying to finagle his way towards his own upgrading. If so, it was clear that whatever service he was providing the empire, it wasn't enough to earn that degree of trust.

The young man, close to hyperventilation, or scurvy, or some other possible life-threatening condition, spoke again. "Excellency we have checked all the modified components, but we've only reinstalled a portion of them. If we focus on those, we should be able to track the rouge upgrades within one orbit."

Kressada, the new bitch queen of the galaxy, softened. Assuming the demeanor of a cheerleader, she smiled and nodded.

"Then please, proceed."

"I... I... will need more personnel. A few more upgrades, and a few colleagues..."

"Anything you require," she said in a darkly honeyed tone. "There's one right over there, eager to follow your orders."

Every hair on my body must have stood to attention. Kressada was pointing directly at me, err, Tragito.

I came close to panic. It must have shown on my face, because Tony and Orlaan were both begging me to explain what was going on, I might even have heard a "gloop" or two out of Fido, but all I could do was focus on the faces in that room; Kressada and her associates, looking at me. Of course, they could not possibly know I was looking right back at them, that this form was any different from the other poor saps stripped of their dignity and willpower to serve these evil creatures. And that I was mentally flipping her off.

I saw myself following the Ullinarian from Command to the lab where the situation worsened. He selected a few of the waiting Olemsi to follow as well, including Oola. Her eyes made contact with mine, or with Tragito's, and joined the queue.

Get out of there as soon as you can, I insisted. *Abort! Just, fucking abort!*

Neither of my Olemsi hosts responded. I switched from one point of view to another; saw them on track to the exterior of the compound and across the yard.

What are you waiting for? Get the hell out of there. If you have to kill the bastard, then do it, just get out!

No one bothered to respond until all the Olemsi cargo was loaded into a small transport. The Ullinarian who had led them from command took to the pilot's seat and prepared the ship. It was now far too late for my friends to escape.

What are you doing? I was getting weak from fear and frustration because no one would answer me.

Oola finally responded as the transport began to lift above the ground.

Jason, I can't pass on this chance, she explained. *The platform is what we've needed to access from the beginning.*

"Scheleene, what is the range of these devices? Will the connection reach the space platform?"

I didn't hear a response, which I regarded as a negative in one form or another. Already, my sight and hearing from inside that transport was fading. *Oola! Oola, what are you going to do?*

There was nothing left to see or hear. I sat in a cave with my eyes closed and Leo sleeping on my lap. No voices sounded in my head—which in this case was a bad thing—and no answers to my question. I was cut off again, with even more people in more places, whose life I may be forced to sacrifice.

CHAPTER 18

Darkness, both literal and metaphoric, settled over the Capitol. We could hear the distant sounds of unrest from our vantage point, but ignorant to what was happening. I waited hours for some signal from Oola, either through Scheleene's device or the com system in our ship. Only silence. Councilor Orlaan proposed returning to the city, to connect with his allies in an attempt to organize resistance. I convinced him to abandon that idea; the numbers were not in our favor. Scheleene continued to lobby for contacting his people, which was rapidly starting to look like the best, if not only, option. Tony still wanted to bomb everything.

I formulated several ideas after a few hours of debate and pacing—mostly pacing. I didn't like most of what was going through my head, but time was running short, people were undoubtedly dying. People frequently died when I was around. I eventually arrived at a single option.

"I have to get in there," I announced, expecting resistance.

Tony was outraged. "Are you serious? Kressada is there.

Probably dozens of others. And what about those Benzonites? I don't have a full library of details like you do, but they look like tough motherfuckers."

"True, but it's obvious they've escalated their plans." I pointed towards the distant Capitol. "And don't forget what they were saying about fixing the platform. If they get those sensors running, they'll find us."

"What do you plan to do in there?" Orlaan asked. I could tell he was still reluctant to trust me, but also cognizant that his trust was of little interest to me.

"I have to access their new network, or whatever means they're using to control your people, and shut it down." I was quite certain I'd sufficiently explained this already, so, my exasperation should have been palpable. If he noticed, he completely failed to react.

Orlaan fidgeted, looking either reluctant or constipated. Maybe both. I happily admit to zero knowledge of his bathroom habits. "Perhaps your friend is right…"

I saw Tony brighten, thinking he had just gained support for an aerial assault. Every bad poker player has a tell, and Tony's was less than subtle; his penis doubled in size every time he held a weapon, thought about a weapon, or heard a reference to any use of a weapon. His heart must have broken when he realized the friend in reference was the land fish.

Tony's *spirit* deflated as Orlaan continued. "…if they have a large enough force—"

"No!" I shouted at the old man sharply, so loud a few chunks of stone shook from the roof. I softened before continuing.

"That may yet become necessary, but let me try it my way first."

"The female already did that," Scheleene objected. "We know that didn't work."

"Oola went off on her own, despite my objection. One more hour won't make a difference."

No one spoke for a moment, everyone apparently considering all the options of which there were very few. Even I wasn't convinced my plan was the best. Honestly, I didn't have so much an actual plan as a general goal. Or at least a notion. Okay, a half-assed impulse and a shitload of desperation.

Orlaan finally consented. I didn't really need his approval, he was in no position to stop me, but I felt, as the only legal and respectable member of the local government, his license would grant my actions legitimacy. After the devastation I had brought to TBNL, I wanted official sanction just to appease my own guilt should things go awry—which was just as certain as the fact that all televangelists pay their hookers with church-issued credit cards.

Orlaan's permission came on a string, however.

"One hour."

"What?"

Orlaan's shriveled form drew tall, almost bold. "You said one hour. I concur. You have one hour to end this debacle on your own terms. If we do not hear from you, or see some observable evidence of success, we allow the Rovalorian to send a distress call."

Fuck. I never intended to make that offer, certainly nothing as specific as a single hour. Oola and Tragito took nearly forty minutes just to get through the mines. Add to that, the very real fact I still didn't have an actual plan yet, twenty minutes to infiltrate, analyze and improvise a course of action seemed rather impossible. Every Harrison Ford character combined couldn't do that.

However, I had no choice but to agree. Perhaps the limitations weren't as bad as they appeared on the surface. Even if Scheleene contacted his people in an hour, the distance between Olemsi Myucuc and the nearest Rovalorian outpost would still delay any military action for some time, and that was assuming they launched without extensive discussion.

"Fine." Tony relented to my authority. "But if you're going in there, I'm going with you, and I'm taking a gun."

"I was counting on that. Get one for Fido, too," I ordered as my only human companion stomped back towards our parked assault vessel. Fido's big pink eye lit up, as if excited about the pending expedition, but I let him down.

"No, my friend. I need you to stay here and protect Orlaan. And don't let Scheleene near our ship until Orlaan tells you time is up. Okay?"

My Gorlack's orb-shaped head bobbed slightly, and drooped near the floor. I could tell he was disappointed. But, being about the most loyal friend in the entire Universe, I knew I could trust him to follow my instructions. He'd rather stay at my side and protect Leo and me directly. I would have preferred that as well, but unlike Fido, I could not trust Scheleene in the slightest, and I was still unsure of Orlaan. This was the only way.

Tony returned with two weapons and handed one to Fido. My sluggy friend pulled himself together and boldly accepted the gun with his front legs. Rising on his other four, and holding his head high, he now towered a whopping eight feet, making for an imposing figure. My group left for the tunnels and I felt quite confident that I would see him again. Custer and Napoleon might have said the same shit at some point.

I led us through the tunnels and remembered, thanks to my digitized brain, the exact route Tragito blazed only a few hours ago. Actually, Leo was kind of in the lead; prancing ahead of me, only looking back from time to time to take the necessary queues.

Most of the route, just as with my previous, vicarious, journey through the mountain, was deserted, the shafts having been worked out years ago. We also made good time.

The main difference between treks, besides the fact I was only a spectator the first time, and no one in this group had done this before, was Tony's behavior. He'd finally normalized after his illicit upgrade and my subsequent correction, which continued to hold. However, I could hear strange vocalizations as he followed close behind, as if suddenly struck by a crippling case of mononucleosis, or he wanted to say something.

"... Um... Uh... Jason...?"

"What?" I whispered.

"You know... uh... that thing we did...?"

Louder this time. "What?"

"You know; that *thing*. In the cell..."

I paused and turned to face Tony with an expression I hoped conveyed both surprise and horror. "Now? You want to talk about that *now*?"

"W... Well, we haven't been alone until now." He fiddled with the controls on his plasma rifle—which did nothing to alleviate the awkwardness of the moment.

"Dude," I began, forcing patience on myself. "Princess Perky Tits is trying to kill us down here, I have an hour to save this planet before Scheleene calls home; an hour before the Rovalorians come-in, probably to reduce this rock to dust, an hour—"

"I know. I know," Tony said, flipping between high power and low. "I just... I just wanted to say I'm sorry. You know; if I hurt you."

"Fine. Let's get going." I pulled away from Tony and resumed my march. Leo continued ahead and was now out of sight. I was about to call for my cat, fearful of losing track of him altogether, when I realized Tony wasn't following. "Psst! C'mon."

Tony started to follow, swinging the riffle and shuffling his feet. "It's just that... when this is over, we could, I don't know, try that again maybe. If you want to, that is..."

"Oh." Wait... Huh? "Ohhhhhhhh..."

My over-stressed body managed to redirect blood flow to a region that wasn't currently the best use of the resource at this time, considering the dire circumstances all around me, like the fear of losing my cat and the likelihood of global annihilation.

Now it was my turn to trip over my own tongue. "I, uh... um... ooohhhkaaay..."

I wished I had a weapon to play with rather than face Tony, but at least I knew my jeans were baggy enough to hide what my *other* brain was thinking. "We can discuss this later. If we don't get moving, we'll never discuss anything again."

Whatever motivated Tony to bring up the topic must have been satisfied because he instantly came together and retook the shape of a soldier. He whipped the riffle up into a proper ready position, and braced himself for the fight ahead. Personally, I think that gesture was gross overcompensation, but it was a resolution nonetheless. Big soldier stood at attention. Little soldier stood at attention.

We're going to fucking die.

I heard a familiar, high-pitched squeal before the mission could continue as Leo came trotting back to us. His tail was puffed to three times its normal diameter, and his teeth were on full display. I had no way of knowing what he'd seen ahead, but I did know better than to question his judgment.

Tony shrugged off Leo's stampede between his feet, and even asked in his normal voice, "What's that all about?"

"Shh," I whispered—actually, it was more like a blast of stale air from an over inflated tire rather than a proper whisper. "Follow the cat!" Swell. I sounded like a Disney movie now.

Tony pivoted on the spot and took after Leo. I was right behind, even as the sound of stomping feet rose from the direction we'd been heading. My precious cat led us a few dozen feet back along our tracks, and then took a sudden right angle into another branch of the tunnels. I had no idea where this might lead, but I was willing to trust Leo's instincts.

This new passage was not very long, and we quickly came

to a dead end. It was, however, cloaked in total darkness, making us essentially invisible.

We all stood frozen and looked back to the main path. A contingent of Olemsi soldiers, like the ones I had seen through Oola's eyes, marched by, escorted by nearly as many Benzonites. If any of the soldiers had looked in our direction, their nanites would have compensated for the darkness and spotted us. None of them did so; in this state, they could only do as ordered, and apparently, their escorts never considered we might be this close.

The sound of their passing faded and Tony asked if we should follow them.

"Absolutely not!"

"But they're heading towards the others. Do you think they know about them?"

"I don't know how. Maybe. If Scheleene sent his message already, they may have traced it."

"It's only been twenty minutes," Tony insisted. "Fido wouldn't let him go against your orders."

I nodded in agreement. "But I don't trust that damned fish. He might have tricked Fido…"

"So, what do we do?"

There really wasn't much to discuss; nothing had really changed, except my schedule. "We continue forward. Stick with the plan."

Tony, under normal circumstance, would have launched into a tirade about the general lack of any concrete plan, and thus, nothing much to stick with. These circumstances, however, were far from normal, as was his reaction. I felt him place an arm around my shoulders and he gave me a tender squeeze. This was such a strange turn of events I almost couldn't process it. Not so long ago, he was apoplectic; a hormone-charged, loose cannon and now all flowers and candy. It occurred to me this is what it must be like to date Mel Gibson.

I also had to wonder how much of this was genuine, or if

his sudden affection was just another aspect of that unstable, alien program. Given the chance, I'd certainly make some further adjustments.

...*Unstable*... Something about this thought embedded a hook in my brain.

"Okay." Tony relented, still holding me in his wildly inappropriate embrace. "Whatever you think is best."

I wriggled free, never gazing at his expression, which I could imagine all too easily.

"Stay close, Leo," I whispered and began leading us forward again. I was more concerned at this point about those soldiers returning than I was with whatever might be ahead. In fact, I was kinda hoping they would return shortly, and without having captured my friends back in the cave. Well, in truth, I was worried only about Fido. I really hadn't developed any kind of bond with Councilor Orlaan, and I didn't very much like the fish—although his presence here was entirely my fault, so I owed him at least a little consideration. But Fido was a loyal friend and his safety really mattered.

The only way to help him or anyone else, however, was by going forward. I crept though the dark mines, nearing the spot where Tragito and Oola had encountered activity, and began to formulate a plan based on the assumption my companions were about to be captured. That seemed inevitable based on what we just witnessed, and I had to be prepared. In fact, it might just be what we needed.

The work proceeded at full speed by the new upgrades, just as it had been with my remote visit to the mines. We crept closer to the cavern below the complex. The gate, previously guarded by two Ullinarians, was deserted except for the throngs of slaves carrying their baskets of ore. They ignored us as we neared.

What did I know so far? Well, I knew the city was in turmoil, and I assumed the army Oola had found was now moving through the streets, conscripting new soldiers by force. If this assumption were even close to correct, most of the Ullinarians would be supervising and coordinating the operation. The fact that the cavern entrance was unguarded supported those assumptions. That would leave only a single Ullinarian technician ahead who'd be supervising the machinery. Tony should be able to take care of him with a single shot.

I peered around the rough wall of bedrock into the cavern. All my plans, such as they were, collapsed in one horrifying second.

Nope. No single Ullinarian technician. Six, and two Benzonites with holstered weapons. The size of the Ullinarian presence wasn't the part I found so disturbing, but rather their activity. The technicians watched while the two guards forced a young Olemsi female into the machinery's interface terminal, left vacant, presumably, since the data bomb.

Clearly, the woman was an upgrade; her appearance implied perfect physical condition, a hallmark of the presence of nanotechnology. Her face reflected both confusion and horror, as I would expect from any member of her species—or any species period—confronted with this situation. She couldn't possibly understand what they were going to do to her, or what they may have done already. I could hear her demanding an explanation, I could feel her anxiety, but the Ullinarians didn't respond. They spoke to each other over her increasing cries as if she were not even there. They were simply mechanics doing a job, and she was nothing more than a component to install.

"What are they doing?" Tony asked. Of course, he knew what they were doing; we had been in her exact position before. What he really wanted to know, same as me, was why they were doing this at all. The data bomb remained in place, circulating through all forms of broadcast signals throughout the galaxy, and firmly implanted in every piece of pre-existing technology. Unless...

"Oh shit."

"What?"

"Hold on..." A possible, very obvious answer, just occurred to me, but I had to be sure. The only way to know was to remain silent and watch the scene unfold.

It did so quickly. The imperial Ullinarians, despite their privileged background, were still formidable. Their height and strength was far superior to any Olemsi, or Human, and they quickly wrangled the woman into the niche. They lowered the headpiece, a series of tubes and cylinders, into place. Her cries immediately ceased and her face became like that of a statue. The whining machinery transitioned into a smooth purr, operating with deliberate perfection.

"They finished the filter," I gasped.

"How? Scheleene said it was possible, but not likely."

I didn't argue with Tony's comment. I didn't trust Scheleene to begin with, and his assessment was not terribly reliable since it was off the top of his tiny little head without access to the material involved. Regardless, the evidence was there in front of us, irrefutable.

"What does that mean for us?" Tony continued, not waiting for me reply to his previous question. "If we interface with any Ullinarian technology—"

"—We might instantly be subject to the primary directives of our own nanites. In other words; slaves to the machine."

Tony grabbed my arm and squeezed. "What about everyone else? What about Oola?"

I shrugged. "Depends. I don't know how this filter works; if they transmitted a program like the original data bomb, then every upgrade, everywhere, is at the same risk."

My mind reeled. I'd been pushing forward with no real plan, and now, I had to face the truth that there was probably nothing I could do. My only advantage was complete control over Ullinarian technology—from the inside. Based on what I'd just witnessed, that was out of the question. Were I to step foot into cyberspace, I would lose not only any advantage, but also my own free will.

"Do you still have one of those data cards?" I asked, clamping an excited hand over Tony's—which remained wrapped around my arm.

"Huh?"

"From the Rovalorians. Do you have one on you?"

Tony pulled away and started rooting through his pockets. "Yeah, I think I still have... here it is."

He handed over the small device, a concerned look of his face. "That thing has limited memory. You needed half the computer space on TBNL when you wrote the data bomb, I don't think you can do it again with *that*."

I was barely listening to Tony, but I heard enough to know he was right. Fortunately, what I had in mind was much simpler, and half of it already done for me. Now that I understood more about what the Rovalorians had been up to, I only needed to make a few modifications...

Tony continued to stare at me with a weird mix of concern, doubt and affection while I finished with the card. Actually, his look might have been caused by the place I chose to store the card: wedged between my ass and the waistband of my underwear. I was about to explain to him, albeit in grossly simplified terms, what I had in mind, but I never got that chance.

A voice boomed through the tunnels before I could speak, or perhaps, it was sounding directly in my skull. I wasn't sure the source of the voice, and didn't really care.

"Jason. I know you are in the mines. I know you are heading for my facility. I know your friend Oola Oola was here recently and is now aboard my platform."

Even without seeing her face, I recognized the satisfied smirk Kressada must have been sporting. "Your Rovalorian pet is in my custody, as well as Councilor Orlaan and the stupid Gorlack. None of them has been harmed... yet. You have very few minutes before I start killing. If you want them to live, turn yourself in, immediately. All of you. That fool Tony, and the small creature. My people have orders to bring you to me, alive.

"No more games. Turn yourselves in, and the killing stops. I suggest you hurry; my patience is expired."

I expected a countdown or something to that effect, but that might be a purely human tactic. And it wasn't necessary; I knew Kressada wasn't bluffing.

"She mentioned Oola," Tony said. "But not the other guy."

"No," I agreed. Kressada either didn't know about Tragito, or didn't care. It didn't really matter. I could do nothing from here, and no way to get near the facility without capture. Surrender was the only option.

I gathered Leo into my arms, marched into the cavern, and surrendered.

Chapter 19

Kressada's smug expression came as no surprise when her Benzonite thugs dumped the three of us at her feet. We were in the same command center where Tragito encountered her earlier, which was also expected. I was partially surprised that I was still alive, but only partially. Sure, I knew how much the Ullinarians hated me, and pretending to be friendly for favors was long gone, but deep down I felt certain they wouldn't kill me right away. First, they'd want to humiliate me, hurt me as much as possible, and if given a chance, squeeze any last byte of useful information from my head before finally pulling the trigger. Indeed, I was counting on that possibility.

I had used the Ullinarian's ego against them once before by giving them what they asked. Unfortunately, I didn't know how much of that event my present captors knew. But if anyone were going to be brought down by arrogance, it would be Kressada. She had ego by the bucketful.

The pole-shaped bitch grinned so wide, I thought she might tip over. It took a moment before I realized my arrival represented only a portion of her amusement. There were other factors in the lab, much more unsettling.

The least disturbing thing was Scheleene, working at a computer console. Thanks to my enhanced brainpower, I instantly recognized the information on his display: the mathematic algorithms of the data bomb. From what I'd witnessed previously, I knew they had perfected the filter, so I couldn't imagine what he was trying to accomplish. I didn't ponder on it too long because I noticed the wizened figure of Councilor Orlaan held against the far wall, an Ullinarian pinned him there with a massive clamp-like hand against his neck.

The worst thing was Fido, showing obvious bruises to his slug-like abdomen. He lay on the floor at Orlaan's feet, all six legs bound together by harmonic flex bands, and another length of the material wrapped around his head, preventing both his mouth from opening, and his eye from closing. A tear formed when he saw us enter.

Suppressing my disgust wasn't easy, but restraining Leo was harder still. He struggled against my embrace, and even hissed at me when he saw his friend's position. I could hear Kressada's silent laughter.

"Glad you could join us," she remarked, finally, having drank enough from my misery. "Find the communicator."

One of the Benzonites began an alien version of a pat down. He quickly found the makeshift device Scheleene constructed and tore it, and a substantial amount of my arm hair, away. Fortunately, the data card beneath my belt was small enough to evade detection. They did the same with Tony, but nothing yielded from that—unless his clumsy performance amused Tony, as a former cop.

Leo resigned his fight and settled into my arms shortly after, but I could tell by his breathing and low, barely perceptible growl, that he was far from complacent. I stroked his head, my eyes never breaking from the gaze of her *Excellency*...

"You should kill them," I heard someone shout. "Now, before they do more damage."

My stare down with Kressada broke and we both turned to the speaker. Prefect Temoosh quaked in a corner, his orange face twisted like a rotting melon. Orlaan attempted to speak, but the pressure from his captive prevented any effective sound. It wasn't necessary to know what the old man said, his meaning was clear.

"Sounds like Orlaan agrees with you," Kressada said, chuckling over Orlaan's muted protest. She sobered, "I still have a use for them."

Temoosh approached the towering Ullinarian, and even stabbed a finger in her direction. "You already tried that, and look what happened. They must be destroyed!"

"And what's in it for you?" I asked. This was a delicate situation I had placed myself in, but Kressada had already slipped and revealed her hand, at least a portion of it. Maybe if I poked the right place, I might get a little more.

Temoosh turned on me. "I'm doing this for my people."

"Really? You climbed into bed with a plutocratic fascist regime, assisted them in enslaving your own people, and think this is good for them? I have to admit; you're well-suited for politics."

"This is not about politics," Temoosh insisted. "Look around. Capitol city is hundreds of years old, and our engineering abilities are the same now as when the first brick went down. We don't advance; we don't grow. I want to see Olemsi Myucuc rise to its potential; a real player in the galaxy!"

"With you in charge," I added. "Hmmph. That makes it all about politics... and probably immortality too, just for good measure—"

One thing I hadn't considered before trying this strategy is that Ullinarians, along with their height, also have very long arms. Even though Kressada was standing a considerable distance away, she was able to strike my face quite hard, and with very little effort.

"Enough of this; you've had your fun. It's my turn." Kressada pivoted dramatically on her heels and swept across the room. "In fairness to the Prefect, you have caused substantial damage; you nearly eliminated our entire military and labor force and reduced the boundaries of my Empire to... essentially the sphere of my immediate body."

She paused long enough to give me a sidelong look. "However," she continued while picking a device from a near-by shelf, "you also eliminated my dear, weak father, which pleases me. This, along with the fractured state of the K'Nostrons, leaves me in the position to begin anew. Unchallenged.

"This has not been without difficulty, as I'm sure you can imagine. Even Volsorice here," she indicated an Ullinarian technician working near the fish, "who's third great grandfather, or something, first suggested nanotechnology as a means of control, isn't entirely fluent in the programming. But now we have a Rovalorian to assist—brilliant creatures despite the smell, and fairly reliably loyal, given the proper inducements..."

Scheleene turned to look at me directly for the first time since my arrival. His left eye was swollen and bloodied. Purple bruises forming beneath his scales. He looked at me for only a second before he went back to work at the terminal.

"You do recognize this." Kressada displayed the device. Although it would look ungainly large in the hands of most sentient beings, in hers it looked perfectly at home. It was a shiny tube, filled with coils of coppery metal.

"With our network compromised, and our live interfaces either dead or escaped, it took us a while to create a new program, which was effective, but far less efficient. That is no longer an issue. As I'm sure you've already surmised, we have perfected the filter your friends overheard us discussing. Yes, I know Oola Oola and Orlaan's bastard child were here earlier."

She glanced at Scheleene. I could not deduce what her expression meant, other than she was immensely pleased with herself.

"I also know they are on the platform, but they will be under my control soon enough. Once we upload the filter to the platform, they will be mine as soon as they interface. It will go something like this..."

She turned suddenly and thrust the applicator to Orlaan's chest. A master nanite propelled from the tip and through his clothing and skin. The old man winced and collapsed. He was still conscious and independent, but weakened by the shock of transition. I could see no evidence of any changes to him, but I knew that nanites were already being manufactured from the materials inside his own body, and spreading. Soon, he would alter to perfect physical condition, equipped to perform whatever function Kressada wanted from him. And if the news regarding the filter was true, which I had no reason to doubt based on the evidence of my own eyes, he would have no resistance.

Tony stood behind me, out of sight, and I could feel him tense. I know he wanted to fight, but instead, he allowed me to lead.

The Ullinarian guarding Orlaan heaved the old man upright. "What do you want with this?"

Kressada studied the Councilor for a moment, with obvious disgust. "Take him to the mines." She even waved a hand dismissively as she turned her attention back to me.

"The really exciting part about this filter," she continued, "is that it turns out you haven't hurt us all that badly. Once we repair the hyperspace transmitter aboard the platform, we can broadcast the filter throughout the galaxy—just like the data bomb—and then all upgrades, everywhere, will return to their rightful place. My ships, my soldiers, my workers, will all be restored."

"Except for your people. I killed them, remember? They aren't coming back."

Kressada came close to me and pressed her hideous face

near mine. "They were only slaves, but with a little rank. I don't need them anymore."

If only Temoosh had been born with enough smarts to grasp nuance, he might have realized what this meant for his own people. Too bad. I surmised he was still designing his never-to-come throne in his head.

"But you need me. You said so yourself."

"I do," she said, turned away and returning the nanite syringe to its shelf. I was surprised to hear Kressada acknowledge her previous mistake. Her confidence must have been truly off the chart.

When she returned with another object, my own confidence waivered. I had no idea what she was holding, nothing in my digitalized brain offered even a hint of what that device might do, or even what it was called. Either this ignorance was programmed in me, or it was something new.

"Until the transmitter is ready, the filter has to be dispensed directly. Like this."

I braced myself, but it was unnecessary. Her long arm reached past me, and pressed the device against Tony. There was a brief, electronic scream, and possibly a jolt. Tony jumped slightly against his captor's restraint, but seemed otherwise unharmed.

"Bitch."

She ignored the comment and instead gave him a little shove—little by her standards, probably. For us tiny humans, it was enough to push Tony backwards, into a bank of computers. Without the liberating commands of the data bomb to protect Tony's sense of self, his nanites reverted to their original design, and sought to interface with the nearest computer. I remember that sensation all too well; even with my individuality and free will intact, the desire to merge remained strong. Like the craving for water or oxygen, this need was seductive, more drive than want, and Tony had no resistance. The very second he made physical contact with the machinery he was subject to program. He fell motionless; already busy performing whatever duties his nanites ordered.

"Impressive, don't you think?"

So far, this was not going quite as I expected, but close enough. I just had to close the deal.

"Well," I began, "everyone needs a backup skill. I guess if you can't be an artist, be a ruthless, racist, mass-murdering piece-of-shit dictator. I've seen it before."

That might have been too much of a push. Even though Kressada certainly didn't get the Hitler reference, she was still pissed, and showed me by snatching Leo from my arms. Her strength was more than enough to snap his neck, and she certainly would have no qualms about doing so. Instead, she slammed him onto a control panel, almost in Scheleene's lap, and applied the filter. Leo went limp and joined Tony inside the network.

"Put it to work on the platform," she hissed to the fish. Scheleene's lower lip trembled as he followed instructions, working carefully around the limp form of my precious cat.

I was still free, mentally at least. This caused some concern, but Kressada made it clear she wasn't yet finished gloating. She had one more screw to turn before finishing me off.

"You remember, of course, I offered information about your home world. That was both true and false. I do know the location of your planet. It means nothing to me. It fell behind the K'Nostron border long ago. We don't know if it has been colonized, but our records suggest it has a perfect climate for them, so I expect your species is otherwise extinct.

"In some ways, I hoped you would cooperate long enough to give me what I needed so I could let you go with the location. Then you could see for yourself what's become of your home. I thought that might be an entertaining punishment, but I would hate to miss seeing your pain."

I had no way to know if what Kressada just said was true, but it was certainly possible. In fact, based on some of what I had learned from Captain Betty, it seemed quite likely. And there was no question that the Earth was conducive for plants.

"Maybe when this is all over, I'll let you go. For as much as I hate you, I suspect the K'Nostrons hate you more. They remember things in exquisite detail." Kressada stood close, breathing on the top of my head like a wolf with a cornered deer. I could smell her satisfaction.

"For now," she concluded, "I need you here."

She pressed the filter device to my neck. I heard the whine and felt the surge of multi-frequency waves. I only had a second of realization before the siren call of cyberspace beckoned, pulling me into that blissful prison of circuits and computations...

Chapter 20

There must be nothing more terrible than to lose one's self, stripped of personal choice, decision-making, love, hope and even fear. Loss of identity. It must be about the same as dying. Personally, I wouldn't know for sure, even though it's happened to me twice. Losing identity also requires loss of awareness, so the absence never truly felt. Yes, it must be a lot like death.

I've never been dead before, but I would guess that coming back to life would be much like what I just experienced. My re-enslavement was short lived, as I had intended. My estimation of Kressada's overconfidence proved well placed. They never searched me for anything other than the communication device, which they already knew about, so the data card hidden in my underwear remained exactly where I needed it.

My sense of self-control disappeared with the active filter, and my nanites reverted to their original directive, specifically to interface with any technology within reach. That included the data card. My modification had been as simple as it was effective. I re-wrote the Rovalorian instructions that made me forget about the alleged tracking device, and instead ordered my master nanite, and thus myself, to forget the last update. If only my PC back on Earth had this, I could have saved myself months of anguish from Windows 8.

I pretended I was still a slave to the network easy enough; I just stood still. Knowing what was going on in the room was quite a bit harder. I could hear everything with no problem, but opening my eyes would be a dead giveaway. There were no cameras in the room as far as I could tell and, from this position inside the network, I knew about every terminal, circuit and wire. Tony and Leo were in here with me, but with their personalities suppressed, I could neither locate nor reach them. All I could do for the moment was listen.

"What about the Gorlack? Should we kill it?"

The voice was unfamiliar and the words were terrifying. Fido was the one wild card in my vague, semblance of a plan. But he was my friend, and, if necessary, I would take drastic measures.

"Probably," Kressada answered. "They are loyal. Although..." Her voice trailed off and I could imagine her studying my friend, measuring what option could hold the greatest value to her goals. "...it might have valuable information about the K'Nostrons. Have we ever upgraded one of these things?"

"No, Excellency," said the first voice, probably the technician previously identified as Volsorice. "They were deemed unsuitable long ago for their lack of imagination and general stupidity. Physiologically, it should be possible."

"Do it. And download the thing's memory."

Despite my sense of relief that Fido was not in immediate danger, I felt a need to reassure my friend. Sensing no one close to me, I risked opening my eyes. Everyone in the room, not integrated to a computer, was watching the technician prepare an injector except Scheleene, who buried his face in the terminal where he was working.

Only one eye in the room met mine, that of my bound friend on the floor. Having no idea if he would recognize the gesture, I winked. Gorlacks do not have lips, or the capacity to smile in any form. This feature, while generally a barrier to communication, now served as a huge benefit. I could see Fido relax, but no one else noticed.

Thankfully, I closed my eyes before witnessing the transformation. Even with his mouth bound, Fido made some horrible noises before falling silent.

"It may take some time for the nanites to restructure its brain," Volsorice reported.

I risked a peek; the technician attached computer leads to Fido's head by slipping the terminals under the bands. He was going to be okay.

"What about the human?"

"Memory download is complete," Scheleene said from his terminal. I'm pretty sure I flinched at that report, realizing that they may have full access to what I had done, and my present liberty. However, if I did react visibly, it went unnoticed. What bothered me more was that I had no idea they were downloading my memories at all. Either I had gone too long outside the network, or it had occurred in the few moments I was under their control.

"The computer is analyzing, but he was in service for a long time on a scout ship that surveyed over fourteen sectors. There is a tremendous amount of data to reconcile."

"You should kill him," Temoosh suggested, his little orange face hungry for blood.

Kressada laughed. "Not yet. Until we completely understand the data bomb, we may need him."

"Cap him at least."

"Definitely not. The data bomb is still in his head; I can't risk that infiltrating the battle system. Which reminds me, what is the status of our campaign?"

Not seeing what was going on right in the same room was frustrating, and I could only assume someone was using a personal communicator. I was still blind to that operation, even though it must have been conducted through the main network. Fortunately, one of the Ullinarian guards was kind enough to report out-loud.

"According to Grand Duke Helmemminon, three neighboring settlements are ready for acquisition."

"What about the Capitol?"

Another pause before another report. "Capitol is ten percent converted. Local resistance is increasing."

Kressada erupted. "Fine time for those idiots to develop courage. Orlaan must have spread the word better than we thought... Tell the Duke to concentrate all effort on the Capitol. We need a full army before any Rovalorians arrive."

So, Scheleene *did* send a message. He must have tricked Fido and transmitted it as soon as I left for the mines.

"Excellency, we could broadcast the filter through the Benzonite ship," Volsorice suggested. "It doesn't have the strength or range as the platform, but it could disrupt any upgrades approaching Olemsi Myucuc."

"Do it."

I heard a door slide open and closed, so I assumed the technician left. When she spoke again, I could tell Kressada had come close to where I stood.

"How are the repairs going?"

Scheleene answered. "See for yourself."

At least this was something I could check without sight. As a fully integrated component of the local network, accessing information was easier than flipping a light switch. I found a river of information streaming from the platform with barely a thought. System diagnostics were complete, faults identified and every maintenance robot on board rebooted and now functioning at full capacity. Leo accomplished all of this in the past few minutes.

"Amazing," Kressada said, sounding almost sane for the first time. "What is this creature?"

"The humans call him Leo. A feline."

"Quite the mechanic. I wish we had more of them." Kressada certainly didn't have the makings of a crazy cat lady, so I knew her admiration was not rooted in affection. However, it did indicate that Leo was safe for the moment.

What still bothered me was that, although I could access all the information streaming from the platform, I could not actually sense the location of the platform. Leo must be performing his duties through the Ullinarian's Imperial communication system, so I was still unable to reach Oola or Tragito, or even confirm if they were still free, or even alive.

One of the guards, the same who previously relayed information from Helmemminon, spoke again. "Excellency, the Grand Duke suggests taking the three smaller settlements and using those conscripts on the Capitol."

"How dare that man contradict my orders," Kressada shouted. Even in my blindness, I could tell she was storming across the room. "Tell him I want—no. Tell him to stand by, I'm on my way.

"Prefect, we need to process the city quickly. Can you convince your people to stand down and submit?"

"Possibly. I could tell them that an enemy fleet is approaching. They may understand the need for preparation."

"Good. We'll both return to the Capitol building. You can address the people and I'll supervise the rest. I don't think my dear uncle comprehends the strategy."

I risked a quick peek. Kressada and Temoosh, along with several Benzonites, were about to leave, but she paused at the door and gestured back into the room. I closed my eyes just in time to avoid compromising myself.

"Watch him closely. If you suspect he's betrayed us, kill him—after Volsorice returns."

Once again, I heard the door, followed by near silence. The

two remaining Ullinarians were talking, but their voices were so low that I couldn't hear what they were saying. It was, however, enough to determine that they weren't really paying attention to me, or probably even Scheleene. I could hear the fish working on his terminal, and that was where I decided to focus my energy.

Only one Benzonite guard remained; but I suspected his knowledge of computers and nano technology was as limited as his sense of hygiene. Still, I was not going to get out of this on my own without some muscle. Either Tony or Fido would be the perfect choice, but they were fully under the control of their nanites. The filter program was obviously effective, and I had no idea how it worked. Details were not located within the network, and I had already ordered my nanites to delete the program.

This left me with only one possible ally, one I didn't really trust. I searched the network to find Scheleene's terminal. My confusion regarding his loyalty compounded upon finding it.

The computer had fully processed my memories. In fact, they had been fully processed for some time, even before Kressada left the lab. I had no idea how Scheleene interpreted the information; being inside the network, my memories appeared to me like photographs and film clips taken as if my eyes had been a camera. I was able to determine that Scheleene was viewing aspects of the data bomb, more than a photograph but rather a detailed schematic consisting of thousands of lines of Ullinarian code.

Really, in this position, I had no choice but to risk trusting the fish, even though Kressada had just threatened his life for doing exactly what I was about to count on him to do. He seemed more like a jellyfish than a sentient, highly intelligent land fish, only I was certain his people wanted to stay out from under the Empire's thumb. The only thing I really could be sure about was his magnificent lack of courage.

First thing I had to do was get his attention. That should be simple with him on a terminal and me inside the network. From my digitalized memories, I extracted an image of the mining outpost where we met from my digitalized memories and forced it to appear on his screen. Scheleene dismissed the picture and returned to the data bomb details. I tried again, this time using his own face when he confronted me on the gangway outside our ship. Several seconds went by before he dismissed the image. Once more, a recent memory, one of the data card in my hand when I made the modification that set me free. With all the flexibility granted by my nanites and the cyber universe I inhabited, it was easy to turn the image into a crude animation, depicting where I placed the card.

Both my makeshift movie and the rest of my downloaded memories vanished from the terminal. I heard Scheleene stand and shuffle across the room in my direction.

"What are you doing?" one of the Ullinarians demanded.

"Just checking," Scheleene said, offering me no information on his intent. "These aren't proper interface modules, you know."

"If you try to help them, we will kill you."

I could hear his breathing very close to me, and felt his flipper retrieve the data card. Unfortunately, he had left the terminal before I could convey any instructions—this worried me. Maybe his intention wasn't to assist, but confirmation that I was awake before getting me killed.

But he did not reveal anything. He had the card, so he knew I was awake, but he was still pretending to check my contact with the computer. I had to send him a clear signal as to what I required from him not knowing if the guards were watching.

"Why would I help them?" Scheleene asked, forcing a substantial rise in my heart rate. "They abducted me. If given the chance, I'm sure they would kill me for helping the Empress. I just want to stay alive."

Abundant computers and related equipment surrounded the lab. Despite the unfortunate lack of cameras, there were plenty of things to make noise, or convey voices. I designed a quick program with little effort that would make a series of mechanical beeps, perfectly matching the Rovalorian's native language. I felt confident that the guards would not understand the message.

"Give it to Tony."

My guess must have been right because no one reacted to the message. The guards, presumably, continued to watch, but the beeps must have sounded to them like part of the computer's normal behavior. Scheleene finished his mock inspection of my contacts and shuffled away.

"He's fine. I just want to check the other one."

My inability to see was becoming unbearable. More than enough time had passed for Scheleene to pass the card to Tony, who should have recovered already. From what I could hear, I assumed Scheleene was repeating the fake investigation—if indeed it had been faked.

"Do you have any more flex bands?" he asked.

Now I was beginning to panic, certain I had entirely misread the fish and his intentions. My mind was racing for a way out of this mess.

"Why?" demanded the guard with the typical Ullinarian disdain. "We weren't told to bind them."

By my best guess, Scheleene ignored the obvious contempt and continued. "It can't hurt, can it? Especially this one; he's the stronger of the two. I would feel safer if he were bound."

The guard grunted. I heard him moving, a metal hinge creaked, and then footsteps across the room.

He must have been standing in front of Tony by now. A sharp *whoosh* indicated a flex band unfurling. Was Scheleene baiting a trap for the guard, or making sure to keep us humans under control? If it weren't for my nanites regulating my health, I might have passed out from anxiety. Any sense of self-control, of which I was not generally privy to anyway, crumbled. I had to see what was happening.

I opened my eyes for a quick peak. One guard was still by the door, but the Benzonite was exactly where I though him to be. Unfortunately, he wasn't looking at Tony, but me, and saw instantly that I was free and awake. Before he could reach his weapon, and before I could take any action, Scheleene forced the data card into Tony's hand.

"—the hell?"

Everyone jumped at Tony's sudden outburst. I used the distraction to pounce on the nearest Ullinarian, even though his size and strength was more than a match for me. To my enormous surprise, Scheleene came to my aid. Despite the massive size deficit, between the two of us, we managed to knock the Ullinarian off his feet.

Tony recovered and assessed the situation quickly. He tackled the Benzonite and remaining Ullinarian like some kind of comic book superhero. Unlike those colorful pinnacles of justice, however, Tony didn't stop until snapping the necks of both opponents.

Scheleene and I were doing pretty good with our own guard, but neither of us had the strength necessary to kill. Fortunately, neither of these guards was experienced in combat; they were former rich kids trying to fulfill a role far outside their scope. We held him down successfully until Tony could join us and finish the job—with his boot. The sound and the splatter from Tony's attack were gruesome, but strangely satisfying.

"I wasn't sure if you were going to help us," I said, helping Scheleene to stand.

He straightened his cloak and brushed away some dust before looking at me.

"They beat me," he sighed. "They threatened to kill me—kill all of my people. I'm not going to run anymore."

"Good," I said, a lump rising in my throat. "Now let's win this thing and go home!"

Chapter 21

The thin plan I'd formed succeeded—completely to my surprise. Moreover, Scheleene had proven which side he was really on, and that gave me real confidence for the first time in months.

"Okay gang, we don't have long," I said, swinging into high gear. My mind spun, so much to do and I hadn't the slightest idea where to start.

Tony might have had an edge on me for once. He checked the doors, and the spaces beyond. "No one seems to be coming."

"Release Fido and you both keep watch," I said, feigning control. "That prick Volsorice will be back soon. Has he transmitted the filter?"

Tony crossed to our Gorlack friend while Scheleene worked a console and reported. "Yes, just now. The signal will propagate like the data bomb, but with a much smaller range."

"I need to design an antidote, are the details in here?" I was about to interface with the computer even without a response. Previously, I had been so concerned with capturing the room that I totally neglected to search the local memory for anything useful. But before I reached the metal skin of cyberspace, I was spared the need.

"It's a simple program," Scheleene said, returning to his terminal. "I've already analyzed the details; a few adjustments will negate its effect."

I paused. "Really?"

His gills twitched. "You may not believe this, but I was preparing to rescue *you*."

Honestly, I did believe him. "How long will that take?"

The scaly, webbed fingers moved across the keys with tremendous accuracy and speed. "Done. But we have no way to transmit this. At least, not until the orbital platform is repaired. I will have direct control from here when it is goes online."

"Will that free the current batch of upgrades? Tragito said he couldn't interface with the control units."

Scheleene shook his tiny head. "The new nanites function on a totally different carrier wave; the imperial wave. Your nanites are forbidden to acknowledge its existence."

That was the last piece of information I required. "Is that why I can't see their communication devices, or detect their signals?"

"Yes," Scheleene said, turning back to his terminal. A few quick keystrokes and his monitor displayed... nothing.

"You can't see this, can you?"

"No. The screen is blank."

"It isn't. But might as well be. The royal family and their closest accomplices use this wave to control their own nanites, the ones that prevent aging and maintain their health. They recognized long ago that nanotechnology could be used against them as well as for them, so the first basic program of all nanites, outside their own use, is to never recognize the existence of anything using the imperial frequency. I can't change that."

"So I can't access any of the imperial systems? Ever?"

For a moment, Scheleene hesitated. "Not in the traditional manner…"

I understood what he was implying, and it contained a terrible suggestion.

Sadly, I looked down at the body of my beloved cat. Only the gentle rise and fall of his chest reassured me that he was even alive. Alive, but locked in the prison of his nanites, and their original function. At this point, he was only a machine, one with instinct, imagination and creativity.

"How long before Leo finishes the work?"

Again, Scheleene consulted the computer. "Not long. I can broadcast the vaccine as soon as the transmitters are online. That will protect all current liberated upgrades, including Oola Oola and Tragito. If they're on the station and interfaced now, they are already re-ensnared."

"Can you transmit the vaccine to the platform?"

"Yes, I have a direct uplink, that's how Leo is conducting repairs, but no. Kressada will know right away that you're free."

I nodded. "You're right. I have to deal with her army before anything else. How long before your people get here?"

Scheleene performed the fish-version of a shrug.

"Gloop." Fido had recovered from his transition. I had no way of knowing for sure, but based on my own experience, he probably felt better physically than at any other time in his life. The nanites already healed his wounds, and he was looking at me with a bright eye, clearly ready to resume the fight.

"Fido, old buddy," I said, gently stroking his enormous, bulbous head. "I have to go get something. Stay here and protect this room. Kill any fucking Ullinarian or Benzonite who comes through that door."

"Gloop. Gloop-gloop."

"Tony, where's that data card?"

Tony still guarded the door, itching for a chance to use his weapons. He held an Ullinarian riffle in one arm, and the Benzonite riffle, which was more akin to a smallish cannon, in the other. His attention turned to me only long enough to toss the device. "What are you doing?"

"Instructions." I interfaced with the card and downloaded a detailed description of what I planned to do. Granted, my plan was still full of moon-sized holes, but really, we only needed to buy time before the Rovalorian fleet, which I was counting on, could reach us.

"Instructions for who?" Tony asked as soon as I released the card. "I'm not letting you go anywhere alone."

"Look, protecting this room is the most important thing you can do right now. Leo has to finish with the transmitter so Scheleene can broadcast the vaccine. I have to try to do something about Kressada's army."

"What are you planning?" Scheleene asked, shaking.

It was a good question, and I had a good answer, but my associates would certainly object were I to give it voice. But they did deserve an explanation, albeit incomplete.

"We have a game on Earth called Reversi," I began. "Two players take turns placing a colored disk on a board. When you surround your opponent, all his pieces in between change to your color. Even when you're nearly defeated, placing a piece in just the right spot can reverse the entire board. That's what I'm going to do with Kressada's army, though I've changed the name of the game. Instead of Reversi, I'm calling it *Fuck Kressada*[15]. Catchy, isn't it?"

Scheleene's pink fish mouth dropped open. "Do you really think you can do that?"

I'm sure he meant reversing the board, not changing the name. "I can... with the right equipment."

---

[15] Fuck Kressada: The name never even once considered by the Tsukuda Original Game Company for their otherwise popular board game, Othello, first marketed in 1973. The Olemsi Memorial Committee, however, did consider this name for their own variation, but ultimately settled on *Kill the Queen*, believing murder a far more appropriate theme for children.

Tony looked far less skeptical than the Rovalorian, but stared straight into my eyes with an expression I'd never seen from him before. "Yeah, I get that. You're not going alone. Fido can protect Leo."

"Gloop!"

"And I'll protect you. I'm not letting you go anywhere without me. Fido, what do you think?"

"Gloop-gloop," Fido said, enigmatically as he retrieved the other pulse riffle from the dead guards and assumed a protective stance.

"How many Ullinarians are in the complex?" I asked over my shoulder, my eyes still fixed on Tony's. Scheleene tapped at his terminal and confirmed only a handful and slightly more Benzonites.

"Without the platforms sensors, I don't know anything outside the building."

That would have to suffice. Neither Tony's resolve, nor Fido's, wavered, and Scheleene's information implied he didn't need more than one gun at the door. I wasn't going to win this fight.

"Fine," I capitulated. "But take these instructions anyway, just in case."

Tony agreed and accepted the data card from my hand.

"Where are we going?"

I shuddered, wishing to think about anything but what was coming in the next few minutes while my nanites forced images in my head.

"Kressada's chamber of horror."

*

Most of the facility remained unchanged since our capture. The only real difference was that the Ullinarians seemed to have all moved to other tasks. The barbaric experiments had ended; with the filter perfected, the need was gone.

I led us to the ground level where a squadron of Benzonites

waited for us. Well, they weren't actually *waiting*. Our arrival came as much of a shock to them as it did to me, which was quite fortuitous. I gulped when facing the half dozen mercenaries, but Tony responded in all his glory. He shoved me aside with the barrel of one riffle and, roaring defiantly, let loose with both guns.

I covered my head while a tsunami of charged particles ripped through the air. Tony laughed, even as bits of Benzonite armor and gray fur splattered around the corridor. Although I didn't bother to check, I wouldn't be at all surprised if Tony jizzed his pants.

"You enjoyed that, didn't you?" I asked, climbing to my feet while wiping the puce-colored blood from my face. Puce. Even their blood was ugly.

"Fuck yeah," he grinned. "Didn't you?"

I did, honestly. But with so much left to do, I couldn't waste time reveling in such a small, albeit satisfying, victory. "Let's go."

We didn't encounter any more resistance on our way to Kressada's human (more or less) warehouse, only a few meandering slaves. Either that squadron was the only security left at the compound, or the ferocity of Tony's defense scared the rest away.

The warehouse, as expected, was now just a huge, empty room, the previously catatonic army now active and moving through the capitol city, conscripting or killing the native population. I didn't come here for a soldier exactly, but I did need something closely associated. I focused my attention on the boxes previously seen through Oola's eyes.

I only needed a few seconds to find what I needed, and holding the cap in my hands made my blood run cold. I couldn't help but stare at the gleaming metal blades of the anchors, and wonder how badly it was going to hurt. The pain hopefully wouldn't last too long…

"Stop."

Tony put one of his strong hands over the device in my hand. His skin felt warm, and surprisingly, so very soft. I didn't want to look at him. Fear? Probably. But not of him. Fear of my feelings.

"I can't let you do this," he said. Releasing his other riffle to dangle on its shoulder strap, he took both my hands in his. "I played your instructions. You can't do this."

"I have to."

"No. You *can't* do this. You have no idea if you'll be able to control Kressada's network once you're inside."

"I accessed Scheleene's vaccine—"

"It won't work. This is an entirely different system."

"Tony..." I finally looked at him. Like me, his eyes had become glossy. I could see his pleading was sincere and his heart was breaking.

"I have to do this. I have to end the suffering. It's all my fault."

Tony forced a brave smile. "It's the Ullinarians fault, not yours. Sure, you've fucked things up a few times, a lot of times if we're honest, but you've always done what was right. You have to keep doing what's right, even if it kills another indigenous population."

"You suck at pep talks. You know that, right?" I didn't wait for a reply. "But I need to do this." I tried to pull the cap away from his grip, only he held tight.

"We both know there's a better way."

I stopped breathing. How much information had I imparted into that data card? I knew there was a more definitive approach than the one I was trying to make, but it was too horrible to contemplate.

Tony released me with one hand and took the card from his pocket. "This thing has a pretty good processor. I've already ramped up my program."

His other hand, still cradling mine, began to radiate heat. I could feel his pulse increasing, and imagine his hormone levels soaring skyward. His pupils began to dilate.

"You can do this," he urged. "In the end, you always do the right thing. That's why I trust you now. That's why I love you."

He released my hand entirely and stood tall.

I felt the weight of the cap in my hand, so light, but with such a heavy burden. I looked at the device for what seemed eternity, regardless of how few seconds my nanites recorded.

I steeled myself, knowing Tony had been right about everything. I wanted to give him one last kiss, spend one more moment in his arms, but I knew if I did, I'd never bring myself to end the war.

"I love you too."

His gaze never wavered through my struggle or my surrender, not even when I plunged the metal blades into his skull.

CHAPTER 22

I only threw up twice on my way back to Ullinarian Command. Even though I was far beyond the raging sounds of Tony's anguish, I still felt every last miserable scream cutting through me. His blood literally stained my hands.

The only peace I gleaned from the experience was that it obviously worked. The slaves I passed while moving through the complex no longer performed their designated tasks. Some of them roamed aimlessly, while others swung their arms around, fighting monsters only they could see. One of them flailed on the ground so violently, he actually managed to dislodge the control device strapped to his head.

He recovered immediately and sat upright. Unfortunately for him, his first sight, while still groggy and desperately confused, was an ugly, scary alien. I grinned and waved hello in return.

"What are you?" he demanded, scooting backwards until he collided with a metal wall. "What did you do to me?"

I held my hands forward, palms upright. I knew from Oola

that this was a gesture of good faith. He had no reason to trust me, but I hoped he was as trusting as his species often lent towards. I was not disappointed.

"The guardians did this to you. Do you remember?"

The Olemsi looked away from me, and surveyed his own body. I wonder how different it now looked to him.

"Yes," he replied, finally. "I remember them taking me from my bed. They put something inside me."

"That's right," I confirmed, creeping closer to the man. "And they put this on you."

I retrieved the control device from the floor and showed him. He definitely recognized the object, because he recoiled at the sight.

"It's okay," I said softly. "It can't hurt you now."

"Are… are you sure?"

I smiled what I hoped would be reassuring. It seemed to make him tenser, so I stopped. I didn't feel much like smiling anymore anyway.

"Yes, I'm sure."

He relaxed—definitely a true Olemsi.

"Will you do something for me," I pleaded soothingly, "something to help all your people?"

His head flopped to one shoulder.

I explained to him as quickly as possible how to remove the control devices without succumbing to their power. I asked him to free as many people as he could, and ask them to do the same. He accepted my hand when I helped him stand up.

If he did anything to rescue the other Olemsi, I can't say. I didn't remain to watch, but rather continued my journey. I passed more bedlam along the way, but I focused ahead.

I reached my destination, and there was a third dead Ullinarian in the doorway.

"Volsorice came back, I see."

My Gorlack friend, who undoubtedly fired the fatal blast, was physiologically incapable of producing a smile. He was, however, capable of bobbing his head up and down while his tongue dangled from a broadly open mouth.

Scheleene wore a more sober expression. He stood by his terminal, where, to my delight, Leo sat, upright and fully awake.

"The platform is functional," the fish said. "I transmitted the vaccine, but I haven't been able to contact your friends."

His eyes scanned the drying blood on my right hand. He didn't ask what I'd done; he didn't have to. Every monitor in the room displayed images from around the city, thanks to Leo's work with the platform's sensors. Chaos of nearly biblical proportions erupted from every corner; soldiers and slaves alike were on the rampage like wild animals. Citizens attempted to defend themselves, most simply went for cover. A few, probably members of Orlaan's resistance, seemingly recognized the opportunity for what it was, and attacked any *Guardian* within reach.

"I have to stop this," I muttered. Although I'd succeeded in ending Kressada's mobilization, I now had an entire army of loose cannons to tame. People were still dying, and it was still my fault. My fault! That'll be the only inscription on my tombstone: It Was His Fault.

"There may be one solution," Scheleene piped up. "But you may not like it."

Have I ever? That didn't come as a surprise. Since the day I first awoke in this strange new life, I haven't liked most of my choices. "What is it?"

Scheleene activated a monitor and pointed at the blank screen. He didn't need to tell me I was failing to see the Imperial carrier wave.

"I can use our vaccine and infect their network with the data bomb. It will kill all the Ullinarians, and free the slaves."

"Oh, hell no!" I shouted. "It'll also kill all the soldiers; that's what happened last time. I didn't know it would do that, but they all died, and I killed them. I won't do that again."

The fish observed me for a second and then waved a flipper at the other images. "Civilians are dying already. We can end it right now."

He was right, of course, but the literal blood on my hand bothered me so much more than the figurative blood.

"Tony is one of them."

Scheleene blinked. "I know. That's why it has to be your decision."

Fucking decisions. I never wanted this kind of power. I never wanted godhood. All I ever did want from life was a 40-hour workweek with benefits, a decent boyfriend (or the occasional anonymous quickie), and a safe, quiet life with my cat. But these damn aliens decided to grab me one day and now I keep finding myself at the center of cosmic events. Just for once, I wish someone else would take the wheel.

But not Scheleene, and not this wheel.

"If I can somehow take control of the army, or at least influence it, I can slow down the carnage, maybe until your people arrive." I grasped at straws. "Can you plug me into the Imperial network?"

Scheleene shook his head. At least, I think he shook his head; it was so small and he had no neck to speak of, so I couldn't be sure until he answered. "Kressada's filter would instantly render you under her control. You would need something to act as a bridge. I can design such a bridge, but it would take hours."

"We don't have hours," I stated the obvious. "What is that sound?"

The fish looked confused.

"Can't you hear it? Thrumming. It's like a…" I had no words to describe what I was hearing, if in fact, it was sound at all. Whatever it was, the sound was barely within the range of my own perception, a quiet, gentle vibration. Not something I could actually feel, but more like the imagination of a feeling. It was strongly reminiscent of Leo's purring.

And Leo was purring. Scheleene had taken to stroking the cat as we stood there, struggling with our dilemma. However, he was across the room, so no way I could be hearing or feeling my cat's expression of pleasure. Another sensation came on top of the vibration, more like sound this time, like jelly squishing between gnashing teeth. Then something else, words spoken in my head, in my own voice.

Jason, can you hear me?

"What?"

"What what?"

I shushed the fish and concentrated. *Yes. Who are you?*

Oola Oola. We've taken partial control of the platform. I see by our surface scans that you've resorted to an old favorite. Can we assist?

Finally, someone I could trust with steering.

"How are you communicating?" I said this aloud for the benefit of my companions who were physically in the room with me. Scheleene, however, looked just as confused as before.

The tracking device. I still can't see it, but Tragito can. He made the connection between the four of us. He's trying to reach Tony now.

Wait! I thought frantically, and then explained this development to the Rovalorian. "Can the tracking device bridge me with the Imperial network?"

Scheleene perked up. "No. But Tony can, if you can get through to him."

"Oola. Have you located Tony?"

Yes. He's halfway down the mountain, heading for the city.

"Okay, connect me."

Just as I'd gotten a sense of Leo and Fido's subconscious thoughts, I was now getting Tony's, a jumble of anger, turmoil, and confusion. Apparently, when he jacked his own illicit upgrade, I scored a triple.

Tony. I concentrated. Nothing like the direct connection

experienced with us both integrated in a computer system. It wasn't even as strong as the makeshift communicators our fishy friend rigged a few hours ago. This was more comparable to shouting across a crowded stadium and hoping someone on the other side was listening.

Tony. Protect the Olemsi. The Ullinarians are your enemy. Benzonites are your enemy. Protect the Olemsi.

"Where is Queen Bitch Kressada?" I asked, while continuing to focus on broadcasting instructions to Tony.

Scheleene consulted the sensor details from the platform. "I can't be sure, but it looks like most of the Ullinarians are sheltering at the Capitol building."

I could tell Tony wasn't receiving my message. The unstable program in his head was overriding the Ullinarian control and blocking me. Tony couldn't concentrate on anything but his aggression, and forwarding that to all the other slaves in the imperial network. Words weren't going to do it. I had to use raw emotion to counter raw emotion.

Kressada, I thought, while simultaneously picturing her amused face when she injected Tony with the filter. I thought about the Olemsi in her torture chamber, and sight of Fido bound on the floor. I thought about the Capitol building, and images of Ullinarians surrounding it with their weapons. I thought about all the civilians suffering right now because of Kressada's cruelty. And through it all, I pictured her laughing.

I never received any confirmation from Tony, I only felt waves of primal instinct.

"The fighting is slowing down," the fish informed me, still scanning. "It looks like the Olemsi soldiers are now moving towards the Capitol building."

"I need to get down there." *Oola Oola, keep guiding Tony, lead the army to the Capitol. Don't let the Ullinarians escape.*

I relaxed my focus, trusting her to keep on Tony, and checked the situation here. The monitors revealed this facility now completely abandoned except for the four of us. The few

Ullinarians still posted here were now running on foot into the countryside, pursued by angry, liberated Olemsi. The young man I freed earlier had obviously done as instructed.

"How long before your people arrive?"

Scheleene shrugged. "Could be minutes, could be days. I didn't get a chance to hear their reply."

"Keep trying to get through to them," I urged. "Tragito and the others should get full control of the platform soon. Will you be okay here by yourself?"

The fish looked nervous, but after checking the monitor and seeing what I had already confirmed, he nodded.

"Good. When you talk to your people, ask them to blockade the planet, but take no further action until you hear from me. I'll send help as soon as I can."

I was about leave when Scheleene called me back.

"Jason, this could work, you know. And..." the fish fidgeted in the chair. "When I enter my next spawning cycle, I'll know my eggs will grow without fear of the Ullinarians. That's a good thing."

"Uh... You're... a girl?"

Scheleene didn't answer but twitched indignantly.

"Well..." I struggled with the huge foot in my mouth. "If you have any boys... don't name any of them after me, okay?" Like that was ever going to happen.

"C'mon guys." And I fled the awkward room with my two best friends.

We make our way back to the caves, passing no slaves or guards. I hadn't bothered to scan this far despite thoroughly scanning the Ullinarian compound and surrounding mines. That, of course, might be why I was so surprised to see a large group of armed Olemsi surrounding my ship.

Fido shoved me aside and reared back on his four hind legs, surprising the Olemsi crowd even more than they'd surprised us. His mouth drew wide as he prepared to shriek, its paralyzing effect being the only natural defense common with

Gorlacks. That and enormous strength and intimidating size. I recognized a face in the group of Olemsi before Fido could deliver his blow.

Well, not so much the face, but the gray robe was unmistakable.

I bade Fido to wait, which seemed to come as a huge disappointment for my friend and addressed the familiar stranger. "Orlaan? Is that you?"

The councilor, now young and vibrant thanks to his upgrade, rushed forward, his palms held forward in gratitude.

"I heard you set us free," he shouted, joyfully. "I was hoping you would return here. What we can do to help?"

"Dude, plenty. Leo, prep the ship."

My housecat bounced across the cave to prepare our advanced, fearsome military craft for flight. I gathered the Olemsi around me with Fido in attendance. By the look on their faces, I could tell all of them, men and women, possibly old and young—though they all looked the same age—were all willing to cooperate. No one here needed coaxing; they knew what the *Guardians* really were, what they had done, and that it had to stop.

I faced Orlaan and addressed all of them. "First, I need three or four volunteers to go to the control room in the compound. Scheleene is there and needs protection."

Orlaan looked aghast, but I assured him. "He—*she* set me free, we can trust her."

The rejuvenated councilor selected several armed Olemsi and sent them on. They left for the tunnels and I continued my address. "Kressada's army is in the city. I've neutralized her control, but I don't have control myself. The population is still in danger. We need to get there, and try to mobilize as many citizens as possible to rise up against the Ullinarians. I don't know what kind of forces they have off world, or if reinforcements are coming. Kressada must be eliminated before anyone comes to her aid."

A murmur of consent rippled through the crowd. The only person still wanting more information was Orlaan.

"What about my son?"

I placed a reassuring hand on the young-looking old man's shoulder. "He's safe. I've had contact with Oola Oola. They're both on the platform, which is probably the best place to be right now."

Orlaan swelled with pride and satisfaction. He then led his people to my ship.

CHAPTER 23

I didn't take too much care loading the Olemsi upgrades into the ship. Basically, I opened the cargo bay and shoved them through the hatch in groups of two or three at a time. If they have a problem with this treatment, I suggest they consider Southwest Airlines[16] and see how well that goes. Even though none of them had ever traveled in a spacecraft, or even an airplane for that matter, I was sure their nanites would heal any minor injuries incurred during the short flight. Only Councilor Orlaan joined us on the flight deck where Leo had already started the prelaunch sequence.

A peculiar light flashed on the control board before I could take my place in the command chair. I'd never touched a single button, lever or switch on the controls; instead I had always operated the ship through direct interface. But I did recognize the purpose of that particular indicator; someone was

---

[16] Southwest Airlines: A mass-transit organization on the planet Earth, noted for their Fend-For-Yourself approach to air travel, as well as the *If-You-Didn't-Want-to-Sit-Surrouned-by-Screaming-Children-You-Should-Have-Just-Fucking-Walked* policy.

trying to signal. The simplest way of interpreting the signal, of course, would be to interface and allow the message directly into my brain. However, if that signal was the filter the late Volsorice transmitted, allowing it into my head might be catastrophic. So, for the first time ever, I touched a button on my board.

"Hello?" I breathed a huge sigh of relief when I heard a familiar voice over the speaker. The young Councilor Orlaan beside me was even more delighted.

"Jason? Are you in your ship?"

"Yes, Tragito. What's your status?"

"Mixed. We have full control of the platform, but an Ullinarian Dreadnaught has entered orbit. Oola says it's the same one that attacked you last week."

"Son-of-a-bitch! Is it the Rovalorians?" I assumed the first time the ship attacked us that it was under the command of raiders, liberated upgrades or Ullinarian survivors seeking the bounty on my head. Then when we encountered it again at the outpost, I assumed it was theirs, or one of their contracts. Certainly, they wouldn't have allowed a functioning Ullinarian Dreadnaught to operate in their space if it was still under Imperial control—I was now fully confident that the Rovalorian had been sincere all along about their intentions. If so, this could be a good thing for us.

No, it definitely isn't here for our benefit. Oola explained directly through the tracking device.

"What's it doing?" I asked through the comm, much easier than Oola's method.

Tragito answered in suit. "They deployed fifteen troop carriers and hundreds of fighter drones."

The connection between numerous recent events finally penetrated my thick skull. The Dreadnaught, the creepy Benzonite stalking me at the outpost and their presence here. They were in control of the warship, and more of them approached the surface.

Orlaan threw himself towards the console and cried, "Son, are you safe up there?"

"Father? Is that you?" I could hear his joy through the speaker. "I've been so worried about you, are you well?"

"Not now!" I screamed, interrupting the family love fest. "What's the capability of the platform?"

"Oh. We have full shields and partial weapons. Sensors are irregular, so is targeting."

"Open a direct network uplink to our ship, Leo can assist with repairs. Keep trying to contact Scheleene's people."

I dropped into the command chair and joined Leo inside the computer. I had the ship off the ground, turned and blasting off into the sky within a few seconds. Now was the time to take a lesson from Tony: no more sightseeing. I kept close to the ground, making us less visible to the drones, which I knew were approaching, while I weaved through the hills leading towards the city. I imagined the Olemsi in the rear quarters, tossing around like balls in a bingo cage, but I was more worried about attacking drones than a few broken wrists.

I had good reason to worry. The city came into view as the valley opened before me. I could see the aforementioned troop ships rising; their cargo already delivered. I accelerated hard as the first volley of plasma blasts struck my skin. My shields could take hours of this, but the city could not; and the city was definitely under fire.

My cannons roared. This came as a considerable surprise to me since I was far too preoccupied to target anything, and Leo was busy helping Tragito by uplink. I then realized I had another presence with me, a warm, squishy presence that worked the weapons.

"Gloop!"

This gave me a real thrill, another arrogant gesture from Kressada coming back to bite that bitch in the ass.

Even though I couldn't understand Fido's language, or the workings of his very alien brain, he could understand mine.

He slashed at the drones with the same zeal as a pack of trick-or-treaters at the first sign of dusk. I assessed the ground troops with my sensors. They should be under Tony's disruption if they were new upgrades. If not, then they must be free agents, working for the Ullinarians by choice.

The answer to this question, and several others, became clear as soon as I scanned the troops. Over two hundred Benzonites were taking defensive positions around the Capitol building, and more moved through the city, culling the local population. Benzonites were brutish, aggressive bastards. I had reams of data on them, none of it flattering. They would kill for anyone for the sheer joy of killing.

The worst part of this scenario was that the Olemsi weren't resisting.

"Orlaan," I called out to him through the ship's speakers. "You have to address your people. They have to fight back. They have to defend themselves."

"How?"

"Put your hand on the controls. Just touch it, and let your nanites do the rest."

I made a hard bank around one of the taller buildings in the city, swinging back so Fido could gun down a legion of Benzonite assholes. I felt Orlaan in the computer, and I knew he would have to experience the moment of euphoria that comes with the first time an upgrade, free from the Imperial directives, merges with a machine. And just like the first time for me, cannon fire shook him free of distraction.

Fido continued to take out drones and Benzonite soldiers alike while I configured our shields to resonate on vocal sound waves. In a sense, I turned my ship into a giant speaker in the sky. All we needed now was a message. Orlaan delivered.

"My people; this is Councilor Orlaan. The Guardians are not our friends. They have never been our friends. They came to our planet to enslave us. To torture us. To use us to harm and enslave others. Their plans have failed, and now they seek only to kill us with the help of the aliens you now see filling our streets.

"My people; we are not a violent race. We are not want of suspicion or doubt or fight. But today, I must ask you to fight. Fight for your lives. Fight for your family. Fight for your neighbors. Fight for all Olemsi everywhere.

"My people, people of Three Rivers, fight for your city. Together, we can purge these invaders from our land and our skies. Fight!"

It took a few minutes for Orlaan's message to take root. I continued to circle the city while Fido worked the guns. Smoke rose from neighborhoods all around the city, and even some from the surrounding countryside. Well-armed Benzonite troops filled the streets, pulling civilians from their homes and dragging them to the pavement for execution. Somewhere, an unnamed Olemsi, who's face would one-day stand tall over a monument in every city park and several commemorative postage stamps, heard the message and understood. She made a fist for the first time in her life, and she swung.

She died in the effort. But others saw her and they learned. They understood the message. They made fists and swung. They picked-up rocks and threw them. They picked-up the long spears used to harvest granby[17] fruit and thrust them. Within minutes, the docile population of Three Rivers was in full revolt.

This took the Benzonites, paid mercenaries, totally by surprise. I had no way to know how long they'd been working with the Kressada, or how much they knew about the Olemsi. Best guess was that they perceived the locals as simpletons, naïve cattle incapable of resistance. The Benzonites had body armor and advanced weapons far greater than the local's sticks and stones. But they were not fighting for their homes or their families, and as such, they didn't stand a chance.

---

[17] Granby Fruit: Fruit that grows on a granby tree.

I set course for the Capitol Building, confident that this particular threat at least, was contained for the moment. Kressada and her regal associates were still alive, and still the greatest menace. I'm not sure what I was planning to do; if necessary, I would level the building to the ground if that would eliminate the last vestige of this evil Empire.

I haven't believed in gods for a very long time, or magic, or fate, or luck. Like Santa Clause or an honest Republican, these are products of wishful thinking, a desperate attempt to force order into a world where we have little control. Perhaps I should revisit that certainty one day.

I maneuvered my assault vessel over the city and the Capitol Building came into view. A blast struck my ship, a bolt of fantastic magnitude. My shields absorbed the brunt of the fire, but the force was great enough to alter our trajectory and, combined with our velocity, drove us into an apartment complex only a few miles from my target.

And, with the impact, I experienced, for the third time in my life, a sensation comparable only with death.

Chapter 24

It wasn't really death, at least not in the conventional sense, but it sure felt like what I image death would be. Interfacing with a machine is, for upgrades like me, the closest thing to bliss one can imagine. The sensation tearing away from that bliss, and the moments of disembodiment that follow, are both confusing and agonizing, much like riding a free falling elevator from the top floor of Willis Tower[18] and crashing onto the grassy lawn of Grant Park.

It gets easier to recover every time this happens, and I did so quickly only to find myself wedged in a corner of the command deck that used to be somewhere between a wall and the ceiling. I also had Leo on top of me, as well as a local politician. Fido was beneath us all, his big, sluggy, boneless body had cushioned our collision, leaving me with only a few fractures, several minor lesions, and a severe concussion. Fortunately, my nanites already started repairing the damage.

---

[18] Willis Tower: Formerly *Sear's Tower*, tallest building in the city of Chicago on planet Earth and, like most gargantuan architectural constructs of the 20th Century, ugly as fuck.

The disruption was much worse for Orlaan and Fido, who had just experienced both their first conscious joy of interface and the trauma of forced removal. I would have taken the time to check on them, but I had far bigger things to worry about, specifically, the condition of the ship.

Not good. The hull had cracked; daylight streamed through interior bulkheads, and the command console lay in pieces, dangling from the wires and fasteners that previously moored them in place. Warning lights flashed from the few systems that even partially remained, sparks showered from power relays while smoke and toxic fumes (not a concern for me or any of my party) rose like an enemy banner waving triumphantly over the battlefield. I heard a female voice, briefly, over what remained of the com system before the circuits surrendered completely and went dark. Even with my enhanced senses, I couldn't glean any information from the transmission, or who had even been speaking.

First, I checked on Leo, who was dazed, but in otherwise fair condition much like myself, and then I struggled out from under the Councilor, who would recover in a few minutes. Fido already squirmed under the pile of the lesser footed creatures on top of him.

I struggled to stand, climbing over politicians and a bit of living room furniture scooped-up from the surrounding building by the gaping hole in the forward section of my ship. I would eventually mourn the destruction of this otherwise impressive vehicle, but, for now, I was more concerned with what was going on around me, which had, no doubt, led to my current wreck.

Oola Oola, I concentrated through the link made by the tracking device. *Oola, can you hear me*

Her reply was as short as it was useless. *Glad you're alive. Bit busy now*. That was all she had to say.

I considered pressing her for information, but my immediate need was to retch, which I did. Voluminously. Even with nanites, head injuries kinda suck. The crash would have killed anyone not blessed with the little machines, and frankly, even with them, we nearly died. Not just from the crash, but more significantly, from the blast that led us to this predicament.

Councilor Orlaan recovered enough to stand with help from my magnificent Gorlack who, unsurprisingly, had already adapted and was doing far better than anyone else.

"What...? What was that?"

"We were hit," I explained tersely. "Must have come from the Dreadnaught. We need to get out of here."

Exit points were, sadly, abundant at this point. Fractures gaped in many locations along the hull, more from the particle blast than impact with the Olemsi architecture, which now cradled the bones of my ship. I carried Leo through the nearest gap, and trusted Fido to help Orlaan. His people had suffered much the same in the cargo hold, but equally protected from injury, and were already gathering outside, having the same access to escape as the rest of us. Indeed, this ship was never going to fly again.

I planted my feet firmly on the city sidewalk adjoining the residential property I had just decimated, and allowed Leo to stand on his own while I surveyed the surrounding.

I've seen war before. I caused it then, and I caused it now. Although this was less my responsibility than before, the damage was already much greater and I couldn't even pretend this was somehow a better scenario. Fuck it. I had been a tool as much as anyone else, manipulated, used and threatened. My ship wrecked, my friend, maybe lover, now a mindless killing machine, and another friend marooned in high orbit. Civilians were dying all around me; a civilization was on the brink of collapse, all because some spoiled brat thought herself better than everyone else. My mind focused on one thing and one thing only while the world burned around me.

Bitch gotta pay.

I grabbed Orlaan by his gray robe and, despite feeling my

blood pressure surging, made sure not take my anger out on him as I demanded, "Which way to the Capitol Building?"

Orlaan pointed over my shoulder. "We can get there by following—"

"—No!" I interrupted. "The Dreadnaught is targeting us. You're indistinguishable from the rest of the population, but maybe we aren't. Take your people and go, marshal as many civilians as you can, and prepare to ambush the capitol in case I fail. We're going forward, and I need you to have my back."

Orlaan paused and stared at me, the sound of gunfire, explosions and general chaos ringing from every direction. There were even the occasional shouts of *Three Rivers* and cries of pain. This was nothing short of an apocalypse, but a fire in Orlaan's eyes suggested something bigger for him and his people. It was not unlike the sense I got from Oola when she refused my demand she not board the Ullinarian platform. For the Olemsi, today might be less an apocalypse and more a renaissance—if any of us actually survived.

Without words, without further prompting, Orlaan steeled himself and rose thirty feet in both substance and stature. I knew that feeling well. I experienced it once before on TBNL when I witnessed refugees become avengers. I realized in that brief second both shame and pride can exist simultaneously in the same space. The Olemsi were not naïve, simple buffoons; they were magnificent. They were honest, kind, egalitarian paragons of warmth and virtue. They were, I daresay, completely and totally... *human*. My eyes watered when Orlaan gave me a decisive nod, a salute of sorts, and turned to lead his people into hell.

Shit. I really should have gotten better directions before that whole *Hallmark TV*[19] moment of moral awakening. This

---

[19] Hallmark Television: A mass communication network on planet Earth, best known for sugary, overtly sentimental programming drivel, while simultaneously pretending this is anything other than 24/7 advertisement for their extensive chain of over-priced retail shops. Their *Christmas in July* moviethons are particularly egregious in blatant commercialism. Thank fucking God this wasn't one of those.

city is in the throes of total war with numerous armies, resistance fighters, and terrified civilians—all of whom directed to fight alien invaders. Meanwhile, I decided to let the most credible local official go, leaving behind one of the two humans, and sole feline and Gorlack on the entire planet alone. How are the natives to know we aren't the enemy?

For a moment, the scope of what lie ahead nearly overwhelmed me. I looked into the three eyes of my two best friends, but I did not see my panic reflected. I saw pride, and courage. I saw confidence, in themselves, and in me. In that instant, I found clarity.

Kressada had a gang of Ullinarian rich kids, a massive army of Benzonite mercenaries and a Dreadnaught in orbit. What do I have?

I'm just a grocery clerk with a cat and a Gorlack.

That bitch didn't stand a chance.

*

We worked our way around the apartment block, deliberately taking a different route than Orlaan's group. The city streets filled with local citizens who had received the Councilor's message, and were rising to the occasion. They carried all manner of makeshift weapons, and attacked every Benzonite, they encountered. Even with the enemy's superior weaponry and experience, the local population was too numerous, and for every Olemsi who died, ten more sprang into action. The Olemsi began collecting Benzonite arms, and the effectiveness of their resistance grew exponentially.

A group of Olemsi civilians would occasionally spot my trio, and wonder briefly what to do about us. To them, we were just as alien as Ullinarians or Benzonites. I worked hard at staying out of their sight, both to protect myself, but also to protect them. I don't know if Tragito's masking of our tracking devices carried over to the Dreadnaught; they hadn't fired at me since hitting the ship, so maybe they couldn't see me after we abandoned the craft.

Not only was the city doused in chaos, but the amount of physical damage already incurred appeared even more shocking. Wreckage from damaged vehicles piled the streets, many of them still burning. Weapons fire razed entire neighborhoods, leaving behind mountains of smoldering masonry, rivers flowing from uncapped water mains, and the bodies of dead or injured civilians were too numerous to count.

I pushed forward, trying to concentrate on my mission; but that was nearly impossible. Of course, this wasn't exactly my fault; the Ullinarians were already converting the population. My presence only accelerated these events. But I know that's only half-true. The war between the Ullinarians and the K'Nostrons was also going on long before my involvement, and had already spread covertly to TBNL before my involvement, but I, metaphorically, fired the first shot. Despite my lifelong desperation to avoid authority and responsibility, I kept blundering into the middle of cosmic affairs, and always with catastrophic results. Were I to survive this crisis, I vowed to find a quiet corner of the galaxy and devote all my time to raising turnips.

The farmer fantasy withered on the vine when I turned the next corner. Half a dozen Benzonite troops surrounded a single figure in a ferocious death match.

Ever the protector, my friend Fido scooped Leo from the pavement and shoved me into a shattered doorway, blocking me from the scene with his own body. He needn't have bothered; the Benzonites had already been disarmed by their target, who himself was armed with nothing more than a broken street sign.

I cowered in the doorway for a moment, not from fear of the ensuing battle, but from the sudden realization of exactly who was doing the fighting.

Tony was barely recognizable. His face was contorted into

a mask of mindless rage, with red skin radiating heat from exertion. Sweat drenched his body, matting his beautiful brown hair, which was partially burned, and even missing in a few places. His entire body displayed signs of injury, and one hand gripping the pole was clearly broken and mangled.

However, he was doing more damage to them than he was receiving in return. The sharp metal edge of the sign, which prohibited parking during the hours of *Shashanee*, completely removed the head of a startled Benzonite in one swing. No technology can fix that kind of injury, and it gave the remaining mercenaries pause.

Fido tossed my beloved Leo towards me before I knew what was happening and he threw himself into the fray. The Benzonites, already concerned after witnessing the decapitation, all looked as if they planned a retreat, but none of them had the chance. With three of his powerful legs, Fido started snapping Benzonite spines like a weed whacker through crab grass. Tony finished off those closest to him.

I clutched my cat and watched the scene unfold, and as the dust settled, Tony glanced in our direction. I can't tell if there was any shred of recognition from him, I suspect the unstable program that now overwhelmed his senses and Ullinarian control, blocked anything resembling consciousness.

And yet, there still seemed a bond when our eyes locked. I may have been transmitting thoughts through the tracking device link Tragito established previously, maybe even sending him instructions. I can't say because my horror and guilt obscured any rational thought.

The connection, if it existed at all, didn't last long. Tony released his sign with one hand and tossed it over his back like Paul Bunyan with his ax. He snatched one of the Benzonite arms—literally, a severed arm—with his free hand and brandished it like a club. He then turned and plowed into the city, searching for more enemies to kill.

Fido waved goodbye with a back foot and rejoined Leo and

me.

My heart pounded out of control, though my nanites were already trying to compensate. I held Leo against my chest, probably tighter than was comfortable for the little cat. Clearly, the situation in the city was far worse than anything I'd expected, but in fairness, I couldn't really have anticipated the Benzonite reinforcements, though perhaps I should have.

At least one thing gave me a small ray of hope; Tony was alive. If the upgraded Olemsi army now under his influence had even a fraction of his killing prowess, the war might be close to its finish. I only had a few blocks left to cross before reaching the Capitol, and from what my ears told me, most of the fighting remained more distant.

I relaxed my grip on Leo, and he purred with relief. Fido watched me with his only big eye, waiting for our next step. But then…

A violent, throbbing pressure wave passed through the city. Smoke and dust danced in the wake and my ears popped.

I turned and looked skyward. The inevitable flash had come and gone before the shockwave drew my attention. But I did see the glowing shell of debris expand. Something in orbit just exploded.

Chapter 25

My chest tightened with waves of grief that eclipsed even the horror of the past few minutes. The glittering debris already reached the upper atmosphere, peppering the heights with glowing metal and smoke trails. Only something truly massive could cause an explosion of that size, something like an orbiting weapons platform.

It was the Dreadnaught.

"What?" I asked aloud, responding to a voice only I could hear.

It was the Dreadnaught, Oola explained again through the tracking device. *We're okay so far.*

I continued to stare skyward, afraid to trust the voice. My digital memory insisted that a fully operational platform could take down a Dreadnaught, but not easily. This platform was only partially functional, and as far as I was aware, not fully staffed. But I definitely heard Oola Oola's voice in my head.

How?

It was one of the other three Dreadnaughts. They just got

here. Hold on, I'm getting a transmission.
I begged for more information, but nothing came. This was a lot like getting a phone call from your long dead grandfather, only for him to ask you to wait while he finishes today's episode of *General Hospital*. Actually, this was much worse. Probably not by much, but close. Three more Dreadnaughts?

No more voices came from the sky, but something else did. First, the few remaining fighter drones came into view, dropping like enormous chunks of metallic hail. More noises erupted from the sky while the drones crashed and exploded on contact, the wail of rapidly descending vessels, dozens of them, about to join the destruction. I immediately recognized the sleek orange/white metal, and the red and green lights of Ullinarian ships. Scouts ships, troop transports, a couple assault vessels and even a few freighters filled the air space above Three Rivers.

Then I remembered: Ullinarians didn't build their own ships, or much of anything else. They were slavers, and as I now know from personal association, aristocrats with few attributes beyond sheer ambition. Rovalorians were their primary workforce in the field of technology.

The sinking in my chest abated as my heart swelled and soared.

"C'mon guys," I said, allowing Leo to drop from my arms and follow freely.

We were already in motion toward the capitol, when Oola came back over the strange connection.

Your friend Betty says "hello."

I punched the air in victory, though it was still a little soon for that. At least that possibility seemed on the table, finally. *Tell them to target Benzonites. Send as much medical help as they can; the population has been hit hard. Oh, and send someone to collect Scheleene.*

Oola didn't respond, but I trusted her to follow through. The streets were already filling with gun-toting land fish by the time I reached the capitol, and many other upgraded species recruited to help. I even saw humans in the mix.

Unfortunately, there was also a large contingent of Benzonites guarding the capitol, along with a few Ullinarian overseers. They were all well armed, covered behind substantial barriers. Rovalorian forces attempted to engage, but the Benzonites definitely had the high ground.

I had to reach Kressada if I was going to end this. She was almost certainly inside that building, or her remaining forces wouldn't be working so hard to hold on it.

I had to find a way to get around them. Yes, it had to be me. I know I could contact Oola, and through her, direct the Rovalorian forces to flatten the building from orbit and end all of this right now. But that wasn't nearly satisfying enough. I knew what I'd done; I still had Tony's dried blood caked under my fingernails. My nanites had recorded all the scenes of death and destruction around me, and would keep those memories alive for as long as I continued breathing. Kressada, or her family, were responsible for so many heinous acts, many of which had ensnared me as well, so she deserved to die. I wanted to be the one to make it happen.

I put aside the moral analyses of revenge; I still had to get into the fucking building. There was already an army attacking, and they weren't getting too far. If only there was yet another army attacking from another direction...

I scurried my friends into the closest approximation of shelter so I could focus. To this point, I still didn't understand the link Tragito had established with these tracking devices, which themselves I didn't remember in the slightest. But I had seen the evidence with my own eyes; I heard the messages, so I had only to trust they the connection was real.

Tony. I need you. I need you all. I focused on the words, because that's simply how the human mind works. But I also focused on the sight in front of me, and the notion of Kressada hiding in the upper levels, reveling in the destruction she had wrought.

I didn't get a response in the conventional sense, nor did I expect one. This connection, whatever it was, was far from ideal. I did receive all kinds of background noise while I concentrated; the occasional frantic thought from Oola Oola, warm fuzzies from Leo, and bits of inconceivable—and indecipherable—genius from Fido. But from Tony?

He was listening, at least as far as that was possible in his condition. A wave of anxiety crashed over me. I felt anger; so much anger, fueled by confusion and despair. It was coming closer, overpowering...

Tony never disappoints when wanton destruction is required. He and a group of crazed Olemsi soldiers, many carrying Ullinarian weapons and all demonstrating the same distress, rounded a corner from the neighboring building. They outflanked the Benzonites from behind their barrier, and took many of them down before they or the Ullinarian overseers even registered their arrival. Rovalorian forces continued their assault, dividing the Benzonites' fire.

Lead them away, I urged mentally, crouching behind what I gathered was the remains of a public post box.

Tony looked around for a moment, as if searching for the source of the words. Or maybe he was making a plan. Regardless of how or why, Tony followed my instructions. He contemplated the severed arm he still carried, and then looked towards the Benzonites. With a defiant, and rather psychotic, scream, he tossed the arm at the defensive guards where it landed poignantly at their feet. He also threw the *no parking* sign for good measure, which failed to strike anyone, but certainly underlined details about their amputated colleague.

Digital memories in my head recalled that Benzonites were violent by nature, and never allowed an insult to go unchallenged. The same information slumbered somewhere in Tony's tumultuous brain. A brilliant move, if that was indeed his plan. After delivering the insult, Tony led his little band back the way they'd come, and the Benzonites, enraged, abandoned their post in pursuit, despite protest from their overseers.

The land fish brigade struck down several mercenaries, enough to terrify the two Ullinarian rich boys, who fled into the now-defenseless capitol.

I jumped to my feet and ran towards the main entrance. Doing this left me exposed to the Rovalorians, but I assumed Scheleene had mentioned me in her call for help. For that matter, I already knew Captain Betty was in orbit with their fleet, so they definitely had to be aware of me, and that I was not an enemy. Hell, they probably all knew more about what was going on here than I did at this very moment.

Regardless, the attacking army ignored my two companions and me as we raced across the street and a burnt patch of lawn leading to the main entrance.

The Ullinarians didn't even bother to lock the front door when they fled, so I flew into the lobby as easily as a Russian Oligarch with a truckload of campaign money could enter RNC Headquarters. I expected resistance inside—to my presence, not the hypothetical cash—but I instead found a pleasant surprise: two dead Ullinarians.

Orlaan and his group had arrived ahead of me but, apparently, by only a few seconds.

"How did you get in?" I asked, both shocked and duly impressed... before the smell hit me.

"We came through the sewer," Orlaan explained. "I've worked here for over fifty years; I know this building better than anyone."

"Great. Where will Kressada be?"

Rovalorian forces entered the lobby. Their commander, not an actual Rovalorian but rather a liberated Avresarian upgrade with lovely crest of sapphire blue feathers, surveyed the scene and approached me directly.

"Commander Burrelus, sir," he said, raising an arm in a form of salute. "We are here to challenge the Ullinarian directive, and serve the local population."

Obviously, but it was still nice to hear. "Commander, glad to see you. This is Councilor Orlaan, legitimate representative of the Olemsi Government."

The bird performed a neat military turn on his talons to face the councilor and saluted again. "Your orders, sir?"

Councilor Orlaan gaped. Even though he had become somewhat accustomed to the company of aliens, addressing a six-foot tall, flightless bird leading a troop of land fish might have been a bit too much. I could sympathize.

I leaned towards Orlaan and whispered a suggestion. "Secure the building."

"Secure the building."

Burrelus clicked his beak and began ordering his troops. I had faith they could accomplish their duty without my help, so I asked Orlaan to lead me to Kressada. He nodded and pointed the way.

I scooped up a fallen weapon from one of the dead Ullinarians and Fido grabbed the other. It felt strange in my hand. Only twice before had I ever held a weapon, both times after my initial abduction, and neither time did I try to use them. However, my hands were anything but clean. Oola had been right when she accused me of using others to do the fighting... and the dying. I'd dodged culpability for too long, hiding behind deniability, or convincing myself that I had no other choice. Not this time.

Orlaan and two of his armed colleagues led us through the lobby and the back recesses of the capitol to a narrow stairway. I recognized it as the same stairs I traversed previously from my cell to that first meeting with Temoosh.

Orlaan, with one of his gunmen, led the way as we climbed, and another slave-turned-soldier following us all from behind. Several dead Olemsi lie strewn in the stairwell, probably simple employees of the capitol, assassinated when Kressada's harvest began in earnest. Scenes like this were no doubt plentiful around the building, and the overall city.

I heard Burrelus's troops moving through the building below us and occasional shouts or gunfire, but their progress sounded methodical and therefore slow. We rose faster than the security force. In fact, we followed the same exact same path as I had before, straight to the upper most level and the very same meeting room.

Temoosh was there with Helmemminon, just like that first meeting. There was no sign of the mock council of elders, or any other pretext of democracy. The presence of the Benzonite commander, the same asshole who menaced me at the outpost, proved this conclusively. He was on a communicator and trying to marshal what remained of his troops.

Unfortunately, he was not as distracted as I might have hoped, and turned his weapon on us the moment we entered. A shower of gunfire erupted.

Chapter 26

Orlaan and his gunman took the brunt of the Benzonite attack. Actually, the unnamed Olemsi got most of it, the blast striking him square in the chest and forcing his smoking corpse into the councilor, who only sustained a minor hit. I rushed forward, raising my weapon, but a stampeding Gorlack shoved me aside. Fido, ignoring his own weapon, charged the Benzonite.

A plasma discharge burned through the air, passing dangerously close to Fido's head. Several more shots rang out as the Gorlack pushed forward his attack. Fido reached the Benzonite and swiped at the weapon as it fired, throwing it across the room and losing one of his middle feet in the process. My second best friend in the universe collapsed, whimpering in agony.

I recovered quickly enough to cover the trio with my own weapon. They didn't know how experienced I was, or not, with guns, so they made no further attempt to resist. Leo hissed with all the anger a cat could muster and leapt to his buddy's side.

The other Olemsi with us joined me and aimed his weapon; he stared directly at the prefect, someone he probably once trusted, and might even have helped to elect.

Both Temoosh and the Duke remained still, holding up their hands in a clear sign of surrender. The Benzonite growled, and stared only at the weapon in my hand.

"Give it up, *Ambassador*. You've lost. Order your forces to surrender before anyone else dies."

Helmemminon shrugged. "There aren't many left. Most of my clan fled when the Rovalorian fleet arrived. You've already destroyed the Benzonite Dreadnaught and our control over the Olemsi army. We've got nothing left."

He was strangely acquiescent, and, stranger still, seemed genuinely sincere. Perhaps he hoped for mercy through capitulation; something I tried once during a traffic accident, which started this whole new phase of my life. It didn't work for me then; it wasn't going to work for him now.

His strategy, or whatever, did give me a minute to survey the overall damage. Orlaan was sitting up now, seriously injured, his nanites already at work. Fido was in much worse shape; he nearly lost one of his front legs, but it was intact, and thanks to Kressada's upgrade, he would soon be as good as new. For now, however, my Gorlack friend lay on the floor, suffering from the painful burns and missing middle foot. Leo checked on his second best friend and started prowling the room.

"Where is Kressada?"

Again, the Duke shrugged. "She's around here somewhere. Probably searching for a way to kill you. You defeated her. Twice. She won't let that go."

"I hope she does kill you," Temoosh shrieked, his sterling white business suit unmarred by the amount of blood figuratively on his own hands. His voice revealed how much he would revel in spilling more.

"You are such a fool, Orlaan," the prefect continued, stabbing an angry finger at the man on the floor. "We could have been the center of the galaxy! With real power and wealth for all our people—"

The Duke, still holding his hand in the air, scoffed. "Never. Eventually, we would have converted every one of you. That's what we've done for thousands of years."

Temoosh continued to rant; I felt my Olemsi colleague's hatred rise, but I was more concerned about the missing queen. Was all this just a distraction to buy time for revenge or escape? I stole a quick glance back down the hall. There were other rooms on this floor, but so far, no sign of Kressada. Unfortunately, I failed to see where Leo had gone.

Helmemminon ignored the ranting prefect and stared straight at me, lowering his arms. "I'm tired," he said. "Tired of all of it. I would have been happy to just settle on this planet and live out my remaining days naturally. Do whatever you—"

A terrible whine, like the sound of a dentist drill hitting raw tissue, cut through the air and the back of the Duke's skull. Blood and bits of bone splattered my face. For as shocking as this scene was for me to witness, it was a mere prelude.

The scenario unfolding before me was not unexpected, but definitely one of the worse cases I could imagine. Kressada entered from the back of the room. She carried a large handgun in one hand, still hot from the recent blast. In her other, she carried my beloved cat Leo.

Leo was alive, but limp. Kressada aimed her weapon directly at his tiny head. He must have understood the threat; I could feel him calling to me for help, desperate for me to protect him just as I always had during our old lives back on Earth. I could feel his pain, but I knew his nanites would eventually compensate, unless, of course, she used her weapon on him. Nanites are effective little machines, boarding on magical, but death is permanent, even for upgrades.

I spared a quick second to glance down at Fido. He'd dragged himself into a corner, still whimpering, but he had stopped bleeding. His nanites were addressing the wound; to what extent I couldn't even guess knowing so little about his physiology. Regardless, I couldn't expect help from him for some time.

I began to panic. The war was over. My thirst for revenge was now secondary to saving Leo. Terror flooded through me; probably a combination of my own fear, as well as that of Leo and Fido as our strange link passed emotion from one to another.

"It's over, Excellency," I whispered, desperate to capitulate as much as possible. It didn't work before and I didn't expect it to work now. But I had nothing else.

"You filthy primitive," Kressada hissed in manner that jacked both Leo's anxiety and my own. "You've taken everything from me. Everything!

"By right, I should be the ruler of the galaxy. I deserve it. I waited a thousand years to take command of my empire! For centuries, I tried to convince Daddy to strike the K'Nostrons and wipe them out. Now they're out of my way. Daddy's out of my way. I deserve this galaxy. And a primitive like you, a parasite fit for nothing but service to my empire, ruins everything."

She clenched her weapon, and Leo, tighter. "I understand what this creature means to you. I want you to watch while I kill it. I want you to suffer."

I had to give her something, anything, any reason to delay.

"You're still alive." I offered. "Kill him, and that ends right now."

Kressada's eyes darted between Leo and me. She was looking for a way out, same as I was. And probably also like me, she was trying to juggle both her hunger for revenge, and survival.

The clock ticked. I could see Commander Burrelus through

the corner of my eye creeping down the hallway with several of his troopers. Knowing how this could escalate the situation, I had to send a message to both him and Kressada.

"I can get you away from here," I spoke deliberately, even taking the extra incentive to lower my weapon. The Benzonite snatched it from me, but remained cognizant of my Olemsi companion who still held his own weapon ready. Burrelus saw all of this, and paused, waiting for my signal.

"Why would you do that? Why should I trust you to help me?"

I nodded, not knowing whether or not that gesture would have any meaning to her. "You can trust that I care about my cat. His life is worth more to me than killing you."

Temoosh stood by in near shock ever since the Duke exploded next to him. This exchange between the rest of us was getting under his skin, and he quaked. "Kill them! Kill all of them!"

His shrieking stopped when my Olemsi friend and the Benzonite both jammed their guns in his face.

Kressada was also losing her nerve, I suspected, as her own behavior drifted from murderous to merely anxious. The ever-present sneer on her face was gone and I could tell her grip on Leo had loosened slightly.

I made a gesture to the Olemsi to lower his weapon. The signal was also for Burrelus to do the same, which he did.

"Commander," I called towards the hallway. "Do you have a comlink with the fleet? Toss it to me."

The Avresarian dropped his riffle onto its shoulder strap and pulled a device from his residual cranial feathers. Instead of throwing it, however, he carefully entered the room, displaying his empty hand while passing me the device with the other. This was probably the best course of action because, despite my enhancements, I still had all the athletic skill of three-toed sloth stoned on valium.

The device was a simple hyperspace transmitter/receiver,

without a microphone, speaker or even visual display, but with a secure clip for attaching to any clothing, feather or fur. Its function appeared perfectly clear to me, so I interfaced and dove into the entire Rovalorian network.

The last time I felt bliss on this level was when inside the Ullinarian network, the day I pissed in their data pool and killed nearly all of them. Fortunately, I became accustomed to the lure of cyberspace a long time ago, and could resist the urge to freefall through all the delightful bits and bytes of digital wonder and instead focus on specifics.

I had no idea who was commanding the fleet; though that information was available to me within the network should I seek it. Instead, I focused on one person who I knew was reliable, and left our conversation open to all others integrated to overhear.

"Oola Oola, are you online?" I spoke both mentally through the network, and aloud, so that everyone in the room, Kressada in particular, could hear.

Tragito here. The fighting has concluded, he thought to me, in my own voice. *But we're still having trouble with upgraded soldiers. Oola Oola is trying to reach Tony. Scheleene—*"

"Fine," I interrupted. "I need a ship brought to me on the roof of the Capitol building. Preferably, a fully fueled, long-range shuttle."

Across the room, Kressada grunted. I interpreted that as approval.

Another speaker came through the network. Again, it came in the form of my own voice, but the actual source was unknown. *We have troop carriers on site. We can extract you—*

"This isn't for my extraction. Kressada is with me. I promised her safe passage."

Are you fucking insane? My voice, but from a different mind. Fortunately, it was a mind I recognized.

"Betty, she has Leo. This is the only way to save him. I will pilot the ship away with Kressada. Can the fleet guarantee our safety?"

We cannot allow that, thought the previous speaker, possibly someone representing fleet command. *Kressada is guilty of crimes without number. She represents a threat to galactic civilization and must stand trial.*

"You're right. But at the moment, I don't care." I was surprised that I actually meant this. Kressada was the embodiment of evil, all possible sins sentient life could ever manifest, all encapsulated in a single form. And I was willing to save her life, no matter how little she deserved mercy. She held a gun to my cat, the one sacrifice I would never allow.

Even without a response, I knew a stronger sales pitch was necessary. Burrelus casually lowered his short, featherless arm towards his riffle. Even my Olemsi companion, still covering Temoosh, seemed to waver.

"All of you owe me," I stated through the network, and to everyone nearby. "Rovalorians owe me. Every upgrade in this sector owes me. None of you would be free now if not for me. And you owe Leo, because I couldn't have set the data bomb, or freed the Olemsi, without him."

Silence from the network. On the other side, the various parties might be debating verbally, or perhaps even through the network if they chose to block me from their thoughts. Any experienced upgrade could easily perform such a simple function. My largest concern presently remained Kressada herself. She breathed fast and heavy, shifting her weight from one leg to the other, swinging from her hips as she scanned everyone in the room. Poor Leo swayed with her movement, his small body dangling from her grip around his neck. If not for nanites, he would already be dead.

"Kressada can't do any more harm," I continued my pitch. "The rest of her people are gone; the few who haven't been killed or captured are on the run. Too few of them escaped to constitute any real threat."

None of them escaped. Betty thought to me, but I kept that information to myself.

Meanwhile, Councilor Orlaan, recovering from his injuries, pulled himself into a more dignified sitting position, the slain Olemsi still strewn across his lap.

"Let her go."

I looked at the Councilor, both surprised and grateful to him.

"Councilor Orlaan, the legitimate authority on Olemsi Myucuc—" (Temoosh huffed indignantly, but considering the number of weapons pointed in his direction, wisely kept his tiny, quisling mouth shut) "—agrees with me."

Two minutes and six seconds passed, during which time I felt so many emotions churn around me, from whatever source. Some were mine, some were subconscious transmissions through the network itself, and some were through the connection established by the tracking devices. I ignored them all; my gaze remained fixed to Kressada. Her confidence was really the only one that mattered.

Very well. We will dispatch a shuttle to your location. Stand by.

"They've agreed," I announced. "A ship is on its way."

Chapter 27

Kressada wasn't yet convinced I had secured her escape, but she also wasn't escalating the situation. She remained poised to execute my best friend. The Benzonite commander still trained his weapon on the obnoxious prefect, watching her Excellency for cues, but none was forthcoming.

Commander Burrelus extended a claw. "I must have confirmation, sir."

I handed back his device and turned my attention to Fido. His bleeding had ceased, but his stump, cradled by two of his remaining feet, continued oozing colorless fluid. His eye was swollen and wet. I had no idea how much of recent events he'd observed, but I suspected he got the gist of what was coming.

Stay with Oola, I whispered through our technological bond. *Look after her and Tony. I will come back for you when I can.*

He didn't respond, not even some squishy, gooey sensation broadcast to my tracking device. He simply blinked once and continued to stare. I think he understood.

Commander Burrelus concluded his silent conference with the fleet and returned his comlink to his feathered crest. "Confirmed. The Rovalorian authority has granted you safe passage from this system, with one condition; if you ever return to our claimed territory, you will be apprehended, tried and executed."

Kressada didn't respond directly, but rather seemed to expect further reassurance. Burrelus ordered the Rovalorians still in the hallway to stand down. They obeyed immediately. My Olemsi companion didn't recognize the authority of a talking bird, though he was now equipped to understand him, and kept his weapon aimed at Temoosh.

Burrelus placed a hand on the Olemsi's shoulder and spoke calmly. "Stand down, son. It's over. Your people are free."

He squeezed the riffle tighter, a tear forming in one eye.

"I understand," Burrelus continued. "The Ullinarians destroyed my planet. They kept me enslaved for years. I hate her as much as you do. More. But her death won't change the past. And as the human said, we owe him and his friend for our freedom."

The man considered; his weapon still held tight swung from Temoosh to Kressada, who responded by doubling down on her threat against Leo, but no further. The Benzonite also held his weapon ready, but he didn't take the threat any farther, apparently hedging in hopes that the offer of freedom was genuine.

"Let them go," Orlaan wheezed, finally breaking the tension. "Just let them go so we can rebuild."

The Olemsi next to me gripped his riffle tighter. I knew nothing about him; what he had gone through, what circumstances led him to his upgrading. Had he witnessed the conscription of his wife? Was he questioning the location and safety of his children? He was definitely angry; it showed in his face and the way he brandished the weapon, and he wanted revenge.

With a final glance from Orlaan, to Kressada, and back, the young Olemsi reluctantly stood down.

"Fine," Kressada acquiesced at last. "But one sign of betrayal, and I kill this thing." She gestured with Leo's body, prompting a whimper and a muted hiss.

My stomach churned at the sight, and a flood of desperation washed through me. I felt heaviness in my arms and legs, as if I was running at top speed. My heart told me it was about to burst, but my pulse remained normal. I didn't know whom these impulses were coming from, perhaps Leo, or even Tony, but they weren't mine. I fought to ignore them, and deal with the situation at hand.

"The shuttle will be here shortly," I stated matter-of-factly. "We should go to the roof to meet them."

Temoosh turned suddenly to face Kressada, throwing his weight on the conference table, which, fortunately for my cat, separated him from the bitch queen. "Take me with you! Do you know what they'll do to me?"

Kressada flashed a wry grin for the first time since this confrontation began. "Better you than me. Keep him."

Temoosh choked on an objection while the young Olemsi happily grabbed him by his collar and returned the point of his weapon towards his chest. Neither Kressada nor the Benzonite objected.

"Fine," Kressada declared, waving her pistol towards me, but never so far from Leo that her threat ever subsided. "Lead the way. If anyone follows, I will kill them both."

I took one last look around the room, making a silent, yet hopefully meaningful, acknowledgement to Fido, Orlaan and Burrelus. I was committed to saving Leo by whatever means necessary, and so far, it seemed, the local powers were going along. I presumably still had contact with Oola on the platform, only she wasn't talking. I felt like I should say something to her, but at a time like this, I don't know what that should be.

Even now, I reeled knowing how much I'd underestimated that woman, indeed her entire species. She had not only risen to the occasion, but she had exceeded me in bravery and wisdom. How do you acknowledge that in a few simple thoughts?

A voice sounded in my head. *I love you too.*

Oola heard my thoughts. That was good enough.

My name is Oola Oola.

I suppressed a laugh, and I knew, even without proof, that somewhere high above, she laughed too.

I felt a little better about my decision, and turned back to Kressada and her Benzonite henchman. "This way to the roof."

*

Twilight crept in above the city on what future generations would remember as the Longest Day. Columns of rising smoke stained the clear sky, and the stench of death rose from the city below. The smell was probably more a figment of my imagination, but the atmosphere definitely reminded me of more of a tomb than a pleasant summer evening outdoors. Muted, distant voices sounded all over Three Rivers: sobs, outrage, and jubilation. The sky appeared empty, all Rovalorian ships landed, and the troops hopefully rendering medical aid to the local population.

I couldn't tell what had become of Tony and the other capped soldiers. No information came through the tracking device, and my ears revealed even less. Tragito controlled that link; perhaps he had severed my connection. I couldn't even sense Leo, which I found particularly disturbing. The Benzonite kept me facing forward since the moment we emerged onto the roof, holding me by my shirt collar with his gun pressed between my shoulder blades. Kressada still held Leo behind me, so the loss of this connection fueled my terror.

The stillness lasted only a short time before the red and

green lights of an Ullinarian shuttle appeared overhead, lowering slowly towards us. Whoever piloted the shuttle definitely had some skill, landing a safe distance away from us without so much as thump on the old timey construction of the roof.

Kressada appeared from behind me when the engine noises subsided into a neutral mode. Leo was still alive, but dangling painfully by his neck, all his fight gone. I gasped and held my breath, stealing myself against panic.

"Slowly," Kressada warned, gesturing me forward with her gun's nozzle.

I obeyed, approaching the shuttle carefully past electrical boxes, skylights, and those round, spinning, vent things that, as far as I know, don't even have a name. Heat from the drive units rippled across the roof, scattering dried leaves and bits of tarpaper. We neared the side hatch. It hissed as the pressure seal cracked, then slid open. A single humanoid figure appeared, eclipsed by the bright interior. Even without seeing her face, I instantly recognized the young-looking woman descending the short ramp.

Captain Betty paused at the bottom of the ramp and raised her empty hands into the air, clearly waiting for instructions.

I was surprised to see her, expecting a Rovalorian instead. Kressada probably felt the same. Of course, unknown to the Queen, Captain Betty first uncovered the operation on Olemsi Myucuc. Captain Betty enlisted me in this endeavor, and who obviously, held considerable sway with the Rovalorians. Kressada didn't know any of that, so had no reason to worry. I knew it all, and for those reasons, I did worry. A lot.

My cat was a hostage, and I loved Leo more than anything else in the universe. I was sincerely willing to sacrifice my freedom for his survival. If Betty was here on some convoluted mission to subvert our escape, it could likely put Leo's life in jeopardy. Even without the weapon, Kressada was perfectly capable of killing Leo; her strength outmatched any human, and my poor cat was in no position to defend himself.

Kressada took an instinctive step back from the new human, and swung her gun from Leo to me. "Move away from the shuttle," she hissed. "Over there."

The bitch queen tilted her head in the direction she wanted the pilot to follow. Betty's face was completely devoid of expression, which is itself an expression, but one I certainly couldn't read.

Betty stopped about twenty feet away from us, standing in a place where Kressada could cover us both. No one moved for a moment, but the tension was palpable, and rising quickly.

"Check inside."

The Benzonite growled as he released me. I felt his weapon retract from my back. Relief, but only slightly. He kept it trained at me the whole time he crept backwards towards the shuttle. I almost expected the lumbering idiot to trip over his own feet, which might give me an opening to… do what? Any action would certainly bring death to my cat. I wasn't going to take that risk, and I hoped everyone here knew that.

My pointless quandary ended when the mercenary reached the shuttle and entered. A new question sprouted. Was the shuttle full of soldiers waiting to attack? Betty's blank expression was conspicuous in the extreme. Non-humans might not understand this, but I did. She was clearly planning something, and it was in progress. But nothing came from the ship; no gunfire, no storming boots, not even a peep from that fucking Benzonite.

Kressada shifted her aim between the three of us, increasingly frantic. I was just as desperate for answers. I mentally screamed for someone to tell me what was about to happen, but I got nothing from the link—except a sudden wave of searing pain in my fingertips.

What the fuck? I wondered, glancing down at my own hands. I felt as though my nails were tearing off! Nothing of the sort, though. What I saw was normal. My arms started to ache; the kind of pain after a day of heavy lifting and my dry clothes didn't match the feeling of my body being drenched in my own sweat, which also wasn't present.

The silence persisted, and Kressada lost what little patience she had. She turned the gun towards Betty, more defiantly than before. "What's taking him so long?"

Betty shrugged casually. "Why ask me? You're his boss."

I nearly retched. Provoking the Ullinarian was the last thing I wanted, at least until Leo was safe, which most certainly *wasn't now*. Kressada was incalculably dangerous at the best of times, and now she was a trapped animal. With a gun.

She turned hard and aimed the weapon at me, her face contorted with rage. "What is this? I swear I'll kill every last—"

"Arrrrrrrrrrrrrr!"

Kressada and I jumped at the scream. All the nanites in the universe couldn't help me process what was happening. My body experienced a massive rush of hormones and emotions, mixed with a toxic cocktail of confusion and a big splash of abject horror.

She spun around towards the scream, behind the spot where Betty had previously been standing before throwing herself behind an AC unit. Tony charged; his hands bloody from clawing himself up the side of the building. He barely looked recognizable, barely human, just a bundle of enormous strength and rage. So much rage that the first blast from Kressada's gun, slamming him squarely in the center of his gut, didn't even slow him down.

This definitely wasn't the opportunity I expected, or even wanted, but I took it nonetheless. I launched myself at Kressada from behind and struggled to divert her aim. Her strength was enormous, but so was my determination. Unfortunately, determination failed against sheer brute force. She got at least three more shots before turning her attention to me.

Tony went silent. I didn't see where those last blasts landed, but all indication was Kressada had found her target. Still, I struggled with her right arm. At least I caused enough disruption that she had to fight back.

She released Leo and used her free hand to reach over her own head and grab me by my hair. I lacked the strength to resist as she pulled me away as easily as plucking an overripe apple from a tree. I flew a fair distance and crashed headfirst on the roof, certainly cracking a few vertebrate in the process.

Dazed, I heard her scream. "Damn you! I knew you'd try something like this. Damn you, damn you…"

I felt my arms flailing while nanites rushed to repair my broken neck. The Benzonite must have heard the commotion and would be here presently. I didn't know if Tony was still alive, or if Leo escaped. I couldn't speak, or protest, or attempt to prove my lack of complicity with these events. I couldn't even turn to face the Ullinarian, who I knew was about to kill me.

Immobilized, I could only stare at the darkening sky above. The stars were coming out, and I wondered how many of them were not stars at all, but part of the Rovalorian fleet. How many of those real stars hosted planets that, thanks to my sacrifice, would never have to face Ullinarian tyranny? I wondered if my friends and me would be remembered as heroes, or destroyers, or forgotten altogether.

A shadow fell over me. Kressada, queen bitch of the galaxy, stood tall, defeated, but still as arrogant as her rank entailed. Her weapon pointed towards my face, no surprise, but she obviously wanted me to see her one last time. She wallowed in satisfaction, gloating that her defeat meant my death. Thank the gods she didn't speak.

Kressada had revealed how little she knew about cats only a day ago, except that I dearly loved one in particular. She obviously didn't know about their predatory skills, or their ability to climb, or their sense of loyalty—something she probably couldn't comprehend in any context.

Regardless of what she did or did not know, I happen to know this; when Leo pounced and scurried up her clothing,

Loose Cannon

she was quite likely surprised, even more so when his claws dug into her skin on the way up. But probably nothing came as a greater shock to the ghoulish monarch than when his teeth, wet with nanite infused saliva, tore into her chin.

She fired her weapon, but by the time she did so, her ability to aim had already been compromised and the blasts exploded harmlessly somewhere nearby. Leo dropped away while she staggered out of my sight line. The sound of her screaming gave me a thrill rather than sense of terror. About fucking time. Sadly, her screams didn't last very long.

My physical repairs proceeded, only I was still in tremendous pain. The sound of Leo purring while doing that annoying head-butting against my face provided some seriously needed comfort, no matter how much it hurt. And it hurt a lot. I still couldn't lift my head, but I heard many voices around me.

Captain Betty's shadow fell over me, but her attention remained somewhere else. I could see the comlink clipped to her own hair, and after a few seconds, I spotted Commander Burrelus and some of his Rovalorians troops.

"Get him onto the ship," Betty demanded of someone outside my view. I didn't know who she was talking to, but her pointed finger was towards my own crumpled body.

"What..." I struggled to ask, "...about the... Benzonite...?"

Betty finally looked at me and smiled. "Oh him? Aw. I assumed the Ullinarian would send someone to scout ahead. I left him a little present."

"Wh... what present...?"

"Did you know arsenic pentaflouride affects Benzonites even faster than it does humans? Poor little teddy bear didn't stand a chance."

I started to snicker, but it hurt too damn much, so I held it back. "What... what about T... Tony?"

"He's in bad shape, but we have a full medical team waiting for him. And you." Betty stepped back while a pair of strong hands pushed under my body and lifted. My head rolled to the side and I saw my rescuer. Fido's burned face looked almost normal already, but I could tell by the way he limped while carrying me that his leg was still a problem. He was alive, however, and, from what I could gather, so was Tony.

My biggest regret at the moment was that I couldn't see Kressada's body. I assumed she was dissolving thanks to Leo's nanites and my data bomb, just like that guard I beat silly back at the brownstone. I'd have liked to watch her melt; maybe give her a good kick in the head just for the hell of it.

Maybe I could get that pleasurable memory from Betty in the near future, but until then, I'd have to be satisfied with survival.

Chapter 28

My medical treatment went smoothly. I essentially only needed a fresh supply of raw materials to speed the self-replication of my nanites. Commander Burrelus gave me several injections of liquefied copper, aluminum, and silicon dioxide, and the little machines did the rest. I felt almost normal by the time our shuttle reached one of the many Dreadnaughts in orbit.

Fido's recovery was even more dramatic. Gorlacks are nearly amoeboid by design, and his nanites not only repaired wounds, but also produced an embryonic foot at the base of his stump. It would require a few weeks to grow, but, eventually, he was going to have all six feet again. How cool is that?

The prognosis for Tony remained unclear, however. I sat in a corner of the shuttle with Leo and Fido's giant head in my lap en route to the Dreadnaught, watching the medics. To me, Tony looked dead. He was unresponsive, bleeding heavily, and still a slave to that block on his head—the one I put there.

We are going to do everything we can for him.

I heard the voice in my head, and it provided some comfort.

At least, in a sense, my whole group was reunited.
Did you send him to save me? I asked over the link. *And block me from knowing about it?*
Yes. Oola confessed. *Your friend Betty and I worked it out together. Neither of us was willing to let you make that sacrifice.*

I felt fury, or something close to that because I was too tired to feel much of anything, though maybe I didn't have the right—the right to feel angry or tired. Betty piloted the shuttle, and for a moment, I considered interfacing and confronting her on the spot. I decided against that. She was driving, and the sooner we got Tony to a proper medical facility, the better his chances. Besides, their goddamn plan worked.

What about the other soldiers?

A few seconds passed before Oola responded. I don't know if she had to check, or if she was simply reluctant to give me painful news. I think the truth was somewhere in between. *They collapsed when Tony did. Many of them died. Rovalorians are gathering the survivors and bringing them for treatment. Scheleene is working on it; she thinks she can remove the caps, but it's quite dangerous. Only time will tell.*

"It always does," I said aloud, so softly that no one besides my cat and Gorlack could hear. "It always does."

*

Many things happened in the weeks that followed *the Longest Day*. Olemsi Myucuc recovered but destined to never be the same again. Scheleene and the other Rovalorians moved Tony after surgery, and the rest of Kressada's new soldiers, to the orbital platform. They managed to remove the caps and purge Tony's illicit program—from everyone but Tony because, just as I'd previously assessed, it was permanently integrated into his master nanite.

I tried to visit Tony every few days, waiting for him to awaken, though there was still some doubt about whether or not that would ever happen. Fido and Leo stayed with him around the clock, but I had work to do.

Unlike before, when the dust settled around the wreck of TBNL, I hid in our commandeered ship, unwilling to face the devastation I brought to those refugees. This time, I accepted my responsibility, and felt determined to help the Olemsi not only recover, but thrive in their new reality. Specifically, I helped to negotiate a treaty between the Olemsi council and the Rovalorian enclave. Former Prefect Temoosh, who now permanently occupied a charming cell in the capitol basement, had been right about one thing: Olemsi Myucuc needed to grow up and take their place in the cosmic neighborhood. They couldn't continue existing in a vacuum, children among the giants.

My work for the Olemsi included several meetings with Captain Betty, who still pressed me into accepting a position with her transport business. I declined every offer. During our last meeting, and my third refusal, I received an urgent call from Oola Oola, requesting I join her aboard the platform immediately.

Shuttles between the platform and surface ran every few hours, piloted by recent Olemsi upgrades, taught by the Rovalorians or their contracts. I noted how strange that felt every time I made the crossing as a willing passenger, especially since I no longer possessed a ship of my own.

I rushed to Tony's room as soon as my shuttle docked, avoiding everyone along the way. I'd gained a certain celebrity status, which I found grossly undeserved. I made too many mistakes to deserve a statue, commemorative postage stamp, or even a limited-edition cup from Arby's. Maybe a happy meal toy.

I saw Oola Oola through the doorway even before I reached the room. She stood just inside the doorway, her hands clasped together over her official state robes. I couldn't garner anything from her expression, which reminded me of what some of my coworkers back in the old days would call *resting bitch face*.

"Is something wrong?" I begged, walking faster.

I didn't receive a response until I entered the room, and it didn't come from the Councilwoman.

"Yeah. I have a huge-ass headache, dickwad."

Tony sat upright on the bed, smiling. His skin looked less gray than on my previous visits, but still far from normal. A thin haze of newly grown dark hair revealed where the cap once protruded, and would remain an unpleasant reminder for some time.

I rushed past Oola to Tony's bedside, and lunged, planting a firm kiss squarely on his lips. He grunted from the impact, but he definitely kissed me back.

"Easy," he said from a micron away. "Still sore."

I backed off, however reluctantly, and dropped into a nearby chair. Leo climbed from Tony's lap and jumped over to mine as soon as my butt hit the cushion. He curled up and went to sleep in seconds. "When did you wake?"

"A few hours ago. Doctors say the healing will accelerate now that I'm up. If you can take medical advice from a talking fish." He finished with a shrug, but his smile never faded.

"You think you have it bad?" I teased. "Poor Fido had a foot blown off."

At the sound of his name, Fido's head rose from the other side of Tony's bed, a repurposed Ullinarian slave support, and glooped happily.

"Is that why one foot is smaller than the others?"

"Gloop gloop."

Fido went back to sleep after his definitive and rather meaningless declaration, and the room fell into an awkward silence.

I looked around as if seeing the place for the first time despite having been there often. It was a grotesque conglomeration of Ullinarian machinery and discarded Olemsi furniture.

The bedding even smelled like Yak[20] piss.

"So..." Tony began while fidgeting with his colorful blanket. I could see a bit of a tent developing, which prompted a similar response in my own southern regions. "...I hear you've been busy?"

"Yeah. I've been working with the Council. We just finished a trade agreement this morning. I assume you've met the newest member of the Council?"

"Oh, yes," Tony acknowledged, his bright voice obviously contrived. "Congratulations again."

Oola Oola nodded with pride. "Honestly, I'm still surprised myself. I was just a farm girl before all this. I'm still not sure Prefect Orlaan was right to appoint me."

"He was," I insisted. "Your off-world experience will be invaluable to your people, and their future."

"Indeed. And you have both provided me with an understanding of concepts I would never have considered before. You have been an invaluable influence."

I know my nanites sometimes prevent the physiological response regarded as a blush, but I felt it anyway.

"We'll be here if you have any questions." I swung my head from the councilwoman to Tony. "I wrecked *Balls of Steel*."

"I heard," he sneered, playfully. "What do you always say about *my* driving?"

"Since you bring that up...," Oola interrupted quickly, her head flopping to one shoulder. Not surprisingly, she completely failed to recognize the difference between a genuine argument, and flirtation.

The real surprise, I thought to myself (thankful that the tracking devices were long gone), was how the Olemsi ever managed to reproduce at all. Oh. Then I remembered how

---

[20] Yak: A domesticated animal on the planet Earth, not to be confused with the ancient religious scholar from Olemsi Myucuc. However, both likely produced unpleasant smelling urine.

both she and Tragito kept studying each other's asses. Never mind.

"…That rather depends on you."

I looked from Oola to Tony and back again. "What do you mean? I already told Betty I didn't want a commission with—"

"No no. Nothing like that," she insisted, swelling with pride. "I made a special deal with the Rovalorians. No small feat, either. They were reluctant to hand over an arrow class assault vessel…"

"Shut your mouth!" Tony bellowed, and then winced from the exertion. "For real?"

"For real. It's docked at airlock nine. You can leave as soon as you're ready. Hopefully not without saying goodbye."

"Of course not!" I leapt to my feet, tossing poor Leo to the floor, and hugged Oola from a safe distance because my own… *tent support*... was becoming rather prominent and I didn't want to offend a local official.

"I have an idea," I announced, backing off and pushing the bone to one side as discreetly as possible. "Why don't you show Fido and Leo our new digs. They can show us after Tony and I—when Tony feels up to it."

Oola's tubular nose twitched, but she only nodded respectfully. After all this time sharing our thoughts, she knew. She definitely knew.

"Well then, gentlemen, I'll see you later. Come, boys. Let's see your new ship."

Councilwoman Eenepret and my two best friends left the room, and I rushed to close the door. It wasn't really a door. This entire ward was makeshift in a wide corridor. The walls were poorly arranged sheets of metal and the door nothing but tanned malbury skin. Good enough.

I pulled the leathery curtain closed, turned to Tony and his tent, no longer concealed and reaching new heights.

"You made a certain suggestion back in the mines. If I remember correctly...?"

Tony rubbed his chin in faux contemplation. "I seem to recall something like that. Do you think that suggestion has merit?"

I pulled at the bone through my jeans, and nodded eagerly. "It definitely has some merit."

He nodded too, and spoke again in a coy, professorial tone. "We should examine it more closely."

I unbuckled my belt, and crept forward. "Very closely."

"You know, this ward isn't exactly private. I'm pretty sure they're monitoring my condition. This bed is capable of interfacing..."

"Well then..." I pulled my shirt off, and then drew the smelly blanket aside. "Why don't we exchange some... *data*... and show these fish how the humans do it?"

Former Olemsi soldiers, recovering all around the medical ward, attended to by the highly evolved land fish all heard the giggles, groans and exclamations from our quarter. Some of them even interfaced, *briefly*, for a look and an education. You'll never find this on Animal Planet.

I didn't care. We'd be leaving this system soon, either to find Earth, or find a place right for us. This wasn't it. Olcmsi Myucuc would never be our home, but would always be a part of us. And for the next couple of hours, Tony and I explored that part, over and over again, until we both passed out from exhaustion.

It's a good thing we enjoyed it too, because then this other goddamn thing happened...

About the Author

Brent D. Seth was born in Bloomington, IL and lived in a whole bunch of places before finally settling in Detroit, MI

Follow me on Twitter: https://twitter.com/brentdseth

Other Books
By Brent D. Seth

Available at Amazon.com

Short Fuse

Gladiolus Tormentus and Other Tales

Made in United States
Orlando, FL
15 February 2022